The Inner Child Journal

of a

Neurotic Parent

By the same author

Spring to Mind

And for children

Tom's Dreamflight

Tess and the Seaside Girl

The Inner Child Journal

of a

Neurotic Parent

by

Zoë Copley

The Inner Child Journal of a Neurotic Parent

Copyright © 2011 Zoë Copley

Book design by Zoë Copley

All rights reserved.

No part of this book may be reproduced in any form or by any electronic or mechanical means including information storage and retrieval systems, without permission in writing from the author. The only exception is by a reviewer, who may quote short excerpts in a review.

Zoë Copley
Visit my websites at:

www.spring-to-mind.co.uk

www.play-on-words.co.uk

Printed in the United States of America by Lulu.

First Printing: 2011

ISBN-978-1-4466-0040-5

For Megan and Jude.

And for Carmen, Trish and Helena,

inspirational women.

And for the inner child in all of us...

You are worried about seeing him spend his early years in doing nothing. What! Is it nothing to be happy? Nothing to skip, play, and run around all day long? Never in his life will he be so busy again.

Jean-Jacques Rousseau

It takes courage to grow up and become who you really are.

e.e. cummings

Sometimes, if you stand on the bottom rail of a bridge and lean over to watch the river slipping slowly away beneath you, you will suddenly know everything there is to be known.

AA Milne

Tuesday, 23 June

I *definitely* need to think about having therapy. I'm at my wit's end with the kids. Gracie has wet her bed every night for the past week. While Freddie, with a burgeoning word count of maybe 100 syllables, is fascinated with the word "shit" (can't think where he heard it!). About 20% of his vocabulary pertains to the toilet or excrement. I'm ready to take any help I can get. I confided as much to Beth today over lunch. I was feeling a little desperate before I met her and was ready to vent my spleen about the children, second rate cleaning ladies who are incapable of mopping the floor properly and husbands with no conversation. I barely got started when she told me that I'm blaming Carla the Cleaner for what really amounts to deep held resentment and unresolved issues with my mother dating from my childhood. Now here I am, three hours later, positively beside myself, riddled with self doubt and fear that I'm cracking up completely.

I blame Beth entirely. Before lunch I was merely sleep deprived and in need of an outlet for my frustrations. Now, as seems to be increasingly the case after spending time with Beth, my confidence is totally undermined. She's starting a new "phase" of psychotherapy this week for which she's "required" to keep an *inner child journal* for the next 3 months. As usual, she wants a buddy to keep her company throughout. She seems to think that if she tells me I'm bonkers I'll oblige her and hold her hand through what may be a confronting journey towards long term growth and change. Seriously: why me? I've never kept an *inner child journal* – not sure what one is – nor know of anyone who does.

Despite which, like a fool, I agreed to do it. In fact I smiled proudly and told Beth that I've been keeping one for *ages*.

What was I thinking?

Just when am I supposed to find time for a journal between washing and drying bed linen, getting to the gym and school, entertaining George's clients and introducing more words to Freddie? But this fib about keeping a journal is at least the fifth lie I've told Beth this month. Perhaps the real problem isn't that I have issues from my past (well, who doesn't?) but that I resent being psycho-analysed by my closest and oldest friend. Every time we get together I find myself pretending to be screwed up and then kidding that I'm one step ahead of her in getting myself sorted out. It's either that or I tell her to mind her own business. The upshot is that I've inadvertently and defensively waded into a quagmire of deceit and paranoia previously only traversed (albeit deliberately) in dealing with women that were *not* my oldest childhood friend. Why? To retain credibility? To compete with her?

I know for a fact that I'm as informed and conscientious as Beth when it comes to most things *self*-help - yes, even parenting. But, let's face it, I don't have her deep experience of *expert* psychological *interventions*. She has me at a disadvantage in that regard and when I'm at a low ebb – like now - she manages to unseat me entirely with her diagnoses and suggestions. So, while I might be able to convince her that I keep a diary, I don't have the first clue what she means by an "inner child" journal. Why do I do this? It's futile to compete with her angst and general anxiety levels. Let alone her budget for therapy. Lately though, when I have a problem to confide, she seems to almost revel in my pain. It's as though she won't be happy until I admit that I'm completely manic and in need of prolonged and sustained psychiatric treatment. This whole thing now has me thoroughly confused and exhausted.

Let's be honest, as Beth knows only too well, I haven't seen a shrink since my university days when Mum dragged me to hers during the bulimia phase. Any fool could see I wasn't bulimic, but since Felicity and her friends were, I pretended to be borderline eating disorder too, to get attention. Dear Dr Greene... so adept at earnestly spinning things out session after session. She knew she'd struck gold when Mum started seeing her. She charged like a wounded bull and made a fortune out of obsessive mothers of moody, sullen, unreachable teens. She did nothing at all in each session apart from say erudite things like "I see" and "go on" while I pretended to have an obsession with dieting (informed solely by Sunday supplements and documentaries on anorexia and Karen Carpenter), while tucking into my stale yet soggy cheese sandwiches bought at the campus refectory on my way to see her. Surely real anorexics wouldn't be caught dead eating (or even picking at) cheese sandwiches. But it *was* relatively early days in the diagnosis and treatment of adolescent eating disorders, I suppose.

Of course I didn't need therapy then and despite my malaise and the feverish nights this week, I doubt it's for me now. No – what I really need is better house help and some uninterrupted sleep. What would I do with a therapist, rambling on without guidance or direction about any old thing that comes into my mind? All that free association is far too open-ended for my liking. One could go anywhere. And besides, I manage – just - to keep abreast of the best parenting ideas and popular psychology books. That's enough, surely, on top of assiduously following all the tips in the papers and magazines about domestic perfection.

I'm no worse than anyone else at this stuff, surely. Either I've fooled all my girlfriends very convincingly that I'm as informed as them or they're so absorbed in their own dramas that they're oblivious to the fact that I'm very often jotting down the names of the latest parenting guru as they drop them into the conversation at the school gate or stealing off with their copies of the new best selling life changing tome. I always could talk the talk if I put my mind to it.

But can it be good for me to engage in so much duplicity in order to seem on the one hand more expert, and on the other, more screwed up, than I really am? To feign mild lunacy to appear more hip and likeable, only then to resent people who think I'm a nutcase after all?

These past few days of sleep deprivation and parenting frustration coupled with Beth's latest fix-all solution, have me questioning myself all over again. Perhaps she's right - venting over coffee is no solution. Therapy? Coaching? A Retreat? Maybe I *am* borderline personality disorder like many of the women at school and the gym; I just didn't think it was getting in my way. But there are days when this definition from Wikipedia applies to me:

> **"Borderline personality disorder (BPD)** *is a psychiatric diagnosis in the Diagnostic and Statistical Manual of Mental Disorders (DSM-IV Personality Disorders). The disorder typically involves unusual levels of instability in mood; "black and white" thinking, or splitting; chaotic and unstable interpersonal relationships, self-image, identity, and behaviour; as well as a disturbance in the individual's sense of self. In extreme cases, this disturbance in the sense of self can lead to periods of dissociation. These disturbances can have a pervasive negative impact on many or all of the psychosocial facets of life. This includes difficulties maintaining relationships in work, home and social settings."*

In any case, Beth is so intent on this journal pursuit that for me not to collude and keep one of my own would be disloyal; even hard-hearted. How difficult can it be, after all? Naturally, I've heard of the "inner child" concept. Indeed I'm familiar with my own. After all, it's said poppet that insists I chop the crusts off sandwiches and the skin off apples and generally resents being told what to do by older people.

However, while I know and love that little darling, I've never felt the need to record her thoughts and ideas in a journal, or indeed in any other form, for that matter. Not that I doubt the therapeutic benefits of writing. I kept a food diary for Dr Greene for several weeks in 1989 until Mum read it and decided I was wasting her time and Dad's money.

But with regards the *inner child* journal I have to say that I'm at a loss as to just how it's written. Is it kept by the inner child as said child would write it? Or from the perspective of the adult, in the third person, about its inner child? While the former would have greater therapeutic impact, it might prove distracting to the actual therapy.

Mine might read:

Favourite colour – Blue

Favourite Number – 7

Favourite food – strawberries

BFF – Beth

Now I only get that far because, frankly, that was the extent of my attention span at 9 (the ideal age, surely, for assessing the needs of one's inner child: past the age of reason, not yet fully self determining, yet basically ready for some self reflection given the newly honed skills of back-stabbing one's friends, being mean to boys and generally becoming really bitchy). But now I'm getting myself muddled up. I don't know whether to write as a child would about the child's experiences – i.e. my life circa 1980 – or whether to use the voice and phraseology of the child that I was, about my current experiences. Or perhaps the point is to harness the thoughts and voice of the child I would be now. It's the inner child, not the former child, after all. But if it's all about the inner child then it may be that such an entity hasn't got a clear voice. After all, by definition, she's hidden, if not secret and repressed. She might be subtle and manipulative, driving one to do certain things. Or she may be shy and retiring – even mute - most of the time.

Or she might be a boy...

I looked it up on the internet and my search revealed nothing helpful. All I know is that time is of the essence. I must start the journal and keep up with Beth.

Unlike some of her fads and obsessions (e.g. wheatgrass, Skittles diet, weekly enemas) I feel this might be useful to me if I just work out where and how to begin. Beth's trying to harness the voice and thoughts of her *damaged* inner child. But I don't think I have one of those; a traumatised inner victim to whom untold damage was done by neglectful and misguided parents and teachers. Unless I'm suffering from extreme, wanton and psychotic denial, (which I can't rule out), I don't feel that there's a victim subdued inside me screaming for attention or a means of egress. Sure, I've some unresolved issues with my domineering mother (who doesn't?), but the issues stemming from my adult life and directly affecting me now will more than keep me busy venting and whining for 3 months. Truth is, I actually think I'm more scarred by my latter years as a whole – the hairstyles, working all night on pitches, the sleep deprivation since having children – than I am by anything from my childhood.

So where does all of this leave me?

Mmm...

There must be something I can write about. My teenage years? A bit of a blur – but happy enough. I was basically ignored by Mum once Felicity hit her teens and Mum became compulsively obsessed with Felicity's academics, extra-curricular pursuits, appearance and behaviour. I don't remember minding at the time – left to my own devices, unless I did anything completely foolish, which was almost never, given what happened to Felicity when she rebelled. Thankfully, by about 9 I'd learnt to emulate Dad's style: low-key and self-possessed. By 13 I was acing my exams without pressure or hassle with only Dad providing support and encouragement. His humour and sense of self containment was the key to his tolerating Mum's issues and the family not imploding. Not that he was a pushover. He was no Mr Bennett. He was very devoted to Mum, but he picked his battles wisely. Clearly, how to manage their eldest daughter was not his choice of battleground. Only the most anal or controlling of fathers would have interfered in some of those offensives and stand-offs between Mum and Felicity. In that regard, Mum's energy and solicitations knew no bounds.

I'll admit to vying for their attention during Felicity's bulimia treatment and during a brief period before that, when I was perhaps 14, in which I may have felt a twinge of jealousy when I missed out on a class trip to see Haley's Comet – it was a camp out - because Mum never signed the permission slip despite a million reminders from me, as she was coaching Felicity for her college interviews. It was as though I didn't exist – or as Felicity so often points out – as though I "could do no wrong" in Mum's eyes. Maybe. Whatever. Being left alone was preferable to being in Felicity's shoes, so I think I got the better deal.

Anyway – what's this journal meant to achieve? If the underlying rationale is to journal or channel all the bad stuff – the accumulation of resentment, disappointment and rejection - then I think I need to find a different voice; say, the inner Aspiring Ad Executive or the inner Jealous Friend. Not exactly the domain of the child. Well, not when I was a girl at least. It's true that several of the little cherubs at ballet with Gracie today might give their adult selves a run for their money. Even I'm scared of them.

Maybe it's all about gaining perspective; seeing the world through the eyes of a child. Goodness knows, 8 years of marriage, 6 of motherhood and many more of work and career have taken a toll. What would my inner child have to say about any of that? If she's really young, she'll likely just put her thumb in her mouth, clutch her favourite blankie and self-soothe. Would the older inner child revel enviously in my beautiful home, husband and children? Would the teenager IM me and suggest a new outfit? All I know for sure is that my inner child must be far more relaxed and better rested than I am right now.

Aaah - perhaps that's the point. She could give me a fresh perspective. I need to give her a bigger role in my life and to heed her more. Ok. That makes sense.

Problem is, today's conversation has left me feeling suddenly very insecure about my appearance as well. Grappling with the myriad issues and demands associated with aging, staying fit and slim and keeping ahead of the pack at charity lunches and in the corporate box at the rugby is vexing me more than it should. I used to scrub up well enough. People have said that I look lovely. I care about my appearance, and yet, it seems everyone is holding Botox parties now. I have completely missed that boat; people know I've not hosted one, nor attended one. And now that I have discussed it with Beth, people will know I am a little scared of doing so. So I look my age, possibly even more and I've not been sufficiently bothered to do anything apart from slather myself in hyper-expensive creams mail ordered after watching late night shopping TV waiting for George to come home from work. Until now!

Beth was less than subtle in suggesting I get myself some filling and plumping before the summer. Is it the sign of a good friendship that she feels she can say these things to me – or a reflection of how truly pathetic I have become? I might just pause here and check out my crow's feet again to see whether she has a point...

Wednesday, 24 June

Ok, ok. To appease my Inner Wannabe, I've drafted an invitation to a Botox party and Nail Spa.

Who am I kidding? I won't host this! First, I'd need a venue outside the home as I couldn't bear for the children to stumble upon Mummy and her guests injecting toxic viruses into their foreheads over Prosecco and canapés. Second, it's just not me. It feels too self-conscious somehow. I know this is how everyone lives, but I don't feel comfortable being seen to care so much about the state of my fine lines, wrinkles and crow's feet. It's too personal, too open. Beth insists she can put me onto the best cosmeticians and has booked me in for a dermal fill next week. I'm sure it will clash with Pilates though. The entire fitness/beauty/health/anti-ageing complex is designed to make my life harder!

Oh wow. I just realised – I'm journaling already! Right here and now. And these completely haphazard and disorganised musings must surely look like the work of a child! I've begun.

There – just do it Verity – and this time it won't be a lie. And best of all, Beth won't get the better of this experience. I can keep up with the ramblings of – if not my inner child – at least my superficial copycat alter ego and her banal and "childlike" yearnings. It may not be the correct way to do it but who'll know? It's a journal – no one will read it apart from me. Mind you, I'm fully prepared to accept that Maria may chance upon it while trying my clothes on when I'm out, so I'll keep it clean. I'll extol the virtues of journaling to anyone who'll listen and hopefully pick up some tips from Beth who will take the express route alongside her sought-after, 7-months-long-waiting-list, well-known, well-regarded and extortionately overpriced therapist, while I putter along in the slow lane behind...

Thursday, 25 June

I just got off the phone with Felicity. Of course, like an imbecile, I forgot the pleasure she takes in my friends' and my antics, and I mentioned the inner child journal ambitions to her. She's been keeping a journal for years. It's actually more like an enormous scrapbook, and she proudly boasts that she started it long before scrapbooking became fashionable. It chronicles all of her doings since fleeing to Rome when Dad died, as well as those of her family and mine, with postcards and snapshots and keepsakes stuck into it. It even has Jessica's lost teeth (since Allan is a prosthodontist they've always been terrifically fixated on all things dental). There are pages in that scrapbook devoted to Felicity's favourite menus and dining experiences and copies of the menus she's offered during her ten years in catering. It's a huge great tome taking up most of the spare room. I know that a large part of my life is also documented there – such a loyal and devoted sister – and some of my better print and glossy ad campaigns (yoghurt, sanitary towels and lawnmowers among them). Naturally, as I subconsciously intended all along, since my inner child is too sweet to engage in any direct criticism of Beth, Felicity shrieked with mirth at the Inner Child Journal and exclaimed:

"Another of Beth's distraction projects! Tell her to get a job."

Felicity, escaping the bulimia thing relatively unscathed and then eating her way around Europe, is now the owner and director of Felicitations - one of the most successful catering businesses in town. She's a walking, talking, beamingly happy example of the benefits of harnessing the crap in one's past and using it to one's advantage. Unsurprisingly, she's not a big fan of therapists and counsellors, given how many Mum subjected her to from age 13 onwards. She puts no stock in talking about the past with regret. She managed to purge her childhood and adolescent demons during those vomiting years of bulimia. She's definitely turned a challenging youth into a very happy and successful life.

But we can't all be as confident and together as Felicity. Even if we wanted to be.

Truth is I have some sympathy for Mum. She was doing her best and for whatever reasons, sought validation for a lot of nonsense that she needed to believe as she strived to be a perfect mother and wife and to create a perfect daughter out of Felicity. These days we all talk about parenting openly, or buy the books. I would never tell Felicity, but a part of me is just like Mum; terrified of missing a little kernel of wisdom that could change my life or that of my children, for the better. I know that I use Beth for vicarious therapy. I'm cheating, looking for a quick and easy guarantee that I'm not doing any damage and confirmation that I'm basically psychologically intact.

I'm a product of this era of self help obsessed, time-rich, pop psychology addicted parenting, and an inner child journal and some occasional and very selective amateur psychoanalytic processing of no doubt repressed resentment and identity issues, couldn't do me any harm. Might even do me some good.

The problem is, and I regret the fact that Felicity will have worked this much out, more and more I feel kind of desperate. Like a soon to be adolescent trying to keep up with its older, hipper, wiser, cuter and funnier friends. And truth be told, I wasn't such a try-hard in my youth. *Au contraire.* I've lost my edge since I became a parent. Being hopeless doesn't come naturally to me. But despite the books and the magazines it's nearly impossible to keep up with all of the fads and crazes. When I finally grasp what everyone is talking and obsessing about, I'm not always convinced by their points of view either. But I barely have time to work out what I do think before the next suggestion from Beth is made, the next celebrity diet takes off, another hot holiday destination has to be booked or the yoga mums start showing off the latest must-have trick or gadget for raising a genius.

I don't have the energy or inclination to do anything apart from pretend. Pretend to believe all these notions. Pretend to be just as eager to jump on the trendy parent bandwagon as everyone else. Pretend to care about ballet shoes. Pretend to believe that organic milk will prevent bowel cancer. It's easier and preferable to looking neglectful or ill-informed. But it's hard work; keeping track of who I lie to and what I've told whom about my child's milestones. I guess I really do need an intervention.

Felicity's advice? Get over myself...

.....

Which brings me to a rather concerning affliction to my right elbow. It's really itchy. It might be a weird eczema! I've never knowingly had an allergy. What if I've contracted some odd adult onset fungal infection from one of the shower areas I frequent? Between Fantastic and Fit, Yoga Babes, the Golf Club, the pool and the Baths of Vespasian Thermal Spa, I could have a multitude of diseases incubating in me at any given time. Up to now I thought I had my mother's ox-like constitution, but who knows? I also thought fungal infections caught in showers would afflict the lower extremities, rather than the elbow. Perhaps it's not the showers, but the mats at the gym. Maybe my extra-long prone holds on elbows and feet (the plank), or the butt tightening exercises which require me to lean on my elbows, are to blame.

I Googled this elbow complaint and in doing so came across a number of foul and nausea inducing conditions. Beth never showers in a public or semi-public facility and never attends group fitness classes. Now I see why. It's not just a holdover from public showers at boarding school. Sickened by the fungal afflictions I searched the elbow's *energy*. According to the internet:

> *"The elbow chakric points are associated with one's ability to be 'flexible' and there is also a relation to that of 'ego boundaries'. The left elbow chakra controls our emotional perseverance, and the right our intellectual perseverance."*

And -

> *"Blocked elbow chakras lead to great self-centeredness."*

And -

> *"The elbows govern our barriers regarding relationships."*

Wow. Very revealing. Ego boundaries might be a good starting point for my journal. I know I need to define some clearer ego boundaries with Beth and my mother. Also, Mia springs to mind with her incredible and boundless sense of self and her insatiable hunger to impose said self on all who get in her way. She may also have some elbow issues of her own; given how large her elbows are. It surprises me that I have an elbow problem at all, though. I think of myself as emotionally and intellectually persistent and persevering, generally. But perhaps too much so? Maybe the fungus falls outside the control of the chakra...

The idea of relationship "barriers" also needs more consideration. I've been meaning to enroll in a Chakra Exploration at the Women's Discussion Centre. I saw it advertised at the café the other day but got sidetracked talking to Emma from Austin, Texas about whether five years old is too early to start cheerleading club. I said - yes – but I'm a tad old fashioned about dressing girls in short skirts and throwing them in the air in front of large, not very intelligent men. The alternative for her child, who she regards as embarrassingly clumsy, would be gymnastics. Seemed a better choice, I said, but Emma was concerned about broken limbs and denting her confidence for the big Christmas ski trip to Colorado.

Then we got onto Emma's thyroid and how it's playing havoc with her weight. I secretly think the saucer size triple chocolate cookies and organic toffee ice-cream combo she favours after ballet might also have something to do with it, but I nodded sagely, and volunteered that stress and insufficient exercise are my own sworn enemies. I only said that to appear comradely and collusive. I'm as slim as I've ever been thanks to a rigorous schedule of Pilates, yoga, weight training, cross training with Michael the Killer Kiwi, personal training with Jorgé the Spanish German, swimming and aqua aerobics. But I learnt after I shed the baby weight when Gracie was born that no one wants to hear about anyone else's diet or weight loss successes. We're only interested in how fat, frumpy, dumpy and ugly other people feel/are. Certainly is easy to get sidetracked at the café notice board.

Intriguingly, Emma and the ballet mums think I'm an expert on illnesses and health worries because George is in pharmaceuticals. Sure, I know a thing or two as a result of some intense investment in the local paediatric practice these past few years. But Emma's friend Kate, is virtually stalking me for over the counter cold and flu meds. She doesn't believe me when I tell her that Pharma Co isn't in the habit of sending home medicine goody bags. But, if she wants some shampoo for those dry, dirty, blonde locks...

She's almost an obsessive compulsive hypochondriac, if such a thing exists. While I was looking through the *Diagnostic and Statistical Manual of Mental Disorders* (DSM) published by the American Psychiatric Association to see if I was bonkers I checked to see whether her disorder actually has a name. It was fascinating reading. Time stopped. I studied the list of "Common Axis II disorders" and got a little chill up my spine. I swear half my friends have most of these covered, between them – and I include myself.

But Kate's a tricky one. I don't think she's a classic hypochondriac because she's not in *terror* of illness, per se. Every time I see her – weekly at least between ballet and the organic deli – and I forget to be rude and say "How are you Kate?" - she regales me with a list of ailments. This week it was backache, sciatica, neck and shoulder tension, heartburn that she thinks might be angina, some tummy upset that's definitely irritable bowel syndrome flaring up and a lingering cough, a hangover from swine flu. I tried to escape saying I had to get home to water the lavender but she completely ignored me and went on to berate me with complaints about the cost of over the counter medicine – as if it were my fault that hay fever spray costs that much. Then she asked me for the 42nd time whether George could get free sample drugs for her.

I don't know what she needs. She seems to be the picture of physical good health. It must be completely psychological. She can't be a Munchausen syndrome sufferer because she's completely happy self diagnosing and seeking *social* attention, rather than professional or medical attention. But attention of any sort is definitely key to her interactions. She makes me feel like a dirty drug pusher at the school gates, only her kids don't go to our school, so it's only in the stairwell at ballet or in the chocolate aisle at the supermarket where she knows she'll find me lurking guiltily on Wednesdays. The only difference is that she pushes *me* around, not vice versa. A few months ago I was so annoyed at her persistent pestering – she followed me and Freddie to the car while we loaded the shopping, still talking as I began reversing, thereby distracting me and causing me to run into the curb, puncture the tyre and then have to await the automobile association's man to fix it – leaving me exposed to her for yet another hour - that I lost it. I told her to try a holistic approach to her health and stop thinking that medicines are the answer. I even suggested she read into the emotional and *mental* conditions that are thought to trigger some of her complaints. Well, that only made matters worse. She now wants tips on hypnosis, herbal remedies (for her "soul") and anti-psychotic meds too.

As if I had nothing better to do with my time than worry about Kate.

Emma must keep her around to remind her how not to be. Not that Kate is depressing – just exhausting. She gets incredible joy from all of her syndromes and aliments. The only topic that gives Kate more pleasure than illness is her husband, who despite controlling the purse strings very tightly, and perhaps wisely, can do no wrong in Kate's eyes. Unlike most people with children, she finds very little about hers to talk about. They're a little dour, it has to be said. But, I feel as if I *know* Brad, the IT guy husband. His foibles, hobbies, diet and friends delight all of us in the queue at the supermarket. Freddie is lulled to sleep by her incessant talking whatever the time of day, while the cashier and I exchange sympathetic looks. We're not required to say anything – just nod, smile and look shocked at the right places. Mind you, it's almost a relief to hear about Brad rather than be pestered for meds. I'm bloody envious that she has such an amazing partner too - surfer, adventurer, encryption expert and amateur James Bond rolled into one. And of course – fantastic in the bedroom. Maybe I *should* nudge a few drugs her way…

When I get a minute I need to find out what was wrong with my ankle chakra last month. Note to self – get the details of that Chakra course. Oh - and buy beads to wear to same.

And I must remember to text Beth to say the journal is going great!

Monday, 29 June

I thought I would have been journaling my inner child all this past week, but I've not given it much thought and now I feel hard done by –

like I'm depriving myself of a deserved pleasure. Now that the children are asleep and George is out at his monthly wine tasting soirée, I can focus on myself once more. I spent today shopping for putty for Freddie. Curtis, one of the boys Freddie's age at play group, has been working with putty for over a month now. His mother, Francine, wants to strengthen his grip and fingers so that he can manage a pencil before he starts school next year. Between the demands of tying his own tie, managing the computer mouse, the pencil, the paintbrushes and the violin bow and practising his scales on the miniature piano keys, he'll certainly need to fast track the development of his fine motor skills.

Francine, despite being the least maternal woman I've ever met, is a little anal about Curtis. Unlike her older children, whom she only mentions in passing – like barely tolerated dogs – Curtis is the apple of her eye. Perhaps it's the old "opposite-sex-youngest-child-so-spoil-him-rotten" syndrome at play. Personally, I think her obvious preference for Curtis over her daughters is a little perverse. Hers would be a great case study for nature versus nurture experts. How do ignored children fare against over-indulged spoilt children? Curtis isn't merely spoilt, he's at risk of ruin and nothing about him is at all endearing. I can't understand her out and out devotion to him. Maybe it's due to the fact that he's relatively simple and baby-like still?

Her girls are quite normal and well-adjusted, despite some issues at school. The second girl has been diagnosed with ADHD, ADDD and something else with a few D's in it, not to mention special learning needs, largely, Francine says, due to lack of fine motor skills and delayed finger development. Benign neglect may have something to do with it too. In spite of this she's still taking up a place at Hillmere Prep, so clearly ability is not the only entrance criteria. I daresay hefty donations account for some of the enrolments. In Curtis's case I suspect that motor skills will be just one of his challenges. Gaining an appreciation that the entire population and its resources are not at his disposal alone may be an even tougher one. Then again, he'll probably never learn this and indeed, it's hardly something that Francine would want him to know, given it would be news to her.

I confess my concerns are somewhat more pedestrian. I just hate to think of too much pressure coming to bear on Freddie in a couple of years when we are vying for places at the better prep schools. The fact George is an old boy may not be sufficient if Freddy is backward. Mia insists that all of the boys at George's prep school (Percy – her stepson aged 9 goes there) are very advanced. What choice do I have but to give Freddie every chance to compete on a level playground, so that's why I'm getting him started early. Between putty, play dough and sand play we should be ok. On the large motor skills I'm less confident though. He's been attending Gymboree classes for 18 months now and still can't manage the balance beam. He simply walks around it or crawls under it, giggling. I've made an appointment for him at the doctor to check on his hips, spine and feet. I wonder if we should order a CT scan of the brain as well and check out the ears – it may all come down to balance. Otherwise we might need to face the fact that he may have developmental challenges. Or it could be genetic. George is terribly uncoordinated. Freddie will be three soon and he's still not hopping!

Meanwhile, Gracie is prima ballerina extraordinaire, much to the disgust of the American mommies. She runs rings around the other girls in Yoga Tykes. Her Downward Dog is sublime and her Bird and Lotus have the other mothers snidely peering at me in envy and resentment. Luckily, I hold my own in Ashtanga, Hatha, Bikram and Power varieties, or I too would feel quite threatened.

But I digress.

This week my inner child has been feeling rather despondent. It's my week to staff the Montessori Tuck Shop and I'm dreading having to go there tomorrow. The nutritional content of the foodstuffs sold is appalling. I decided last year after a bitter argument with the then president of the Parents' Association – Jeff - to stop upsetting the applecart – pie cart in this case – and simply ban Gracie from buying anything apart from fruit at Tuck Shop. I then went silly and volunteered to work there every few weeks hoping to influence the children to buy the healthier offerings. I was overcompensating for being so critical and convinced myself it was in Gracie's interests for me to meet new people, curry favour with the movers and shakers in the upper classes and get to know her playmates. It's been disappointing in every respect.

First, I'm rostered to work by myself – a frightful bore that leaves me run off my feet – and a punishment for speaking out, I suspect. Second, none of Gracie's classmates have Tuck Shop, so just exactly who I think I'm cultivating is still unclear – fat kids with parents who can't make sandwiches? Finally, try as I do, I can't ignore the saturated fat, salt, preservatives and emulsifiers, not to mention E numbers and carcinogenic additive values in the meat pies, baked goods and hash-browns. The only almost health giving option is artificially coloured and flavoured pink milk. What sort of parent sends their children to school with money to buy this toxic rubbish? It's worse than feeding them supermarket own brand pet food.

Freddie calls it Duck Shop and George has a less kind work for it. I want out! George's sister, Sophie, was actually the person who got me thinking about the ethics of school canteens. Living in the UK where school dinners have been "revolutionised" in the interests of improving the health of school children and reducing the incidence of childhood obesity, Sophie is an expert on school dinners. She's an expert, per se, actually. Her children are anything but obese and she's a health nut and a know-it-all, so I can take some of her remarks with a grain of salt, but even so, a salad sandwich or a tub of yoghurt wouldn't go astray.

I offered to swap my Tuesdays at Tuck Shop for Helen's Thursdays in the library. Helen's an earth mother. She gardens, grows her own fruit, herbs and veggies and embraces moderation in all things. Accordingly, she sees the merits of a little junk food from time to time. She's expecting her fifth child and has an insatiable appetite for carbs at the moment. Since she can't eat while on library duty, she's very amenable to a swap with me. I love seeing at her at school and hearing her views. Time spent with Helen is a wonderfully refreshing experience. She's outspoken, yet loveable. She's brave and warm and emotional and getting to know her has been one of the highlights of Montessori.

Helen was single-handedly responsible for affecting the anti car-bullying campaign last term. Three Year 2 girls (daughters of *dentists*) were making life hard for some children who had joined the school mid-term. One family relocated from California and the mother rode to school on a scooter – a large green one. The girls teased the son of this woman venomously about his mother who "only had a scooter". This was the tip of the iceberg. After all, Scooter Mom *was* leaving her children open to some comment with that sort of behaviour. The bigger problem was that a number of girls were picking on children whose parents drove small, older model cars from Japan or Korea. The mean girls didn't actually know the brands of the cars, they just knew they were old and small and not very prestigious (no doubt hearing their mothers comment from the luxurious leather seats of their air-conditioned behemoths). The taunting and ridiculing transcended the car prejudices of course, with taunts directed also at girls with healthy appetites and shy boys, but it was the car taunting that opened the huge can of worms – far more serious than mere teasing about size and smell ever could - as it seemed to constitute an attack on the parents, as well as the child.

In response, Helen initiated a campaign to get more children walking, scooting or cycling to school. The opportunities to compare cars became few and far between as many parents jumped on the bandwagon in the hopes of being environmentally friendly – or being seen as such. Hey, I drive an SUV too, but I'm not a hypocrite. It's a hybrid. I personally don't think I need to green up my school run, even though I applaud Helen's ingenuity in overcoming the bullying by driving forward an eco-friendly agenda. My own approach is to park a long way from school and walk in to collect Gracie, rather than drive up to the gate and wait there ostentatiously with my engine running and carbon emissions mounting up in my notional balance sheet of carbon crime. A number of parents now follow my example rather than face the car-bully backlash. I'm not sure what I think of all of this. I got swept up in the momentum, at the time, and supported Helen, but I think the girls in question are a product of their homes and it's their parents and their attitudes that really ought to be chastised not the rest of us who drive German or Italian cars. There endeth the lesson.

The fascinating thing was how quickly Helen's idea was embraced. Typically the parents are reluctant to make changes in how things are done at school. They're very invested in the status quo. I know I haven't been at Montessori very long, but my three suggestions in Gracie's first year to change the fundraising events in small but – I thought - meaningful ways, were completely "ignored". Mrs Blythe, the principal, was more than happy to have some fresh ideas, but the backstabbing and coffee shop gossip that ensued when I said - jumping castles are unsafe; why not a slip 'n' slide at the summer fete? – really made the first few months there quite fraught. Even Helen remarked that she was taking a huge risk with her car campaign. I suppose though, that the global warming zeitgeist was on her side. One needs to choose one's battles carefully, apparently.

Helen has countless examples of crazy and irrational behaviour amongst the parents at school. She's very plugged in – people tell her everything and one of her close friends works in the office. Some of the parents are so demanding and critical; marching in all day long demanding redress for this or that wrong, solutions to yet another problem of their own making and requests that their child be afforded some sort of special treatment. They act as though the school is their private business. One family have requested that all class field trips be scheduled for mid term rather than the final week of term, as is usually the case, because they take their holidays early and their children are missing out on the trips. Seriously!

But back to the library plan - I think it will be beneficial to shift my focus to reading and covering books and dusting. I just have to make it happen under the radar, as this year's Parents' Association president, Wendy, will have my Jimmy Choos (old and mouldy) if she finds out. Wendy is manic and controlling and nothing can happen without her say so. Throw into that frightening mix the fact that she was poisoned against me by the outgoing president, Jeff - stay at home Dad and desperate housewife extraordinaire – following the Great Tuckshop Menu To Do, and I can be sure that any discussion of a change in roster or role will be fraught with controversy.

If I just quietly arrange things to Helen's and my liking though, Wendy will almost certainly step up at the next Parents' meeting and take credit for the new arrangement in a blaze of micromanagement glory. In another life I would have been amazed that anyone could care, let alone stress these tiny details that don't matter to anyone, but if I've learnt one thing it's this – the less you have going on, the bigger deal you make of small things. It's the law of "Inverse Importance". Thus, I completely see how my unilaterally changing role will threaten her. On the one hand, doing anything without her permission is a slap in the face. On the other, the ease and speed with which Helen and I could make the change could be seen as a reflection of her amazing management and delegation skills and overall style and success as

President. So much angst over such a bad set of options - working with dusty kids' books or lard.

Wendy and I have a weird relationship. She's caught between a rock and a hard place, because despite her suspicions of me, she perceives herself to be in my debt because George (or Pharma Co) is her husband's law firm's biggest client. She usually quakes in her platform wedges and too short skirts billowing in the breeze when she sees me coming, for fear that upsetting me or Gracie might jeopardise Paul's partnership prospects. I must tell George to spread the legal work around the lesser firms for a time, just to keep her baited and thrashing about on the hook. If Paul makes partner before Gracie gets a place at another school, Wendy will have no further use of me. Am I scared? Damn right. We each hold power over the other that I, for one, did not seek. I can't say I blame her for resenting me. It's never easy to suck up to people one dislikes for the sake of one's husband's career.

Wendy, in spite of her dress sense and rather large backside, is one of those people who gets a huge kick out of being involved at the school. Combining a passion for interfering, a skill for organising and an incredibly advanced ability to suck up to governors and staff, she enjoys huge influence and favour. The school is her life. I've never been in the school without encountering her there too. She's in charge of everything, goes on every class trip with her daughters, whether required or not and all manner of decisions seem to be channeled through her. Worst of all she's completely insecure and paranoid so that even with all of that "power" she's desperate for attention and approval and is always seeking out confidantes to whisper her little secrets to.

Her latest ploy was to set up a Facebook page for the Mortimer Montessori Parents' Association (PAMM). Now she only communicates with parents through this medium, unless one is unlucky enough to see her in person, that is. The Facebook thing is perverse. First, not everyone uses Facebook so it excludes and marginalises people. Second, she posts meaningless self-serving drivel about herself and her daughters (weight loss tips, spelling test results and photos of recent purchases) and almost nothing about school or the Association or its events. Generally, anything we need to know is printed in the school newsletter and handed out each week by Mrs Blythe, in any case. It's obvious the Facebook thing is another self promotion tactic.

I finally signed up with a false name in order to "Like" the bloody PAMM when Helen kept talking about the fantastic recipes her chums were posting there. Fearing I might be missing something worthwhile I reluctantly got onboard. I refuse to use Facebook legitimately because I know Kate and several women from the gym and yoga have all "Friended" each other and would find me to friend too. It's bad enough running into some of them socially or at the shops, without having to see pictures of them all over my laptop and read the banal and dreary details of their kids' first day at school/swimming/karate/juvenile lock up *ad nauseum*. Anyway, I had to laugh when Wendy accepted my friend request under the alias "Loosy Lude". In fact Loosy has over 47 friends now, no profile, nor photos and absolutely no personal info. But she likes PAMM, yoga and "The Good Wife". Go figure.

I'll admit that I enjoy certain elements of getting involved at school, like meeting new people and rolling my sleeves up to help, but it seems contrived, if not desperate, to see the school as a complete occupation. Admittedly, I don't have a role of the gravitas and responsibility that Wendy holds (voluntarily, mind you, since no one wanted to do it when Jeff stepped down), but I wonder if I lack the perseverance, tenacity and political will to do it well, in the first place.

Note to self: sign up at Gracie's next school for important political role before alienating any parents.

But it's not just politics – it's the art of living vicariously through one's children productively that I have yet to master. Politics and having too much time only gets people so far. Actually living through one's kids is also a requirement. I know Wendy delights in the successes, dramas and activities of her 8 year old twins, but I'm not really privy to her plotting and politicking. Helen is my source. She was heaving with laughter as she recounted the tale of Wendy at the Montessori cocktail evening last year – I was tipsy, talking with George and Lucsious Larry and his wife Rose and missed the whole thing – when she offered a group of listeners her unique perspectives on child psychology and excellence in parenting. It seems that she has a secret yearning to become a counsellor for neurotic pre-teens, so worried is she for her girls and so convinced that society is creating an epidemic of depressed and disturbed adolescents. She offered to run workshops in her kitchen for parents. The crowd thinned out after that. Thank goodness Helen has her finger on the pulse. Wendy shuns and avoids me as often as she seeks me out to further her husband's career and without Helen I wouldn't have copies of the eating disorder books Wendy was recommending that night. Just in case. For Gracie, that is.

But the fact remains, if I can manoeuvre into a library role I might get a chance to fast-track Gracie's borrowing schedule, while keeping tabs on the older girls and what they're reading. George said that I need to keep my focus on the home rather than the school. But until we get Gracie a place at Hillmere Prep, school and home are inextricably linked. I have to do everything in my power to get her through the entrance interview next month; cultivating her interest in books will help enormously. If library duty and sewing bees, baking for the fete and leaving sweet delights in the staffroom fridge can't secure us a good reference from Mortimer Montessi, I don't know what will.

The rest will be down to her on the day. We've been rehearsing her little speech about herself morning and night. She's still stumbling over the "tête-a-tête" sentence which is coming out sounding vulgar. Her speech and elocution coach says not to worry – we still have a month. It's hard though. Especially late at night when I'm awake worrying about Chakras, George's career, Freddie's verbal range, what brand of putty to buy, whether dark chocolate covered goji berries count towards my antioxidant calories for the day and what to wear to George's mother's 70th...

I'm trying to slow down my breathing and focus on living in the present and enjoying the children more. They won't be little for long. My Mindfulness for Mothers course stressed the need for us to live each moment and appreciate the beauty of now. Needless to say the teacher of *that* course is not looking at Hillmere for her toddler. It's all very well for her to tell us to slow down and just watch the anxious, worried and paranoid thoughts pass us by. Easy enough to do if you don't have to deal with Wendy and Jeff, swearing toddlers, school interviews, Tuckshop food and stressful schedules. Besides the Mindfulness lady is rumoured to be a *home* school maniac in any case.

Oh dear, George is back – I hear his uneven footsteps on the parquet downstairs. I hope he's not plastered. He comes home from these wine tastings full of ideas about buying boats and chalets in Canada and racehorses. He can speak to Mum about race horses and we'll catapult ourselves into her good books once and for all. Nothing would please her more than my buying into her business, even tangentially. Thank goodness we don't see a lot of her. We already live way beyond our means. And what a blessing that these men's evenings happen only once a month or we'd have no money left for school fees, holidays or my fitness regime. I must humour George though. His dreams are valid and symbolic of him as a man. I respect that. Suppose I need to act like I do. Sigh.

Saturday, 4 July

We're just home from a Fourth of July party at the "estate" of Emma from Austin, Texas. I knew most of the guests, predominantly other friends from ballet and anxiety counselling; an alarming number of them being expatriate Americans whom Emma has met at Embassy functions and alumni events here. Emma and Carl have three daughters aged 4, 6 and 9 and an amazing house. Each child has her own suite with playroom and bathroom, walk in robe and bedroom, all converging on a shared media space. It was inspirational. The party consisted of cupcakes (!) and champagne on the lawn overlooking the river (for the adults) and circus themed excitement for the children on the terrace by the pool. Carl is in computer and internet gaming and has made a fortune. Emma was describing his various avatars and their favourite games.

I somehow expected that people with so much cash might have a more engaged approach to the real world. Carl spends most of his spare time updating and playing these games in cyber space, while Emma spends most of his money. But they do throw a fab party. Perhaps she has honed her hostessing skills in some on-line parenting/partying and wife-ing game. I'll look for it online tonight, once the children are asleep.

Kate and Brad were there too. Kate managed to buttonhole George for a good hour to discuss her health and the future of pharmaceuticals. I heard her asking him to put her name down for any drug trials Pharma Co might be doing.

Several of the party guests were discussing their domestic arrangements. By which I mean house help. I must tell George that we are beginning to fall behind in this arena – my self sufficiency is economical and admirable from our perspective, but in these circles we may be seen as tight. The ballet mums have between them live-in nannies, night nurses, gardeners, cleaners, maids and hairdressers, housekeepers, cooks and meditation gurus. It's a full time job just organizing the staff.

One woman – Sara - cannot endure live-ins so she has an entourage who arrive daily. Personal trainer first, then stylist, hairdresser and personal assistant. She's contemplating starting a business advising people on schools and extra-curricular activities for children. The must-do list for the under 10s. Her husband apparently has doubts about the likelihood of this making any money so she's desperate to prove him wrong. Based on what I saw at the party she already has an i-Phone full of contacts, many of whom were calling her for tips all afternoon. I overheard four calls while sipping Moet and clearly the real value is not the "tips" but the access she has. She knows everyone in the business from day care centres, to gym crèches, from caterers to algebra tutors, Mensa members offering brain gym training for the under 7's (must email Sophie to see if she has heard about that – is that even legal?) and Olympic medal winning gymnasts giving private tuition. One call from her and your place at "Toddler Tennis" or "Pottery for Poppets" is assured. Not only is she able to secure sought after places in the best clubs and societies, she can get tickets to everything in town, long after they're sold out, and I don't think she's getting them on e-bay.

Sara's girls, aged 6 and 10 have been members of the Opera appreciation society since birth and have attended the season and the ballet since they could sit up. I heard the older one tell Gracie she could have her ticket to *Rigoletto* as she has seen it before and it's even more boring than *Carmen*. Gracie said maybe her mummy could let her come to a movie with us, to which the girl said, only if it's "culturally broadening".

Sara and I struck up a conversation about style classes for pre-teen girls (i.e. anything from 2-12!). There's nothing out there like this yet, apparently. She congratulated me on Gracie's outfit – post circus costume – and suggested I set up a blog or virtual dressing room to help mothers and girls find their signature look.

Mmm. Very gratifying. It would appear I have a string to my bow after all. I kissed the career goodbye when I found out I was expecting Freddie, deciding that when the children were older I might return to my first love, literature, and write historical novels. This had been my romantic girlish dream before I was lured to the big time and got on the corporate treadmill. But now, given the industry of mother and child oriented services and products lurking in the better village streets and at the end of the mouse pad, perhaps I *should* venture into this market place with my own offering.

I secretly think that style classes will not fly, though saying so to Sara would be foolhardy given her connections and her promise to make some calls regarding tennis for Freddie. It's just that I know how secretive and protective people are about fashion. Plenty of the mothers around town have stylists advising them on the school run look, the after gym supermarket shopping apparel and the school reading volunteer garb. But they seek this advice quietly and privately. No one admits they lack style or need expert guidance. It's a funny thing that. The line between embarrassed or enviable is a very blurry one. Certainly, in my circles, Botox parties and addictions to Diet Coke and Diet Pills seem to be less shameful than a paucity of fashion sense. It's only through Mia's gossip, courtesy of her personal shopper, that I know that a "reading mum look" exists. Goodness knows Wendy could benefit from a session or two on how to dress for her role as Parent Association President and General-Busy Body. So no, people are very defensive about their look and their children's appearance. And often downright rude about it.

I remember when I first started to go to Baby Music Appreciation when Gracie was 16 weeks – it was on my day off each week – many of those mothers would look us up and down with incredible animosity when any of my friends in the group paid Gracie or me a compliment about our dress. I was a corporate big shot - or so I thought – and had the wardrobe to match, so it was no wonder I was the envy of the mummies. But they weren't happily envious, like men tend to be, but snide and catty. Two of the women were in "Café con Leche" after a class and didn't know I was lurking nearby, waiting to meet Beth. I overheard them putting the knives into me:

"That conceited cow from the city with her bespoke tailor made pant suits and silk scarves! She should spend a little less time on her looks and a little more time with her child. That poor little girl doesn't even recognise her mother."

That was patently untrue. I had the most wonderful arrangements right from birth for Gracie – she spent more time in the office than at home during that first year. I only left the company when I realised that the family friendly policy of part time work expired when the first child turned 3. One day a week at home worked so well for me with Gracie. But there was no way I could manage the account load I was expected to carry (even full-time) with *two* small children. Not only that, but the wonderful and clingy Trudie - The Nanny, was leaving us to get married and travel the Andes, so my becoming a Stay at Home Mum was the obvious and natural choice to make. That family policy was in fact a blessing in disguise. Thanks to leaving the ad business I was able to truly embrace motherhood for the first time, revel in my second pregnancy and fully engage with all of the wonderful opportunities that small children bring about.

That was, in fact, the genesis of my "doing it from scratch domestic goddess" phase – making bunting, quilts, rugs, samplers, pottery and clothes. The baking courses all through my third trimester with Freddie have stood us in great stead ever since and the seaside themed mosaics in the children's bathroom always lighten my heart and elicit superlatives from the mothers and nannies of all visiting children. Some of the frescoes in the garden are still dinner party openers among the Pharma set as well. Not only was I able to explore my creative side, but for a while there I was the talk of the town. So resourceful, so productive and so original! As well as being a domestic goddess, I never let myself go like those women in "Café con Leche", bitching about me while tucking into their pastries and full-fat *leche*. My kids recognise me *and* I can still wear all my old work pant suits!

So, long story short – I can see that having a business that caters to the needs of mothers is a fantastic idea. But style classes is not the right thing. I wonder if I could market my literature degree or my passion for chocolate and core strength. Not sure how yet, but it would have to be a high-end offering. I won't upset my children's routines undertaking work outside the home unless it's extraordinarily well paid. Or charitable, of course.

Oops, forgot – tomorrow is the Mindfulness for Mothers Charity meditation fundraiser for tsunami victims. God, what will I wear?

Thursday, 9 July

I've spent the past few days scoping out the viability of an online business to do with chocolate. It's hard work, this entrepreneur-mum thing. I realised fairly soon it would involve huge sacrifices and getting a lot more help. I can't bear to have to interview for more staff now – the process of replacing Trudie was like a military campaign. We were lucky to find Maria at all, in hindsight, given that she was leaving the Drummonds after 5 years and really looking to get out of childcare entirely. The lengths we went to in order to secure her were quite extreme. George wooed her with promises of her own suite if she moved in. Finally she agreed to work for us provided we contributed to her rather high housing costs, across town. Leticia Drummond was astounded that we were able to swing it. Her four children had just about finished Maria off. I should think Maria has had a pretty easy time with us, since the Drummonds left (or fled?) the country – setting up hotels in South America, no less. Maria is discreet and has never run them down, but by all accounts (mostly Helen), the Drummond Four were unteachable ragamuffins. Gracie and Freddie, in contrast, are very straight-forward children. And we pay her a bomb as well.

Anyway, I don't have the head space right now for establishing a business. It's not really my thing. Moreover, at the moment, with Hillmere selection pending I can't undertake anything else. My one big external job is to help George's mother source entertainment for her party and help plan her eco-campaign to promote environmentally friendly use of the urban streetscape which she's launching at the event. I doubt my green credentials are quite up to that, but it might be fun to use my brain again.

But I know my limitations. The kids' activities and the demands of my mother-in-law and husband make for a pretty full week. My hands are raw from the gardening I did over the weekend at the school working bee. George took the children to his mother's for some creative art and craft with her sculpture consultant. Sophie had hers tutored by him last time they visited from London. Sophie's a bit much – boring and intense – but she really knows how to extend her children. Seriously, how could I even consider begging for places at "Pottery for Poppets" when Mrs G has the real thing, Ludwig, in her conservatory every month? I only regret that I can't really brag about it. The last thing we need is for Hypochondriac Kate or President Wendy to take him over. These artistic types are often very easily corrupted by a little patronage.

The children had a wonderful time too. Their creations are monstrous but lovely, and will eventually find their way out of their bedrooms and into the bin, but for now, we have a suspiciously phallic high rise office building - "Daddy's work" - sitting atop Freddie's bedside shelves and a row of garish grotesques on Gracie's window sill. It's a little frightening to confront these gargoyle-like faces when putting her to bed. I'm concerned that she might be channelling something rather dark and ominous. A manifestation of her internal demons possibly, because there's no way she's been exposed to any gargoyle imagery on my watch, apart from leafing through Felicity's scrapbook of photos from her travels in England, perhaps. Poor Gracie. Her aspect is increasingly gothic and temperamental of late. I can't think why. Note to self; arrange appointment with Emma's anxiety counsellor for Gracie. Emma's Honour has been transformed by that woman and Emma even reports that Honour is craving sugar less since seeing her. A few play based chats, some crayon drawing, a princely sum of $1700 and Honour is a different child. Almost poised, in a rather rotund and freckled way.

Anyway, my poor hands are utterly blistered and chapped after raking, pruning and weeding and then planting dozens of multi-hued perennials. They look even worse than my elbows during the weird eczema thing. It will have been worth it when the accolades flood in and the abundant blooms in the terrace garden of Mortimer Montessori spring forth next term. My only fear is that my efforts will not be duly recognised in time for Hillmere selection. Despite all of the assurances of the Working Bee Committee that Mrs Blythe would be there to note my contribution, I caught only a passing glimpse of her as she pulled away soon after I arrived, hidden behind the largest pair of Gucci sunglasses I've ever seen. Glad our fees are helping to maintain her sartorial elegance. Since she would not have seen my efforts at all, it was most prescient of me to have designed and made gorgeous little plant markers last week (a holdover from the doing it from scratch phase). As a result, the "Donated and planted by Verity and George

Fortescue" signs should assure me of further goodwill in my quest for a glowing reference for Gracie for Hillmere.

The only fly in the ointment now seems to be that Gracie is underachieving academically. I was convinced this was a blip when I saw her teachers last term. George dismissed my worries saying that children will be children (thanks for that George!), but it's never that simple. Gracie is clearly gifted and exceptional. They could well be jealous. They may be intimidated by us as a family. Or Wendy may have sown a seed in their minds. They may simply not have the resources or wherewithal to channel her creative and interpersonal genius appropriately. I feel reasonably confident that Hillmere will focus more on the soft skills, her physical accomplishments (and the financial side of the equation), rather than mere academic output. Surely, they will; she's only 5, after all.

All of the focus on Gracie means I've neglected the urgent issue of Freddie's potty training. It transpires that he picked up the expletives from Curtis and Mia's son, Toby, at play group. He told Maria. I've suggested (anonymously) that we institute a ban on foul mouthed toddlers at play group and am boycotting the sessions until the matter is resolved. Missing a few weeks has done Freddie so much good. He's speaking in sentences now and sounds like a three-year old rather than a member of a dodgy road crew and he only says poo and wee now. Helen was quite right to advise me not to draw his attention to the profanities. And poo and wee are fine words for him to use anyway. If only he wanted to do poos and wees in the toilet. Gracie stopped wearing nappies at 20 months. With Freddie Maria won't force the issue for fear of losing his love so it looks like I need to step up as bad cop. The things we do to keep a good nanny.

I've been reading up on potty training, positive messages and the psychology of excretion and trying to keep the whole thing relaxed and calm but I feel exposed by the puffy little nappy bottom in his trousers whenever we are in the garden and I see Clothilde, next door. I can almost hear the voices of her French friends – all mother's who are members of their exclusive little *societé* - "*Le Petit...*"(*Merde* I suspect) trilling about *le toilette*. The French are so chic about everything. Their babies sleep through the night from birth and as far as I can tell never actually poo. I can't imagine them having a moment's worry about anything as gross as stinky nappies.

Not that I have membership of "*Le Petit...*", so I'm only speculating as to what they really talk about. So many hours peering longingly at their on-line catalogue of French children's clothes, wishing my son could keep himself as clean and pressed as continental children and I'm still none the wiser. As well as offering a mail order clothing line, "*Le Petit...*" is a members only club of expat French women who meet monthly to discuss and workshop the state of everything that matters to them. I've managed to discover that topics range from hairstyles to dance, holidays to the new dark chocolate in the better stores. Clothilde hosts "*Le Petit...*" get togethers every couple of months when I go a little crazy and peek through the shutters trying to catch a glimpse of them. I'm even doing French on-line in the hope of catching something they say. Perhaps lip reading will help too. Anyway, Clothilde always cites "*Le Petit...*" as the source of all her best secrets in the kitchen, the laundry - and the bedroom - for that matter.

I'm desperate for more particulars or even a tiny tidbit of chic know-how, but they're as cagey as the Masons and I know nothing!

Sunday, 12 July

Mrs George dropped in today to wish Gracie luck for her interview at Hillmere, bearing Belgian chocolates and advice. She has offered to make some calls for me if I need further help. I have to admit this is tempting, but I really feel that Gracie needs to make her own way. If Grandma can open all the doors for her she'll never value the effort it takes to achieve for oneself, nor prize the success it brings. I've always had a little bit of anxiety about being too much in anyone's debt, even Mrs G's. Also if the rumour mill gets hold of news that Gracie got in through the back door, it would just about finish me off.

I must now start my research into chamber orchestras and acoustic guitarists for Mrs George's party. I suggested a jazz ensemble but she turned her very patrician nose up at that. Anyone would think I suggested a rapping DJ or French onion dip. Thankfully she has fully outsourced the decor and catering. After the bunting and cake debacle at Freddie's "seaside" themed first birthday party, I'm reluctant to take on too much responsibility. Who would have thought the older siblings would do that much damage with a bit of fabric. The Gordons still avoid me at Montessori all these months later. It's not as though I intended the bunting to become a means of tying their daughter up and keeping her away from the buffet. Nor did I intend for her to trip and flail screaming into the cake – or more accurately the 246 cupcakes handmade and individually iced and decorated and assembled (by me) in the shape of a sailing boat – thus destroying the *piece de résistance* of the entire event. It's *I* who should snub them.

How could one predict that those older children would be so cruel? Though one can hardly blame them – such an easy target. Every party she's attended since she could crawl has seen her hovering over the sweets bowl gorging herself. The mere sight of a jelly baby has her in conniptions, and no wonder, given the extremes of sugar deprivation that her rake of a mother puts her through.

Luckily, the photographer got some very good "before" shots of the garden replete with umbrellas, bunting and sails billowing in the breeze and cake centre-piece untouched and pristine, before little Katie Gordon was wheeled off wearing it. The irony is that I spent a small fortune on that fabric and the beginners sewing classes because I was so deeply committed to making everything myself. I could have sourced the whole shebang at Kmart, as many do, and still have had the dubious pleasure of seeing Anna Gordon at Pilates for the next year. I didn't sleep for over forty hours in the run up to that party. I attended to every detail; pinning up flags, planting and arranging potted flowers, preparing nibbles and seaside themed party bags full of home-made taffy and rock and preparing that edible masterpiece. The whole scene was reminiscent of Monet's *The Terrace at St Addresse*.

What was I on during that time? I gave my life over to the ideal of domestic self sufficiency and being the most creative, practical and gifted homemaker. Sure, the roman blinds in George's study are themselves a study in workmanship, but glass blowing was a bit extreme, even for me. While I curried a lot of favour at Montessori with the sheep costumes for the Christmas play last year, I'm eternally grateful that Freddie's party was such a disaster or I would be baking and freezing a million profiteroles now for George's annual staff picnic/garden party. No, the Katie Gordon cake debacle was a blessing in disguise. As it is, I lose far too much sleep on the whole theme of entertainment, even when I employ caterers and outsource the hard lifting as I now do.

Which reminds me – must call Felicity to discuss the menu for George's Do. Beth is still pushing me to do some filling and plumping with that party in mind. I just can't seem to make her see that much as I'd like to look 25, everyone knows when it's fake and I would prefer to age gracefully. It's bad enough Mum having her hands done and then spending most of her time in the sun or riding horses. There was never a better put together equestrienne on this earth. Being married to a senior executive of the country's second largest pharmaceuticals conglomerate does not mean I have to go about looking like I'm sampling *all* his products. Evidently Kate and Beth don't agree.

Wednesday, 15 July

Gracie has finally settled down after an intense and emotional evening of cramming for the Hillmere interview tomorrow. The anxiety counsellor was pretty firm in his view that the interview is the source of her recent troubles (the moods, the poor attainment at school and the most recent – pinching Freddie - phase). While Dr Bennett claims not to see this sort of behaviour in pre-adolescents, he was adamant that her issues are symptomatic of extreme stress. I *knew* Gracie was advanced. Even as a newborn she had a knowing look of incredible intelligence. She's an old soul. Nevertheless, I don't want her to be self harming at 8, so I need to help her work through this anxiety. I'm really worried about this self harming thing. Yvette, from my ad agency days, called in tears from Paris, just last week. Her eldest has been cutting herself at school – with a compass, no less. She's only 13. It's heart breaking. I've decided to use this entry in my inner child journal to unbundle my feelings about the schools admission process. Maybe if I can get clearer about what I want for Gracie I can be fairer to her.

Hillmere will be so wonderful for her. It offers the best in musical, language, and extra-curricular tuition, wonderful school trips, deportment and elocution classes, dance and movement courses and a virtual guarantee of a place at the better universities. The only downside is the pressure on her at such a tender age. Will she burn out and give up? Perhaps there is both too much competition to get into the school and too much competition to excel once there. Maybe she could afford to cruise for a while and just stay at Montessori for two more years like the majority of the children do. Helen's brood have been very happy and well adjusted there and the older two have gone on to a very acceptable primary school. Clearly keeping the options simple and low-key can pay off.

Truthfully, I'm very conflicted about this. I do subscribe to the view that children should be children and enjoy freedom to play and invent and create. By the same token most of the other children Gracie's age, even the less ambitious ones, have twice the hobbies and interests their parents have. Even without Hillmere to prepare for, keeping her out of activities and classes would be wilfully handicapping her.

After the interview tomorrow we can take stock and perhaps she can scale back some of the activities. I know that she gets tired. Most Fridays she's not even prepared to roll on the floor at Kinder Gym. But, it'll be very difficult to select an activity to drop. She loves ballet, art, science club and yoga, music appreciation and "Mini-Chef", while swimming and the high dive are just for fun. We already dropped water ballet after the near drowning episode. I was able to withdraw without penalty from Toddler Travel Languages as well and now Maria speaks Spanish and French to her. We have yet to take up chess – that was to be George's "thing". And I'm pleased we did not pursue Cantonese. Both Mia and Beth say their nannies can't keep up with the homework in Chinese. So that just leaves violin and Tai Chi. Perhaps she can choose for herself between those two. After all, Hillmere will be offering so much music.

But, what if she doesn't get in? I can hardly bear to think that scenario through. I've been very discrete about the application and told only a few people that we're trying for Hillmere so there'll be limited damage control to do if we're unsuccessful. And there's still the Frobisher Academy to try for. It's not Hillmere, but it's academically strong and it would extend her. Sophie suggested Frobisher's to me last year when they were considering returning here from London. If she'd consider it then I know it must be a strong academic school. Sophie knows everything about schools and academic excellence. George Skyped her the other week. They had an in-depth one-sided conversation from her son's swimming gala, while she quizzed the second child, Claude, about waves - sound and other kinds - and how noise and light travel. He's 4, but according to George, on the ball. Maybe hot-housing *is* the way to go.

I don't know what to do. Have we left it too late? To hear Mrs G describe Sophie's regimen with those kids, mine will look like imbeciles next to hers should they ever come back. Secretly crossing my fingers and praying that the lure of London and Europe is more compelling than any backwater lifestyle upsides she might discover here. Nevertheless, if Frobisher is good enough for Sophie then we would be lucky to get Gracie in, her giftedness aside. Apart from Frobisher, there are not many other options. If she stays at Mortimer Montessori another two years, we'll still have to face a move then or risk her getting lost in mediocrity and striving. Perhaps we'll have to move across town? Sometimes I think it would be easier if George made less money. Then our choices would be so limited as to make all this stress unnecessary.

I shall put these negative concerns aside and channel lots of positive energy Gracie's way for tomorrow.

The day will be full on. Meditation first thing with Asana, interview from 9-12, lunch with Gracie afterwards, swimming with Clothilde, then I have a pre-session at Beth's therapist. Beth is insisting that I look haggard despite my journaling and I need to unbundle more effectively. I am only going to appease her – it's either a therapy try out or a dermal fill! She won't take no for an answer, and frankly, I don't have the will to fight her. Finally, the day will end with drinks at the new tapas bar downtown with Beth and Mia.

Note to self – Maria needs to cook George's dinner. Or at least defrost the coq au vin.

Saturday, 18 July

I can barely find the energy to type this. What a week. Hillmere was the most gruelling and intense experience of my life – let alone Gracie's. It was abundantly obvious from the very start that she was overwhelmed and underprepared. The intake at age 6 is only 16. She has no chance. They asked her what she thought of the government's plans to tackle global warming. Half my friends couldn't answer that. Let alone their five year olds. The only area in which she clearly shone was the physical. She was poised and wonderful during the demonstration of her dance, gymnastics and yoga abilities. I know already that the spelling and maths were hard for her. She completely bungled the Speaking Task – secret topic mind you – 2 minutes on *Why I love school* – (she just talked about painting and being allowed to make messes in the art rooms) but to her credit, she finished the tests and even smiled through the whole horrible morning. I nearly lost it when they asked her to spell Othello – seriously!

That was the straw that broke the camel's back. She won't get a place.

I have to admit (to myself, not to Beth) – Beth's therapist helped me to see that Hillmere may not be right for her (or me). Hillmere is just not in her destiny. So I'm starting to regroup and plan for that eventuality. She's a gorgeous and talented child and will thrive wherever she goes. I have to acknowledge that preparing for Hillmere was extremely intense and I've pushed her much too hard for the past 9 months. And yes, having someone to talk to about this who is not herself currently engaged in a similar process was very therapeutic.

Mind you, I'm still none the wiser as to where the Inner Child Journal comes into the treatment (didn't like to ask), but it *was* only the first session.

Having said that, I don't know if I'll go back for more. While I do need to get more clarity about my goals and how to work towards them, I think I can do so on my own. Therapy is beneficial in lots of ways, but somehow I can't help feeling that the underpinning assumption is that one has to be a bit screwed up and I just don't want to believe that about myself. I have a set of healthy neurosis that enable, rather than impede, my passage through life. Certainly nothing that a glass of Sauvignon Blanc, an entry in the journal or a good chat with friends cannot fix. Let me caveat that – a good chat with the *right* friends.

Whatever should happen with the schools admission process, Gracie is like a different child now. It's as though a huge weight has dropped from her shoulders. As we drove out of Hillmere's imposing wrought iron gates she looked back and said:

"Mummy, I don't think I would like to go to school there. It's boring to have to talk about the world all the time." The past two nights she's slept so well. She begged me to let her miss violin yesterday and announced there will be no more talking French with Maria.

I'll happily acquiesce if it helps her relax and enjoy what she's doing more. I don't want her burning out before Frobisher interviews next month. Frobisher has a very different approach. They meet us and chat for 30 minutes. The written application is key and as that's already submitted, I can relax.

The worst part of the whole gruelling nightmare of a day, though, was Mia's smug face at drinks after that terrible interview. Georgiana (first marriage – better genes) is now in fifth grade at Hillmere and by all accounts is doing very well. However, despite the grand name, Georgiana is very plain and serious, so proof that one can't have it all, irrespective of Mia's conviction to the contrary.

Mia is without a doubt one of the most self assured, strident and dogmatic people on this earth and while she would do anything for anyone – provided she was wearing Prada and Todd's and the children were off her hands at the time, and best of all so long as she could regale all and sundry with the tawdry details later – she delights in the troubles and worries of her female friends. It's beyond mere Schadenfreude. She truly revels in the idea that she is luckier, funnier, wealthier, better dressed and more spoilt than anyone she knows. While all of that may be true, her days are filled with up-market banality. She has nothing to talk about apart from her stylist's love life, her manicurist's botched face lift and her boring, not really friends', problems. After a session with her I feel like taking a shower. Goodness knows I have nothing more interesting to say some days, but I'm not smug, superior and complacent with it. She said to me last night, as I recounted the stress of Gracie's interview:

"Darling, relax. No one expects your little moppets to get into these schools. You were a hot shot at university and married quite well, but George isn't exactly an oil painting, nor a rocket scientist. I know you can afford it but frankly, there's something a little nasty about getting rich off Viagra and diabetes drugs and then sending your children to school on the proceeds. Also you're not like us. Mitch made a mint in New York, we've got homes in three countries and I divorced a cattle station heir. I *have* to get my kids into these ridiculous academies."

I could have poured her fourth flute of Veuve down the ample enhanced cleavage and all $785 worth of faux lamé gold singlet ruined in one fell tip. But a restraining glance from Beth stopped me and I just knocked the rest of my glass off with a (I hope) wry smile.

"So true Mia", I said graciously.

Yet, here I am, journaling it! She's too much. Worst of all, I know she's probably right at so many levels. And to cap it off – she will waste no time gossiping about me with the next poor sod she meets. I abhor the idea of fraternising with her at every school fundraiser. I shudder at the thought of seeing her ever again given what she said about George and me.

The knowledge that for months I made Hillmere my sole focus and goal is gut-wrenching now. Poor little Gracie. Why did I do this to her? What made me think she needs *deportment* - in the twenty-first century? Perhaps I should go away for a while and return transformed into some sort of whole foods, raw diet, greenie, hippie mother who can get away with her kids being average and hapless because she's saving the planet and curing cancer. That has to be better than an alcohol induced fuzz of a life or worse still, a rollercoaster of cocaine induced highs and lows such as Mia's set enjoy. Is my own ridiculous quest to keep up with the women like Emma and Beth really any better? Perhaps hypochondriacs like Kate are in the best place after all; far more concerned about their bodies and their health than their kids' schools. So much healthier!

It's dawning on me that my problems lie partly in my cultivating the wrong sorts of people. I need a new crew! Say Helen, the earth mother. Or Hard-Done-By-Harriet from play group, who I somehow became friendly with when Francine and Mia were being particularly toxic earlier this year. Harriet is a breath of fresh air in the world of competitive parenting. She has never once attempted to outdo another mother. Innocently thinking that this meant she was more together and a source of fresh perspective I suggested a play date.

That was a mistake. It soon became clear that she is not into competitive parenting because her ploy is to seek attention through competitive victimhood. Indeed, her mantra is "woe is me". No one has it worse than Harriet. She gets less sleep than anyone I know, has more stress than anyone alive, struggles to make do on less money, has less support from her family, has a husband who is humourless and harder working than anyone and her children are the victims of the most bullying. Traditionally known as a whinger, Harriet breaks the mould, in that she seems to revel in her misery. She not only delights in feeling bad about her lot in life she seems to take comfort from the fact that everyone else is relatively better off than her. Indeed to hear her speak of them you would swear that everyone else was put on the Earth solely to make her feel worse about herself. If anyone attempts to moan about their lot, she immediately relates their issues to herself and concludes that they have nothing to complain about, but must be trying to make her feel worse. In fact, she often comments that these people think she's beneath them, given how readily they discuss their problems in front of her; she being so badly off to start with. I actually think it would be very bad for me to befriend her. When Harriet starts in on a complaint about someone who thinks they have it bad but are incredibly lucky compared to her, my eyes glaze over and I start to lose the will to draw breath. It certainly puts my stress into a fresh perspective.

For example, Freddie is an angel from Heaven when compared with her youngest son, Hilary. The name alone tells the story. Hilary is a Handful for Hard-Done-By-Harriet. For anyone else his high-jinks might be regarded as trying or precocious but Harriet is making him worse. She drones on about him while he sits next to her, clawing at her face, listening avidly, hanging on every word, knowing that all her negative attention is preferable to hearing her complain about everything else in her life. He gets his reward for being troublesome when she reprimands him and interrupts her monologue with criticism of his noise levels, failure to share or messy eating.

Over the past month he has had a growth spurt, physically and mentally, and has suddenly mastered the art of noisy and tearless crying, falling and wailing without actually bleeding or bruising, and bullying and pushing the other children just enough to invite the longed for attention from his mother, but not enough to precipitate payback from the children in question. Very intelligent.

She never has a smile or a kind word for him. If she were my mother I would run away. I would pack my nursery backpack and head for the hills. Indeed there would probably by a few mates that I could persuade to join me. I would set up a commune for the children of neurotic, whining, miserable parents that never should have had children. That poor child is condemned to a life of complaint and unreasonable expectation. Nothing he does will ever meet her standards. Given how miserable she is with her life at large, he will no doubt grow up to be a frightful bore, or a sociopath.

Ok, so not Harriet, but, between play group, Gracie and Freddie's schedule of activities and Montessori, not to mention my own interests, I'm not short of female acquaintances; working mums, stay-at-home mums, working-from-home mums, part-time-sharing-custody mums, lesbian mums, grandmother mums, nannies-who-really-do-all-the-mothering mums, stay-at-home-dad mums, 40-going-on-18 mums, 30-going-on-50 mums, wanna-be mums, coulda-shoulda-woulda-been mums, sourced-from-the-sperm-bank mums, yummy ones, slummy ones, big-fat-tummy ones, the ubiquitous screaming-in-the-supermarket-aisle ones and my personal favourite – speaking-loudly-in-false-posh-voice-to-show-off-how-great-I-am-at-this mums. I know loads of women and with few exceptions none of them are any less child focused than me.

We all obsess about our kids, research the ideal diets, exercise, stimulation and education for them. We all lie awake worrying about what to put in party bags. We all stare at them in wonderment when they do anything new. We would lay down our lives for them in a heartbeat. We would not be mothers if we didn't. Sure, those working ones, like Yvette in Paris and Clothilde (if you can call social director to "*Le Petit...*", working), seem to hold the obsessions at bay. No doubt they are pretty good at hiding their aspirations for their children because they have fulfilled some of their ambitions for themselves. But the ones who work and have not fulfilled their ambitions (Sophie is a good case in point) are still just as obsessed with ballet and giftedness and who is reading the most advanced book (or in Sophie's case translating it into Latin), as the next under-stimulated, full-time mummy.

All this competition and striving for schools is no better for the mothers than it is for the children. George agrees – not because he has any profound understanding of what Gracie and I have been through, mind you. He's just tired of me being so distracted. Honestly, he's very infantile sometimes. It's like having three children. He needs so much nurturing and attention. I concede I've completely lost sight of his needs lately. To remedy this I've enrolled in a new adult education programme – *Introduction to the Male Psyche* – which I hope will teach me new ways of engaging with him.

Ooh. Perhaps I'll make some friends on this course.

Monday, 27 July

I've just come home from the first class in the Male Pysche course. I cancelled my monthly Mah-Jong with Clothilde and two of the girls from *"Le Petit..."* to attend so I'm even more annoyed than I might otherwise be. I'm struggling with Mah-Jong, I have to admit. I asked Clothilde if I could join her group in a pretentious bid to differentiate myself from all the book clubbers.

Let's face it, we've been book clubbing for donkey's years. It's so terribly clichéd and predictable. Half the women watch the film and pretend to be readers, while the other spout forth all the erudite critics' drivel they download from the internet, thinking it validates them as intellectual heavyweights. They either read a diet of self-help trash or choose the most boring books on the best seller list in order to further throw one off the scent; a ploy along the lines of "no, we're not airheads who never picked up a book until we heard about thirty-something celebrities that read", all the while confirming just how poorly read, ill-informed and adolescent they truly are when 20 minutes into a book discussion their conversations veer so easily into the banal gossip of the neighbourhood families, their husbands' bedroom statistics or who is shagging whom in Hollywood. What hogwash. At least at Mah Jong the struggle to keep abreast of the rules as explained in French creates about a thousand new opportunities to combat dementia and pass vesicles across synapses. It's like an electrical storm in my brain!

Nevertheless, after an evening of *Introduction to the Male Psyche* I actually think a discussion of some gimmicky pop psychology tome might have been a better use of my time. Complete nonsense. Worse than *Intro to Flower Arranging*. I'm such a sucker. It was pitched so low. The average age of the attendee was 23; nerdy girls with no hope of catching a man, opting for adult classes over just living and getting out there to meet some drippy mate who will hold their hand and tell them they're beautiful when clearly they're not and never will be, at least on the outside.

Naively believing this course might be intelligent or insightful, I mentioned that I was enrolled to take *Intro to the Male Psyche* at the school pick up yesterday, to amused smirks and knowing looks from the other parents there. Even Luscious Larry had a look of benevolent condescension on his otherwise rugged and handsome face.

"Verity, surely you're an expert on the male psyche by now," giggled Tedious Tabitha, all tight t-shirt and painted nails, protuberant backside wobbling as she flirted with Larry, before flabbily poncing off to whisper loudly to Wendy who of course was single-handedly sorting out the school office, that:

"Verity must be having marital troubles – she's going on another night course". Not that I care if they think that, given I know for a fact (virtually), thanks to Mia, that Wendy's Paul is an habitual Viagra user. Seriously. I know Wendy would be hard work, but impotence?

Tedious Tabitha – so inconsequential - if her uncanny grasp of the obvious were not so astute, one might tolerate her a little more. Every aspect of her life is explained in boring, minute detail – how she boiled the eggs for breakfast, where she buys petrol and how she gets the kids to brush their teeth. My God. It's all I can do to stand there. Poor Larry. His body language is so open and welcoming but seriously, he needs to get more discerning while waiting at the gate. Life's too short to hear Tabitha's soliloquy on where to buy strawberries.

It's very frustrating that no one is prepared to discuss anything apart from their kids and their problems at pick up. I'll have to revise my park and walk approach to collecting Gracie. I'd be better off in my air-conditioned bubble listening to pop music, than standing around making idle small talk to these people who have less imagination than a cricket bat. I might start sending Maria to pick up in my place. Tough call. Nanny collecting will set tongues a-flapping of course.

Pick-up frustrations are tiresome but even worse is that this earnest attempt to enliven my own marriage and gain greater awareness as to how men generally and George, in particular, think, was such a waste of time and indeed, *pre-emptively* perceived as a waste of time as well by all of those parents at school, none of whom knows anything about psychology, psyches or adult education, for that matter. My problem is that I'm too quick to divulge my business. I hereby resolve that I'll no longer tell anyone what I'm doing. I'll be mysterious and guarded. I shall have "appointments" and "prior engagements", instead of broadcasting the news of my great session at the gym or my next night class or what I read in the paper. If asked outright what I've been doing, I'll say "having lots of meetings" or "working the phones". No more name dropping either. I'll start shopping across town and occasionally be very late to pick-up, dinners and coffee meets with a made-up excuse such as "Held up in town, so sorry".

The truth is, I just don't feel right at the moment. I feel lost and frustrated. I've Googled all my symptoms and can't get a clear read on what could be wrong with me. I almost called Kate for a diagnosis earlier. George is never around. Between work and business dinners and his men's nights out, he's home to see the kids only two or three nights a week. Gracie is now refusing to attend any and all of her classes and is pointedly taking double the normal time to do everything I ask of her. Meanwhile, Freddie is pooing everywhere but in the pottie. Maria is threatening to leave us for an American woman at ballet who has offered her a Vesper and an i-Pad if she signs on. Who are these people? On top of that, I have three humungous purple spots on my chin and I missed my detoxing yoga class today due to an appointment for Freddie at the child psychologist who for $350 tells me *he* is fine and maybe *I* need to relax!

Aaaggghhh!

Now I have no choice but to open a bottle of wine and shop on line for the next hour to anaesthetise the pain!

Tuesday, 4 August

I'm convinced George is having an affair. He's like a bear with a sore head and even more worryingly, he has started going to the gym again. I saw him checking out his profile nude in the bathroom mirror this morning, sucking in his stomach and admiring his newly tautened biceps. Not that I'm complaining – he looks better and is doing brilliantly in the office. But he's never been much into gyms or scheduling workouts, more a casual jog, spontaneous bike ride kind of guy. Something's definitely up with him. Mia told Beth that she thinks he has at least one mistress based on her sighting of him in that new tapas bar last week. He was with two male colleagues apparently, but they seemed to be very interested in the waitresses; reminding Mia of her first husband's fall from grace all those years ago when she had him tailed by her private detective brother-in-law. How seedy. Beth has his number if I want it.

What's most curious is how Mia manages to find herself all over town, at all hours of the day and night, while seemingly remaining so engaged with her current husband and *three* children. She has fantastic help, it has to be said, round the clock. Money does talk, after all. Normally I would just laugh off her suspicions but this preening and recent self-consciousness on George's part is starting to really worry me. Also, regular exercise should be making him happier, not more irritable. It's all very perplexing.

Perhaps the private detective idea does have some merit since the extra-curricular class idea has crashed and burned. After the second class of Male Psyche 101 I dropped out. I could have done it with a little more subtlety, I admit. I fell asleep during the second hour. The topic was "Boys will be Boys" and the lecturer was covering guns and cars as emblems of manhood. I nodded off – for only a minute or two, I swear. Freddie had been up most of Sunday night vomiting putty, bird seed and sand. He's been rebelling against small motor skills development work all week and obviously decided to act out his frustration by eating all the offending substances that Mummy and Maria were forcing him to play with. So yesterday after several loads of washing (done by Carla, but supervised by me, because she's incompetent), doctor's visits and seeing Felicity to discuss the catering for George's Do next weekend, I was close to collapsing by the time I arrived at the Women's Discussion Centre for the course.

I stumbled in 10 minutes late, was greeted by a stony and pointed silence from the dais, and went on to upset the class by interrupting to ask the teacher whether we would be covering sport as an emblem of manhood (personally, I think sport and cars are far more relevant in our part of town, than guns, but hey ho). I then forgot the name of one of the attendees (mousey, floral and forgettable), at the tea break, having no recollection of meeting her last week. She was very annoyed (and possibly unhinged) as she flounced away, fighting back tears, slamming into chairs and muttering to herself. I know George and Gracie react like that to me sometimes – but strangers?!

Well after tea, during which no one else spoke to me and I was forced to undo all my good work at the gym and eat stale chocolate digestives in order to look busy after Floral Girl stormed off, the crap about men needing fast cars continued and before I knew it, I dropped my leather notebook and silver Mont Blanc pen with a clatter on the floor as I fell asleep, my head hitting the desk. The bang woke me up just in time to save said pen from the greasy hands of the uptight chick dressed in black sitting in front of me. Thank God I woke then. While I could have used the shut-eye, I wouldn't want to be seen muttering or dribbling in my sleep amongst that crowd. It was evident I was bored out of my brains. The 27 mice turned to stare at me, shocked and appalled by my rude disturbance and the lecturer suggested I absent myself unless I was ready to pay proper attention. I said I would, but it was more peaceful in her lecture than at my home given the regurgitation propensities of my son; speaking of which, would they be prepared to cover the arena of male excurgitation at large, I inquired ironically, whereupon I was asked to leave. Immediately.

Then it was *me* flouncing out slamming into chairs. My demands for a refund were met with an icy and prim "not on your life, madam". So I drove around the so-called "discussion" centre car park screeching my tires and brakes for the next 12 minutes to get back at those crazy women chauvinists inside. My head still hurts from where I hit the table. There's already a bump and a chunky blue bruise on my forehead. I stopped at the organic pharmacy on the way home to buy arnica, narrowly missing Kate on one of her over-the-counter-drug sprees, but it's not really helped. I look as though George has been beating me.

George was delighted to see me - Freddie asleep in his lap. His quiet night in had been ruined by the children, Maria having left early with a temperature. I was blamed for the fact George had to take care of his son in an Oscar worthy passive aggressive display of Masculine Psyche – the ins and outs of which are still a mystery to me having wasted 4 hours and $450 on the scintillating topics of fast cars, gangs, male bonding and beer. So, now I'm waging yet another cold war stand off against George. I refuse to be resented by him for his having to parent his children for two hours mid-week. And after all of that, I still have no idea what's actually wrong with him. After the angry handover of Freddie it was George's turn to flounce off – to his study. Sometimes he behaves like Francine about her eldest two - as if the children were irritating pets he had agreed to buy to indulge me. Yet another topic for discussion with the psychologist – could *his* attitude be affecting Freddie's toileting?

George seems to think that he deserves a medal for going to work and a red carpet and hero's welcome on his return. A ticker-tape parade every Friday night? *I'd* work if I could make the money he makes for doing as little. I don't mean he doesn't earn it, but it's not exactly front line or dangerous. I daresay the learning for me is that I should think twice before signing up for courses. How dare I not have back up babysitting organised! Or rather, I should stay home every night and massage George's feet, minister to malingering nannies and tend to the attention-seeking ploys of the children, while mincing about in suggestive night clothes.

Oops.

George just reappeared. Overcame his sulk in record time. Sheepishly asked whether all is going to plan for his client party on Saturday.

"Yes George, dahling," I cooed. "Don't worry. I'll do you proud, as always, my sweet." Auuughrh.

Saturday, 8 August

Well today was the Do. George invited 85 of his closest clients to the event – a garden party – and spouses and children were also invited. It was a huge undertaking but it went swimmingly. Felicity and her amazing team did a magnificent job with the food and drinks and everyone complimented me on the event, the children, the garden and the weather (not to mention the mosaics in the guest bathrooms). I took full credit for all of it, not revealing the army of backroom helpers who got us to the day and who are still downstairs cleaning and sorting crockery and glassware. I deserve a little credit for all I do and put up with around here.

We invited Luscious Larry and his wife Rose since she heads up a very well-regarded medical practice in town. Larry's so sweet. The nicest and least emasculated stay-at-home dad I know. I met some lovely new people too, which was a bonus after the past few weeks of stress and worry. I'm long overdue for some fresh company. I've made arrangements to show a new girl around town this week. Desirée, mother of two angelic girls – she said – they were not in attendance but home with Nana, newly arrived from Boston. She's married to Phil who, while a little long-in-the-tooth, will report directly to George. Desirée is about my age, from the east coast of the US, but she grew up in the UK. She's very well put together, utterly natural, funny and charming. We made plans to meet up this week and see an exhibit at the Gallery.

George was very pleased with how the day went and was quite his old self this evening; jolly and funny and flirtatious and very appreciative of my hard work. I almost forgave him for his being (to borrow the expression from Freddie) "such a shit" these past few weeks. Well, I did forgive him - he is the love of my life after all - but he'll need to earn his way back into *all* of my good books. I'm not losing my granny nightdress on account of one pleasant party. However, I do see that I need to be more mindful concerning George; to appreciate him more. Just a few minutes with Desirée made me rethink my cold hearted view of him. I realize that he's very fragile in lots of ways, and he needs more nurturing and cosseting. Desirée is convinced that all men need to be treated like children. I'm not sure about that – Larry doesn't - but I know George is under a lot of pressure at work. I feel very silly suspecting him of an affair or anything untoward. He's just been working too hard.

Inspired by Desirée, I will try to be more wifely and cheerful.

Friday, 14 August

Desirée is just great. We've spent most of the week together – art gallery, cancer fund-raiser lunch, hairdresser and taking the children boating on the lake after school today. Her daughters *are* angels - Rafaela and Gabriella to be exact – and love Gracie. We all had an amazingly relaxing time together. For the first time in months I feel as if I've heard a new idea! Desirée is inspiring. She has no help, other than an occasional ironing lady, a cleaner 4 hours a week and a babysitter. Yet she's very calm and Zen-like about everything. She raised her voice one time – when Gabriella almost knocked Freddie into the lake while I was retying Gracie's hair ribbon – but otherwise is completely unphased by anything to do with mothering. She tells me her mother was a fabulous role model and loved and enjoyed all aspects of parenting and spending time with her children.

How I envy her that example of parenting. Sure, I can emulate Desirée's style in certain respects but how can I ever undo my past – my mother? Experts say that 50% of a person's mindset or approach to life is accounted for by genes. What hope have I got? I've worked very hard to overcome the legacy of a propensity towards perfectionism and control; with success, I should add. I absolutely refuse to raise the children in the way Mum raised Felicity and me. Her idea of fun was watching "60 Minutes" with me. Now her idea of a good time is grooming her horses and choosing hats for the next race day. I accept she's a caring and devoted grandmother – though how hard is it to capture the attention of a three and five year old with a paddock full of horses, a paddling stream and a huge house to enjoy?

Despite which, she has very little to say that's of interest to me. Most of our conversations – the weekly courtesy call, every Wednesday morning – descend into critiques of my life. I completely zone out. I go to my "happy place" and become very still while she goes on about my latest error in judgement or suggests things I should be doing with my time. Perhaps my non-engagement with her only makes things worse. Felicity says I need to give her a role in my life. No vacancies right now.

Mind you, this has been going on since I met George, exacerbated by my decision to stay home when I was pregnant with Freddie. She thinks I sold out when I gave up work; fears I will be widowed young as she was – relatively speaking - and be lost without a career or interests outside the home. Apparently I am bereft of ambition and motivation. Meanwhile, she approves of Felicity, puts her on a pedestal; Felicity is hard working, entrepreneurial and successful. Her husband is vivacious and laconic (i.e. overweight and jolly), while George can be "hard to connect with". Seriously. George connects with everything.

Naturally, Felicity's not complaining – anymore. Mum's control, domination and indoctrination of her – Mum was completely done in by the time she got to me – as to the importance of domestic perfection, academic excellence and exacting standards of cleanliness and exquisite preparation, has been the foundation for the success of "Felicitations". So sure, Felicity has nothing to moan about now. She forgets though that she fled the scene when Dad died - needing 7 years abroad to find herself and rebel against Mum's control before she found what she really wanted to do with her life. Now with her incredibly "successful" husband (making a fortune whitening and brightening the smiles of women like Francine, Wendy and Mia) and cute Jessica, who just happens to be a "gifted horsewoman" already, she's the apple of Mum's eye.

I don't deserve the criticism though. Mum has had nothing but pleasant and solicitous kindness from me. By the time she noticed me, during the bulimia thing, her work was virtually done for her. She didn't need to put in any energy at all. For a start I was four years behind Felicity, feeding on the scraps and hand-me-downs and learning quickly what to do to keep out of Mum's way. Study hard, be sensible, practice diligently, use impeccable manners. She seemed to have neither the need nor the inclination to take me on after the Felicity Saga ended. Of course, the timing was perfect. Three days after Dad's funeral, Felicity flew to Rome.

Mum had no choice but to accept me just the way I was then. We were close for a while, given the circumstances. And we had a few things in common; literature, tennis, old movies. But I was neither young nor impressionable. Even if Mum had wanted to mould me into the Ideal Daughter, and Dad's premature death and Felicity's departure hadn't robbed her of her *raison d'etre*, she knew there was nothing she could change in me, anyway.

Funnily, those years with Felicity away were the best time in our relationship. Mum was gentler then, kind and caring. She stopped being controlling and exacting and just let go of so many little things that she used to think were important, leaving me to my own devices. Felicity says I'm Mum's favourite because she came home to find Mum so altered - softer and vulnerable. But the reality is that it was only when Felicity came home, settled down and started focussing on her business that Mum seemed to recover her resolve, regain a sense of purpose and meaning. It was as if, seeing Felicity working hard and building something, Mum felt her parenting efforts had been worthwhile after all.

Felicity's return validated all of that work. Mum recovered her sense of purpose and regained her passion for life. It was then that she bought the farm and began riding again. All of that steel and strength that got her through Dad's cancer and all of the dogged persistence that saw her through Felicity's adolescence when she pushed Felicity and rode her harder than her toughest thoroughbred for more than 10 years, came back, flinty and hard. It was as if she'd been in hibernation.

For the past decade she's worked like a demon to build the ranch, one-eyed about success and excellence and obsessed with the animals and her local fraternity of horsey people. I applaud her. She's channelled all of that restored energy into creating something amazing. She breeds champions, looks unbelievable and is respected by everyone in racing. One would think that might be enough. But no, despite all of that, she can't leave me be. The day she bought that farm she started in on me – the one project she has yet to complete! And she's barely stopped since.

I've lost track of where I was going... Oh yes, Desirée is going to be a great asset to my circle. I must be sure to keep her well away from Francine and Mia though. And steer her through the troubled waters at ballet. No one should have to take on that lot on their own.

Freddie has been doing so well this past week. His potty training seems to have taken a positive turn. Maria and I are filling up his star chart so fast that he's due his prize – a new mini-electronic whiteboard with magnetic side. He said he wanted new Duplo – something with dinosaurs - but he has so much of that plastic stuff. It's pretty pedestrian really. George has agreed to come with us to go shopping and have high tea afterwards at the Drummond Bar. We love the Drummond Bar for family celebrations. It's all the more special since the Drummonds left the country (I heard that the tax office is after them for unpaid stamp duty and sales tax) and Maria joined us.

George wants to buy Freddie a mini Porsche Cayenne (one of his clients did this for his three year old when he aced a kindergarten admissions interview). I'm trying to impress on George the importance of him not buying Freddie's love. Freddie's too young for the Cayenne. I learnt enough at Male Psyche 101 to appreciate that a car is key to Freddie developing an appropriate sense of his own masculinity and will be integral to his bonding with George, but it's just over the top at this age. What will he have to look forward to when he starts school? Big game fishing?

Freddie has just appeared bleary eyed and half asleep at the bedroom door and clambered into bed beside me, all cute and soapy smelling. Such a darling little man. He starts Montessori in just a few months. My baby will be a big school boy with a back pack and a lunch box (no Duck shop for him!). A little part of me thinks it might be time to talk about another baby. I mentioned that to Beth. She practically yelled at me:

"Get a grip! Get a new kitchen, redo the garden. NO more children!"

I'm not sure though. I love the baby stage and Maria is great with the little ones. If only I knew what would be best. Desirée shares my wistfulness about more babies. She always wanted 4 children but Phil won't have any more. She's reconciled herself to this saying that since

Gabriella is now 4 the baby days are really behind them. Plus, Desirée is studying part time and doesn't want help. Not that it matters. Phil adamantly refuses to discuss it and is threatening having "a snip" if she so much as looks at a crib or an ovulation kit. Phil's old. And he's a worrier. From where I stand – and I barely know him – he seems like a bit of an old woman. Worst of all, he's awkward around his own daughters. That always sets my alarm bells jangling. I don't think he's a bad man, just a bit weird and way too intense. She could do a lot better, but love is blind.

Monday, 17 August

Desirée makes everything look so easy. Should I enrol at uni again? Perhaps a proper course is just what I need. Desirée is studying Classics. She already has a Masters in Law. What would I do? I want to tap into my creative side. But how? Interior design is too obvious. Half of the children at Hillmere have parents in interior or garden design, while the parents of the other half either travel for a living, retired at 40 and do goodness knows what with their time or are terribly socially responsible and save the children and the rainforests all year round.

Maybe I should learn another language or become a Pilates instructor. Or a personal trainer. George says physical training is beneath my dignity. Jealous of all the men I would meet if I had a life outside the home, no doubt. I know I dismissed the idea of having a business last month when I was thinking about the style/chocolate website, but maybe I was too hasty. Have I lost all ambition? Is Mum right about me? I'm going to take this question as my wish to meditation with Asana next time I see her.

Beth called today to "compare notes on the Inner Child Experience". Yeah, right. All I heard about was hers. She was really calling to moan and to apologise for being so distant and to convince herself that the rumours about my lovely new BFF are unfounded. Her inner child has needed a lot of maintenance and nurturing this past month and so she has been "in Siberia" as she puts it. She has withdrawn Zach from nursery school on the grounds that they were serving biscuits for afternoon tea and watching TV. Oh and they didn't appoint her to the board of governors after a very committed period of campaigning. Can't say I blame her on that score. Now she has to get Zach into another Nursery before he begins Prep at Fauntleroy Junior next year.

Never one to let a few worries stand in the way of an indulgent treat, Beth offered to take me to Baths of Vespasian – her favourite spa - to share in a little therapeutic pick us up after her big inner child month. I acquiesced willingly. She's so desperate to compete with Desirée for my time. Moreover, she's completely out of humour with Mia. After five too many Cosmopolitans at a spina bifida cocktail evening last week, Mia told her that I'm following Desirée around like a lapdog and then apparently invited Beth's husband to the opera - in Venice! They're no longer speaking – Beth and Mia - that is.

I told Beth this would happen. She's very flippant with Yves. She thinks it makes her seem more French. She's not French. He had French and that went badly. This time he did not want French. When will she see that he loves her as she is and no amount of therapy or lap bands will alter her intrinsic beauty or value to him? She has a heart of gold and wants earnestly to make everything in the world right and good. Who could ask for more? I shall tell her on our spa day.

As for Mia! She needs help. Her personality was not great to start with, but it's getting uglier as she ages and the drinking is out of control, even for her. According to my sources at ballet – goodness knows I've been avoiding her since the post-Hillmere interview drinks party - she does the school run drunk at least three times a week after her lunches and alcohol infused life painting sessions. She thinks swerving into a gaggle (can't think of a more apt collective noun) of handsome school boys in boater hats is de rigueur for the wife of an exotic ex-trader who races fast cars. Her own step-son is mortified. He's too young to know why. Meanwhile her youngest, Toby, Freddie's Play Group Pal, and the child she spoils with every treat imaginable, has upset most of the other mothers with his foul mouth. Needless to say my suggestion of remedial treatment for the swearing duo of Toby and Curtis is now being heeded. Mia is not one to swear so I'm at a loss to learn where a three year old has picked up this expressive vocabulary.

Maybe Mia is spreading herself too thin. Between the three children, at least 8 charities, the lurking and unforgiving first husband (threatening to sue for custody of their daughter), maintaining her army of staff, recovering from two nose jobs, breast implants and a propensity to flirt with tradesmen fixing non-existent problems around her huge sprawling urban ranch (she got the house in the divorce from former cattle station heir - the station itself was repossessed by the banks), and ex-Wall Street commodities trader husband number 2 (Mitch), away months at a time racing cars and yachts thus leaving the beautiful aforementioned boatered son from his first marriage to Mia's influence, she is perhaps, a tad overcommitted. Maybe some intense eye contact with Yves is enough to set her off. Goodness knows Yves has teased us all down the years with those lashes and sinewy forearms...

Where was I?

Oh yes; delighted to oblige Beth and refuse any and all invitations from Mia, and if required generally run her down to anyone who'll listen. In fact, I think I should escalate the cold war I began with her after her rude remarks about George not being an oil painting. *If* she even thinks that. Was she actually creating a red herring? Is she after George too? Why isn't she after George; he's no Yves, but he's every bit as manly and good looking as her architect, more manly than her hairdresser, more available than Mitch and almost as manly as her pool boy!

Thursday, 20 August

I've been neglecting my journal again. While I'm still none the wiser as to what the Inner Child component could fully deliver, I had begun to see this process as helping me identify and work through my feelings of anxiety and worry, frustration and consternation; to clarify my thoughts and ideas as well. I have to confront the Frobisher interview tomorrow. Poor Gracie is refusing to go to it. I've promised her a new blue and silver tutu – pink is so passé now – as a bribe, or I should say, incentive, for attending.

I overheard some women talking at Yoga Babes this morning. They were chatting all the way through the Hot Yoga cool down – such as it was. Very irritating – talking corpses. Apparently, there's a tummy virus going around the schools now with peculiar bird flu like symptoms that leaves the sufferer disoriented and faint. I swear I've had that several times! It's coming on now. Perhaps it's nerves or anxiety, but I feel sick to my heart. What will we do if Frobisher won't take her? I'm so grateful for this journal. I have no one else to talk to about this.

I can't discuss it with Mum – she won't see the big picture. George is in some other place and has no patience for me or my concerns. Beth is goodness knows where. She talks a good game but she's not available. She's lost in some childhood fuzz of sadness and morosity; obsessed with therapy and the children. Felicity's too busy and far too pragmatic to spend time discussing things with me. Clothilde is far too French. Emma and Carl will be back in Texas before any really significant schooling decisions have to be made. Helen from Montessori is fab, but she's got more on her mind, let's face it. But for my journal and Desirée I would be entirely alone right now.

At least I'm clearer that therapy isn't for me. Certainly not the psychoanalytic intervention that Beth favours (I went to that quack of hers twice to oblige her, but Desirée was so diffident about it that I just felt self indulgent afterwards). I'm spending loads of great time with Desirée. She's showing me how to enjoy doing nothing so much more. She actually reads voraciously at night. Phil spends most evenings in his study working so Desirée has always turned to books and study as her outlet. I'm trying this out and have rediscovered some of the books I loved at university. I can't imagine why I've not been reading all these years since Gracie was born. I've had more time these past three years not working than I did before and yet I convinced myself that my reading days were behind me.

I had tea with Mrs G today. Her party plans are coming together beautifully. She forgives me for dropping the ball with the entertainment. She was very frank and told me straight out that I'm unfocussed, but she understands that I've a lot to contend with right now. What a relief. I hadn't intended to avoid playing a part in arranging the entertainers; my subconscious (or perhaps my *inner*) rebellious teenager just knew that I wouldn't do it to her satisfaction and would disappoint her, so I was procrastinating and putting off facing the task. Not that I struggle with small tasks like this. Just with pleasing very demanding and exacting people. I suspect she only asked for my help out of politeness – to be inclusive – given Sophie's coming home for the party and Mrs G knows I'm not close to Mum. But, with the issue out of the way we had a rollicking good time. Mrs G is a very amusing and inspiring woman. I'm amazed at her capacity to take on projects. She writes, she plans, she hosts things, she attends things and she has hundreds of friends who trust and rely on her.

Between Mrs G and Desirée, I really have no excuse for feeling lost. I'm going to mindfully emulate them. Mrs G has spent her life playing to her strengths. She takes on nothing that bores or fails to excite her. She really has it sorted. In fact, a few minutes with her and one forgets all one's worries and believes everything will be absolutely fine.

George should call her tonight. Though I doubt he'll have time or energy for it after the day he had today. There's been a spate of internet porn problems at the office. Somehow as head of Business Development and Strategy, it falls to George to manage it. If it were not so serious it would be very funny. The porn that is – not George having to formulate a strategy. Poor George. Given he can't pack an ice cooler for a BBQ in the garden without making a list first, I'm not convinced he's the best man for the job. Anyway, someone has been crashing the Pharma Co HQ server on Thursday nights, for the past three weeks, overloading the system with images from lewd sites sourced from Amsterdam. The culprit(s) seems to have logged into a computer using the password of a temp worker who's definitely not to blame, as her security card report and the CCTV footage at reception show her – a homely looking 58 year old widow – leaving the office at 5 pm sharp. However, between 7 and 8 pm there's been a massive influx of porn to the system via her login on a terminal in the former typing pool – now being refurbished.

Now that George and his assistant have traced the physical source they have a plan in place to catch the actual culprit in the act, should he or she try to do it again. HR, IT and security are all standing by! I can hardly wait til next Thursday evening to hear the next exciting installment.

Friday, 21 August

Frobisher was amazing. They accepted Gracie! She did so well; she was calm and poised and sweet and delightful. They were so natural and easy with her. What an amazing and forward thinking environment.

She'll thrive there. The grounds, the buildings, the staff, were all wonderful. I almost wish I could go there too. And I really wish I'd told people we were going for it. *And* that we got it! Now it'll look like it was a second choice, last ditch attempt due to Hillmere failure. Damn. Maybe they won't care. Maybe only I think like that – or maybe I've learnt to do so, at playgroup copying Francine and Mia. In any case, I'll sleep so well tonight knowing that Gracie's primary education is now sorted.

We arrived at Frobisher in good time and were greeted by the Head Mistress, Mrs Melloy – very elegant and poised. She met us in the middle of a horseshoe shaped gravel drive beside a sloping, shaded lawn leading to the river beyond. She was the least headmistressy person I've ever met, Hillmere included. She showed us into a sunny playroom full of toys and bean bags, children's artwork and a table set up with paints, pens, glitter glue and stickers galore. Gracie was in Heaven. She very politely asked if she might play and left us talking for 10 minutes before the interview properly began.

Mrs Melloy offered us refreshments, which we declined. Nerves, bladder issues etc. Then she just chatted freely with Gracie for 20 minutes. They talked about the summer and their favourite places, times of day and animals. They talked about ice cream flavours and colours and which letters are girls and which letters are boys (have not thought of that in 30 years!).

After a while, two little girls aged around 9 appeared and offered to show Gracie the garden and the year 1 classrooms. Gracie didn't hesitate. Mrs Melloy and I followed a little behind the girls and she told me about the school and its ethos and some of the orientation events that would be on offer if we were to accept a place for Gracie. I stopped in my tracks.

"Are you offering us a place?" I stammered.

"Why of course," she replied, smiling.

I almost hugged her! It was the happiest moment of the year thus far. We stayed another hour touring the arts facility, the music rooms and the gym, then meeting the year 1 teachers and seeing the classrooms and the children working. It was delightful. Education has never looked so calm and relaxing.

As we were leaving Mrs Melloy shook my hand and said:

"May I call you Verity? Verity, Gracie is a delightful little girl. But she's only a little girl and she needs to experience some freedom and some fun as well as challenge and stimulation. Will you relax and let her be a child a little more?" I was rather taken aback and yet it was perfectly sensible and I smiled with relief.

"Of course Mrs Melloy," I said demurely. I would have agreed to swim backstroke up the Ganges at the point, had she asked.

Now that the dust has settled and we've shared the news with George and Felicity and Mrs George and we can visualise life at Frobisher next year, I have a chance to pause and consider what Mrs Melloy said to me as we were leaving.

Could she really tell on the basis of two hours acquaintance and my written application that I've been pressuring Gracie to grow up too fast and to do too much? That I need to relax? Could she tell that we were desperate? Did she assume anything by the fact George was not there? What did she think of me, really, to have said that? Does she say it to everyone? She must have seen and experienced every kind of mother now after 25 years in education? Maybe she has a bar chart or a pin board where she puts us after that first interview. Maybe she says something pointed yet different to each mother, testing us, curious to see what we do and how we react. Perhaps it was part of the interview. What if I'd argued or defended myself? Does she think I'm crazy and pushy and ambitious and totally unfulfilled as a person?

I'm not going to sleep tonight after all!

Wednesday, 26 August

We're off to the beach for a long weekend tomorrow with three of George's colleagues and their families for our annual Pharma Co Spring weekend get together. Half dreading it. Just not feeling up to it this year. I keep going over in my head what Mrs Melloy said. George is torn between coming with us tomorrow or joining us at the beach on Friday. He hopes to catch the Porn Person in the act (of downloading(!)) on Thursday night. IT and security have managed to identify 37 employees who've been in the building with access to the floor and the desktop that was used on the past two occasions. The mature lady temp has been questioned as to who she may have disclosed her login and security details to – so far she can think of no one, but she admits to having written them down and left them in her top draw, the key to which she keeps in a coffee mug on her credenza.

Too many suspects to monitor directly.

But back to the beach get away. The weekend is going to be trying. Thankfully, Desirée and Phil and the girls are coming this year, though not until Friday. The other couples and their children have been going with us for three years now. We first went when I was bursting with Freddie, almost going into labor by the pool three years ago when Harry – George's best man and long time friend – regaled us with stories of George trying out for rugby in middle school. It's no wonder Freddie is so uncoordinated and always falling over. Gracie clearly gets her grace and poise from my side of the family.

Harry's eccentric; heavily overweight and an absolute darling who George has known and loved since kindergarten when Harry – not then overweight – arrived fresh off the boat from Lancashire. At the time, George was the only child that could understand his accent, so they became fast friends. Harry is a serial obsessionist. Last year his hobby was making his own beer and we had to sample the home brew all weekend. From anyone but Harry it would have been excruciating. This year he's promising to share with us his new passion – cooking. He's a frustrated failed chemist who wanted to develop cures for cancer and vaccines for malaria; instead he works at Pharma Co with George, managing risk. He describes this as schmoozing with lawyers while the "poor sods" suffer untold side effects from misuse and over prescription of Pharma Co's drugs. He's a wonderful father and devoted husband and hugely comical. I'd go to the beach just for him.

Unfortunately, his wife Claire, is bitter and hard, worse with each passing year and resentful of me because George is *not* fat, is paid more than Harry and because we managed to have a second child, while all their attempts have been fraught and unsuccessful. Anyone as mean and sour as Claire must be barren.

Then there are Tim and Hannah, also from Pharma Co. Hannah is head of HR. Their children,. Jack and Peter, are hilarious and attract trouble like little magnets. They are five, exhausting, terrible and beautiful. They are the opposite of Harry and Claire's son, Wilbur, who is, frankly, a bore. I know that's uncharitable. He's only 7, after all, but his personality is as dull as dishwater. He's scared of the waves, bugs, sunshine, heights and play. Harry tries to jolly him along and he does relax somewhat the more time he spends with his dad, but given most of his time is spent at a pretentious academy in the suburbs or with his toxic mother, he has his work cut out for him to be normal.

Claire was George's college girlfriend – which may also account for her iciness. He's the "one that got away". They broke up in third year when George took an internship in California and wanted to be free of her. She worked her way through his friends over the next four years until

Harry (at that time slim and athletic) fell in love with her. She was beautiful and funny then, apparently. I didn't meet them all for another five years, by which time I think the rot had set in and she was already obsessing over starting a family and extending the house. She's joyless and cold. She makes an effort for Harry but it nearly kills her to go to these weekends. Indeed, she mightn't even come on this trip, given what George mumbled to me last week about Harry's intention to come with or without Claire. Fingers crossed.

Better start packing. Have no idea where the beach play toys are. Maria tidies like a maniac whenever we return from a day at the beach or time at the farm with Mum, and I never manage to work out her system. Toys are with swimmers. Towels are with umbrellas and goggles. But never in the same place twice running. I'll search the playroom, garage and laundry and goodness knows what else I'll find in the process. Most likely I'll be shopping for new stuff on the way.

Oh, I just thought of an upside to the weekend - George will be able to show off his newly toned torso and bulging biceps.

Sunday, 30 August

Whew. That's over for another year. It was ok, all told. Not nearly as bad as I feared. Claire was there, micromanaging everything, controlling the conversation and dominating the children. The ocean view apartment was palatial, with maid included in the rates, but Claire spent more time directing the maid on how to chop shallots and arrange flowers from the local farmers' markets than she did in idle relaxation or conversation. The children and I drove down after school on Thursday. We spent a quiet and pleasant evening with Tim and the boys. First thing Friday we were joined by Phil and Desirée and an overexcited Rafalea and Gabriela who had yet to see the beach since leaving the US. Harry, Claire and Wilbur arrived mid-morning; Hannah and George drove down together after lunch. George stayed back late at the office Thursday night to catch the Porn Person. But all was quiet. No downloads, no illicit emails, not even a crude joke.

I devoted Friday before George turned up, to the children. It was my hope to overcompensate ridiculously for all the stress and pressure of the past few weeks – the interviews, the potty training, the frantic over-stimulation aimed at enhancing Gracie's admission prospects. We've all been at sixes and sevens. We spent some lovely unstructured time on the beach just playing in the sand. I confess, I was so relaxed that the benefits for Freddie's motor skills and whole brain development did not even occur to me all weekend – indeed, not until now. Now I'm even more pleased with the unstructured time. In the course of digging holes and driving trucks through tunnels and over sand ravines and *corniches*, I realised that the beach is an amazingly satisfying place for a physical workout.

I managed to burn at least 450 calories I should think just digging holes. I'll ask Jorgé what he thinks when I see him tomorrow at the gym. I was really active in the sand. The trick is to use no equipment, just bare hands (my nails are atrocious of course!), abs and back muscles and really flex the biceps as you pull the sand up and out of the hole. The hole must be deep, dug in semi-dry sand, not near the shoreline – preferably close to high water mark. Burpees and push-ups done in soft sand are a must, as are lunges. Above the high water mark, the sand's uneven surface further challenges the core, giving one an overall workout to rival that of any self respecting personal trainer. Finally, for cardio, the dune running is excellent, ideally done in intervals with some squatting and crunches thrown in for good measure. After all of that exertion one needs to cool down – some swimming is essential, followed by knee-deep striding in the shallows. This works wonders for toning the upper thighs and calves.

I was sharing this strategy for fat burning *á la plage* with a captivated Desirée and an amused Hannah, when Claire graced the scene in a plunging floral one piece and a ginormous white hat. We'd not seen her all morning since she preferred to stay indoors managing the kitchen, the maid and Wilbur who tried on several outfits that he might wear to the beach before they finally appeared. Harry begged her to come to the beach only to be dispatched on an errand to buy new napery for the holiday apartment at the local interiors boutique – strict instructions to buy nothing tacky or local. With him gone she seemed to come to her senses and emerged like a pale and stricken Venus being born from the dunes, the maid carrying out a chair, umbrella and bottle of water for her. Well, despite being late to the conversation and the last person to be qualified to comment on sport or outdoor pursuits, Claire was having none of my fitness viewpoints. She quickly pointed out that the key to a beautiful and toned body lies in inner calm, yoga, whole foods, Pilates and water ballet, with regular colonic irrigation and water therapy (getting blasted with an industrial strength hose apparently). While I'd be happy to offer her some extra water therapy of a more rigorous sort, I pointed out that water ballet was a little challenging in the Pacific Ocean and that one could not exclude the health giving benefits of some cardio and weight bearing training. She dismissed me with her trademark condescending smile and muttered, "Perhaps; if you want to build up bulk, of course". She thinks she's elfin and gamine, but she's not – just gaunt and sallow. She would not know an upward dog from a cobra if they bit her in her boney butt, but she sat there all sinew and veins telling us to stop talking about muscles, effectively destroying my precious morning with the children. She's the quintessential kill-joy.

Fortuitously, at Harry's suggestion (poor darling has become an expert in repairing moods and relationships left stricken in Claire's wake), we decided some antique shopping was the order of the afternoon. We split up and took separate cars; Desirée and I and the girls conveniently getting lost in the next town and spending a charming hour sipping iced coffees (no fat) overlooking the waves and lengthening shadows while allowing a suitable time period to elapse before returning to rouse Freddie from his nap for more sand play and paddling. The next two days passed relatively uneventfully apart from the fishing debacle.

Note to self – never, ever, rely on Harry to catch dinner again.

We were forced to wait til 10pm on Saturday night to sample – barely taste – the teaspoon of flesh on the scrawny bones of two minute whiting caught by none other than the remarkable Wilbur. Harry stood in a gutter of freezing water for three hours while Wilbur nailed the poor blighters and then patiently watched and advised as he scaled and filleted them. Who lets a 7 year old loose with a filleting knife? Claire, of course. The ordinary fishermen and farmers of the area and George who went to the market for us, deigned to supply the rest of the meal, thank God. After that session in the water not even Harry could bear to cook, so Claire's ministrations in the kitchen bore fruit, at last.

The men (apart from Tim who slept) played golf on Saturday afternoon. I was tempted to join them, but Desirée's face at the thought of an afternoon alone with Claire and Hannah, sent me back to my room to change out of plus-fours and into swimmers. I've always like Hannah. She's very clever and authentic. She's worked very hard to climb the ladder at Pharma Co, but equally manages to be a wonderful and involved mother to her crazy, fabulous sons. Desirée, however, finds her completely intimidating and almost prefers the threat of a traffic jam spent alone with Claire. There being safety in numbers, the four of us lolled by the pool while the maid played with the children. I caught up on the world of interiors news, while the others chatted idly nearby.

Surprisingly, Claire was not that bad on Saturday. First, she actually joined us at the pool. I think she warms up after lunch. Perhaps by then her system has accepted it's still being starved and she finds it easier to be congenial. Or perhaps without Harry's boyish humour and attempts to jolly her along she feels she can let go somewhat. Or maybe the Camparis she secretly downed on a "bathroom" trip lightened her load. She lied and said it was Berocca in the bottom of the glass but we're not as stupid as we look! We discussed working women and the sacrifices and compromises made in the quest for career and family. It was all terribly fascinating. I learnt so much from Hannah about the politics of power. The game has changed considerably since I was managing accounts four years ago. Claire even seemed interested in this conversation and told some witty anecdotes about winning over some male clients while working at one of Pharma Co's subsidiaries.

Meanwhile the men had one of those ridiculous rounds of golf where no one plays well and everyone would rather be somewhere else. George blamed me of course. Apparently having a wife along keeps it civilised. Phil, I now see, is a terrible bore at the best of times, and outplayed the others, who were in silent and foul moods on their return. Which might explain Harry's willingness to stand in the icy water with Wilbur all evening. The children had the best time of all that day - building forts and teepees in the garden til dusk.

Desirée was very quiet all Saturday evening. I asked her about it while we were sipping a pre-dinner drink – Tim mixes a lethal cocktail - and she looked decidedly uncomfortable. Could be big house parties are not her thing? Perhaps in that sort of setting she feels exposed or scrutinised. Not that *she* could come up wanting; it was merely the dull, all-knowing Phil that left us underwhelmed. Having said that, a few Grasshoppers certainly livened him up and he seemed in very good form for him, even cosying up to Claire at one stage, suggesting a dance on the terrace. I went to bed at that point. Too much sun and Sauvignon and I had plans to quietly address those sand dunes the following morning before we drove back.

So, all in all, not a bad weekend. I think it did the children a world of good to have a couple of days of free and unstructured play. George enjoyed getting out of town. He drove home with the children this afternoon and was not at all bothered that I decided to stay on a little longer for one last swim. The fact that he stopped at his mother's on the way home no doubt eased any burden he may have felt, as she took care of their dinner and bathing, and will drop them home in the morning before Montessori.

I thought this turn of events, namely a night without the children, would prove beneficial for George and I, but he's fast asleep on the sofa in his study – the golf muted on the flat screen.

Thank goodness I have my journal to turn to...

Tuesday, 31 August

I've been contemplating some of the stories Claire was telling over the weekend. After a good deal of consideration and a thorough discussion of this with Jorgé yesterday, I've decided that Claire is not so bad after all. Jorgé is better than the best girlfriends when it come to gossip and analysis. He really should become a therapist. He listens very attentively, never forgets a detail and is as discrete as a priest in the confessional. Claire, we have decided, is high maintenance, but in a self-sufficient way. She's never needy and if she doesn't like something or someone she just changes her situation or that of everyone else to suit her better. Truly admirable. And Harry clearly sees something in her. George once did. Even Wilbur's getting better. He was breast fed til he was three and Claire was still singing him lullabies when he was 6, which might account for their weirdly connected bond, but apart from needing to have a lot of parental attention most of the time (certainly not his fault) he's quite sweet. In fact when he lets himself relax he's almost normal with other children. He even taught Freddie how to grate cheese. Anyway, since I'm finding myself feeling charitably towards Claire, it strikes me that some of her ideas are quite interesting. For example:

1. Career women are unified by one feature – they are all plagued with guilt.
2. Mothering is the most important job on earth and should be remunerated.
3. Fathering is the second greatest job on earth.
4. Not enough is done to prepare women for the commitment and responsibilities of marriage and motherhood.
5. Children need more, not less, parental supervision.

I tried to engage George in a discussion about these points earlier, since he and I have barely spoken properly in weeks. He wasn't the least bit interested. He's due to meet the Chief Executive tomorrow about the Porn Person, among other more pressing concerns, and fobbed me off with a wave saying:

"Verity, call a friend. I don't have time."

So, here we are again – just me and my journal.

As luck would have it, I can't be bothered analysing those topics by myself. It's not the same as chatting to someone, so I'll work out what needs doing around the house. If I learnt one thing on the weekend away – besides how to smile through gritted teeth – it was that one can't put too much money into one's property.

We've done nothing with the house in almost two years. I really want a summer house at the bottom of the garden, though. Now that Gracie is getting a little older I'm tempted to make a start. It would give her quite an advantage at Frobisher. But as for the main house, the kitchen could do with some attention. We need to reconsider its aspect and the whole central island work bench concept. It's very dated – it must be four years since we had it done and I've been meaning to call in Felicity's kitchen designer for months but never seem to get around to it. I'm leaning towards French Provincial but Mrs G is very keen on Soho Loft. Beth is a great fan of white and has just done a wonderful "Room of her Own" a la Virginia Wolf in her former home gym. That room has been amazingly adaptable. She now has a media space with all the latest stuff, one of those architect tables that she uses for her paper making and design work – little ink etchings of birds to decorate her personal stationary. She says her therapist suggested it as a way of unwinding and slowing down her mind. It's like origami I suppose, though my time spent doing that was more frustrating than most of my other hobbies, indeed a huge source of stress, if truth be told. Anyway, her Room is very pristine; white and harmonious.

Personally, I prefer something with a little colour. A Tiffany blue cushion might enliven it somewhat, but she insists that her Room will not have cushions. I want to incorporate a rustic flavour to my redesign of the house. I've embraced all things Mediterranean in my cooking and aspect to date; now I want to travel north and perhaps borrow from the *très* elegant limestone floor and washed wood themes of many of the Loire Valley Châteaux we stayed in during our pregnancy trip 6 years ago. Desirée has shown me photos of her house in Boston – Scandinavian. I love the Nordic design features. She says the house was like that when they bought it and she barely touched it. It seems too good to be true, but I'm inclined to believe her. While she's very cerebral, she's not aesthetic, despite her wonderful appearance and appreciation of art.

Speaking of all things Scandinavian, the new manager at Mummy's Word is Swedish. Mummy's Word is a glorious little café/play space where I meet up with some yoga mothers on Tuesdays with Freddie. I've missed a few meets lately so I'm looking forward to getting back there and finding out what Britta is channelling in terms of Nordic style.

Things seem a lot better with Gracie since the weekend away. She's returned to her usual place at the top of the class in her phonics play and number skills. Mrs Tait beamed with joy as she told me that Gracie was back to her old self. Sad, beleaguered and tense Gracie is a thing of the past. Even the reluctance to share the fuzzy felts and plasticine has stopped. Not only that, she's the Star of the Week this week for welcoming a new boy so warmly. As a reward, I've promised that she can stay overnight with Mum. Mum's always offering and I've never let her go alone. Gracie is so proud of herself and is already counting the sleeps. I'll drive her to the farm next Saturday and then head back to focus on Freddie.

His third birthday needs some consideration. Some of his Gymboree friends are planning parties at venues now. I thought we'd do it at home, as usual, but I'm hearing talk of Toddler Track days! Am I just too conservative? It seems too early. Should I buck this trend? I would look like a flake to George if I booked up a track day party considering I banned him from buying the Porsche for Freddie – and worst of all it would leave Freddie exposed to ridicule at his own party, as he wouldn't have had any driving time before hand!

No. I'm resolved. We'll keep it simple and have a farm themed party. I have the perfect Max Mara gingham shirt for it!

Gosh, my knees are killing me. I think I overdid the "Soft Sand Lunges" on the weekend. I'll have to squeeze in a session at the reflexologist tomorrow between Mindfulness and aqua-aerobics. Or I could cancel Library roster on Thursday. I must say the whole roster thing at Montessori is really starting to get old, now that we have Frobisher sorted for Gracie. I mustn't burn out on the school help front before

Freddie starts there. Perhaps I need a higher profile, more executive role. Something less hands on, perhaps...

Thursday, 3 September

I can't believe it's already September. I've done nothing about Christmas yet. This was to be our year to travel. Easter Island is George's preference, while I favour a walking wine tasting tour of the Marlborough Region of New Zealand. I know that's low key – even a bit pedestrian - but I don't want nannies on Christmas holidays with me. Anyone prepared to work over Christmas is not a good influence on my children. We can manage to get to New Zealand without full time help. And, if it all seems too much once there, we can easily find local babysitters. I saw it in the brochure. Now I just have to persuade George that sipping Sauvignon Blanc while watching the children play is going to be sufficient rest and relaxation for him. Personally I have a really strong hankering to see a glacier. I think I need more drama in my life.

Speaking of which, Emma from Houston called earlier to tell me that her daughter Honour is starting a new diet – she's still too tubby for Emma's liking. Emma wanted my opinion of it given I'm slim and George is in pharmaceuticals(!). I did not point out the lack of logic there. I was a little distracted throughout the call, though, as I was watching Freddie in the garden. He's developed a worrying tendency to kill insects. Is this the first sign of sociopathic tendencies? I asked Emma whether her older son ever got his kicks killing bugs. She insisted it's a rite of passage for small boys and nothing to worry about. Still, it's so sadistic and cruel. I'll book an appointment at the psychologist again. It's weeks since we saw him so we're due another chat anyway. It won't be hard to come up with a few more issues to discuss. I might ring Mrs G and ask whether George ever did this. Or maybe Sophie? *She* strikes me as the type, actually.

Friday, 4 September

Oh my Lord, what a day.

I don't know where to start. George just called from the office. The Porn Person is Phil.

The very idea of boring old Phil, seemingly a dull prematurely elderly wet blanket, devoting hours of his life to the pursuit of porn? I can't get my head around it. I need to call Desirée, but what to say? It's like when Beth's Dad died in year 11 – drive by shooting while on business in LA. We had no idea what to say to her. It's incomprehensible. George is still at the office dealing with the Fallout. I'll wait up for him tonight. It might be the right time to hit him with the New Zealand plan; he won't be thinking clearly for a day or two, especially given that Phil was his deputy and his star recruit. Gosh, I hope George isn't implicated in this. No – he'll be fine. But he'll be vulnerable until this blows over. I'll make my move on New Zealand, the new kitchen, re-landscaping the pool terrace and getting more help around the house.

.....

Just got off the phone with Desirée. Phil called her an hour ago. He's being detained in the office by HR (i.e. Hannah), the CEO, risk (aka Harry) and security. The preferred plan from Pharma Co's perspective is to keep it quiet. They're offering Phil the option of a payout - a golden kick out the door - or therapy and a transfer to the new research lab in Latvia (a role they've been trying to fill for three years). Desirée doesn't know what they'll do. It seems that she knew about his interest in internet gratification before now. They argued about it as recently as last week, hence her stony silence at dinner at the beach. She gave him an ultimatum just before the downloads at the office started. Get the obscenities out of my house and away from my daughters or find yourself another family! Well he took them as far as his new executive suite, it would appear, and then tried to hide them by using the temp's login after hours. Sly dog dirty old Perv!

Desirée is livid. She appreciated my call. She fully expected to be iced by me and all of her new friends on account of Phil's behaviour. I consoled her – only Hannah and Claire will know and a couple of security guys. And she was not that keen on Hannah or Claire, and the security guys don't exactly frequent her haunts. It looks as though the damage can be contained. George has mercifully kept the word to a very small number of employees, all whom have signed confidentiality clauses tonight. Phil can take his cash or take the new job, dignity intact. No one will ever be the wiser. Lucky Phil. The only catch is the non-compete clause which effectively rules out his working in this country for the next three years.

Poor Desirée. She's torn between dumping him once and for all and leaving her girls fatherless, and standing by him through therapy and rehabilitation. She's adamant she'll not go to Latvia. But she can't really refuse if she agrees to stand by him, as far as I can see. Also, Latvia is not too far from Stockholm... But it begs the question whether he can indeed be reformed. Don't they say – once a useless perv, always a useless perv? Or have I got that muddled. George'll know.

For me the hard part is that I can't tell anyone else. George insists I'm equally bound by the confidentiality clause. But I'm bursting to talk to someone. Maybe I could call Yvette in Paris. She doesn't know any of the players and has loads more on her mind than this to start with. Or I could go to confession, I s'pose. Or I could just be good and keep this journal. Better start locking it up...

Wow. You just don't know anyone. It's always the quiet ones though.

Sunday, 6 September

George and Gracie are just back from Mum's. Gracie had a lovely time. I dropped her down after lunch yesterday and she had a brilliant afternoon swimming and helping Granny and the grooms with the horses. Granny made her a delicious dinner, she collapsed into bed and woke up early to feed the chickens and have a little ride on the resident Shetland pony. I barely spoke with Mum. She was with a very handsome and, for a horse person, charming and elegant trainer when we arrived. She took Gracie out to the stables with her and told me to stay or go as I pleased, but not to worry, Gracie would be fine. I had a persistent vision all the way back home, after a therapeutic little browse in the local shops and a pick-me-up purchase at one of the local galleries of a beguiling sculpture for the rose garden, of Gracie never coming home. I visualised Mum kidnapping her, bribing her with horse and pony rides and fairy floss and the life of the children in *Black Beauty* or *My Friend Flicka*. In hindsight we really all should have gone and stayed the weekend; rather than me driving four hours yesterday and George doing the return leg today. We're now tired and have not spent any time together all weekend. I'm reminded of Mia who once advised me that never seeing one's spouse is the secret to a happy marriage. That and plenty of Veuve, money and Botox, she might add.

But the aim of the weekend was to let Gracie experience a sleep over at the farm without us. Not the same as staying over at Grandma G's apparently. George and I should have found a B&B nearby and had a night away together. Next time I'll propose it, though I doubt George would have been willing this time, anyway. He spent yesterday between work and his mother's.

Mrs G is readying her garden for the big party and has been very keen to have George's input, even though she has an army of staff and garden consultants to hand. Mrs George and Mr George, when he was alive, were always gardening. It was their "thing", even as a very young couple, long before it became chi chi. George was brought up out of doors, before people knew about skin cancer and eye damage from the sun. In fact Mr George died in the garden three years ago. It was an early spring night. Mrs George had been away for a few days on one of her environmental jaunts – she took the train to reduce her carbon footprint. Had she flown she would have been back two days sooner and would have spent that time with Mr George. As it was they were in the garden after dinner, taking a stroll and catching up with one another's news, when Mr G just collapsed beside her. A heart attack.

The consolation for George was that we spent a lot of time with his dad that week since Mrs G was away and Mr G was planting a new border to surprise her with on her return. We'd been helping – which was really George helping – heavy lifting and trips to the garden centre – Gracie digging in the dirt with them and me lying in a nearby hammock, about to pop with Freddie.

While his death was sudden, George has those memories of being with him. He died in his favourite place with his beloved wife of 42 years. Three weeks later Freddie was born.

Mrs G was amazingly strong. She has dedicated her work to him every day since. It was Sophie who had the hardest time grieving. She was a long way from the family – had been for over 10 years - and while she kept in touch and visited every year, sometimes more, she was not close at the time he died. She hasn't let it get in her way but she is hardened by that, if anyone already so hard and driven could be made less soft by anything.

Mr G was like Spencer Tracy. Funny and serious in equal measure. He was very intelligent and thoughtful and admired and respected universally. He was a doctor and his foundation for research into parasitic diseases thrives to this day. I think George harbours some regret that he didn't follow his father into medicine. They used to joke about the role of big pharmaceuticals in the development of more virulent bacterial and parasitic diseases; that George was undoing all of his father's work. It was light hearted and loving but it also contained some truth.

Dear George. He carries a huge sense of duty towards his mother. I don't know where he gets it from as neither of his parents ever pressured him to be or do anything. He was always motivated to please them and yet nothing he could have done would have disappointed them. Mr G was, and Mrs G continues to be, the most enabling, generous and loving parents imaginable. Sophie is an anachronism. Given the example of parenting that she was raised with, it's truly remarkable that she has become such a pushy, controlling, high achieving and ambitious mother. Whereas if *I* were like that, it would be no surprise at all.

Tuesday, 8 September

I finally made it to the coffee after yoga today. I had an appointment to take Freddie to the child psychologist but cancelled it at the last minute when the girls said they were going to coffee. I'm feeling sorely out of touch with my network and a huge part of me cannot yet face the chance that I'll be told that Freddie needs an intervention. He must be acting out some anger issues with all of the recent bug bullying. I don't want to face this just yet. By the same token, those serial killers and mass bombing types are always the boys who started young, torturing animals or playing with fire. Emma might be right; he could outgrow it. Helen says I should not worry unless he starts maiming cats and other domestic creatures that are generally regarded as cute and cuddly. Good gracious.

I was reassured when I saw Freddie interacting with the other children at coffee. He and four other little ones played beautifully nearby. Maria came too – thank goodness – as, even before the recent spate of violence towards insects, I'm often on tenterhooks with Freddie. He can be very boisterous. He has a wonderful extrovert aspect about him, but he also loves mischief and can rev up the other children into being quite noisy, even a little crazy – hilarious sometimes – but one has to appear to mind and I find myself rebuking him a lot, which, when the fun is all innocent, seems so unnatural. If Maria comes with us she can usually take him outside and let him run off some energy. In fact this has started a bit of a trend and several mothers are now bringing their nannies with them. It's invariably a good idea to have the nannies where one can keep an eye on them in any case and it definitely takes the guilt out of neglecting one's children for the duration of the coffee and chat.

Cecile, one of the yoga mummies, was almost lasciviously purring over how impressive George looked when she saw him at the garden centre last weekend. It was last Saturday while I was driving Gracie to the farm. He went to the garden centre with Freddie to buy plants for his mother.

Apparently George cuts a dashing figure through the gardenias and magnolias and Hard-Done-By Harriet, who also happened to be there at the same time, buttonholed Cecile at the cashier to find out who the man with Freddie was. While Harriet recognised Freddie, apparently she didn't recall me ever describing George in a way that would have aptly depicted the man Freddie was with. Indeed, she was most taken aback to learn that he was in fact my husband and not some dashing brother or newly divorced or widowed single friend. I suddenly realise that I've been doing myself a huge disservice by not talking George up more.

Assuming all the women of my acquaintance would not be particularly interested, I've never really gone to town about George's looks, or personality, for that matter. I appreciate him and think he is quite lovely, but love is blind, after all. Certainly, to recollect Mia's opinions, I would be most foolish to think any different. However, I stand corrected if Harriet and Cecile are to be trusted. Indeed Harriet appears to be most put out by the fact that George is, as she put it, "such a dish". She said to Cecile that I'm always very competitive, and she finds me rather smug about all my good luck in life. I have to say that's a bit of a stretch even for Hard-Done-By-Harriet. Indeed, it's not as if George fell from the sky and landed in my kitchen ready to be wed. It was through sheer hard work, compatibility and my father's good temperament (which I inherited in spades) that I secured George, and while I'm on the subject, I should say that George did pretty well to catch me!

I suppose I should take it as a compliment that she wasn't in fact surprised that I have such a fetching husband. Better that I am regarded as a competitive bitch than one who snares good men without deserving to. At least, I think that's the best way to interpret Harriet's remarks. Cecile was at pains to explain it away, as just Harriet's snide way of speaking and probably motivated by jealousy. Yet another topic upon which she can feel hard-done-by, no doubt.

I shall mindfully choose to take it as a compliment. It's very gratifying to hear that my friends think my husband is attractive. I wonder if I shouldn't start talking about him more. Won't tell George, of course.

Saturday, 12 September

Saw Desirée and the girls today. We held a tea party in the garden, ostensibly to break the ground for the new summer house, but really to discuss the Porn Situation. We're relieved to learn that the porn involved no one under age, no boys, no animals and nothing sadomasochistic. It was pretty run of the mill stuff – adolescent - apparently. The main issue was the server overload – i.e. the sheer volume of it.

George was an absolute darling with Desirée and assured her of Pharma Co's complete support for her and the girls. Phil is away. He agreed to go to Latvia and has begun an intensive programme at a retreat four hours drive from here as the first stage in his rehab. I would kill to know who else he meets there. Desirée is holding it together incredibly well. She told her girls that Daddy is working at a client's site for a few days and they seem to be none the wiser. Mind you, Gabriella said to Gracie:

"My daddy is away looking at breasts," to which Gracie nodded sagely and said:

"All daddies do that."

Good gracious, what have I missed?

Well the summer house ground breaking was quite a non-event as it happened. We did dig a small hole which Freddie filled in with several buckets of water, collected from George's micro-irrigation system strung up through the arbour and pergola, then stamped down and sprinkled with bucket loads of petals and leaves. But all is not lost, as I have George on board for a new kitchen and updating the pool. He went out while Desirée was here and came back with a delivery van full of new garden toys for Freddie. Over-compensating for something, I suspect. I just hope he's not up to any porn antics of his own.

Beth called during the afternoon's shenanigans, ostensibly to discuss her outfit for Mrs G's party and it was very hard not to let her in on the secret. She's already jealous of Desirée, so news like this would give her heart. I suggested a spa day for this week in order to prove my complete and loyal devotion to her. She's been morbidly focussed on her children's diets of late. She seems obsessed with the calorific content and undisclosed trans-fats of all the foods she feeds them, not to mention the pervasive advertising ploys aimed to lure children towards junk food. She's mounting a campaign at the local farmer's market, the organic shops and the entire range of mummy oriented places she frequents in the hope of pressuring everyone to pressure everyone else, to eliminate this insidious and corrupting influence on our young.

While I'm determined to help her, I've yet to reconcile all of that with my children watching me suck down a Coke Zero TM some afternoons. Usually, after I've secreted a wodge of dark chocolate (rich with antioxidants and fair traded, I hasten to add) under the organic carrots and brazil nuts (selenium) in the shopping trolley on our weekly educational romp through the supermarket. Perhaps Helen has been influencing me, but I feel quite serene about our diet these days. I've actually decided that my role is not to police their eating but to inform them enough to help them make good choices for themselves. And until they have money of their own with which to make bad choices, it's probably moot. I've more on my mind, thankfully, even if it's only Desiree's problems and my house.

Anyway in the hope that I can help Beth to chill out a little, I'll ask Helen and Clothilde to join us at the spa. Beth needs to get some perspective about all of this and I know that Helen's brand of self deprecating and laconic humour about all matters family or foodie and Clothilde tutting in her French accent will soon sort Beth out. I just don't want Beth to become a serial OCD sufferer. She obsessed about having a cross gender child when her boys were in utero, then she obsessed about their sleep issues and neural development. Bronnie – a ballet mum – had a similar tendency to worry and was carted off to Greenwood Psychiatric last year after a particularly bad spate of illnesses her daughter had over the winter. We don't discuss it at ballet, but I heard murmurings at the American avatar family party back on the Fourth of July (keep forgetting to sign up for that game Emma's husband designed online) that she was diagnosed with Munchhausen by Proxy and has been struggling to get access to the children ever since. It's tragic.

Beth would not harm the kids, but she's controlling their environment so much that they're getting resentful. They exchange glances and look away when she starts in on their weight or outfits. They're 4 and 7, and boys, for goodness sake. Aren't they meant to look like they play in dirt all day? After all, they're only *half* French. They're too young to be dealing with this drama. She needs to stop journaling her inner child and worrying about her parents' mistakes during her childhood and start focussing on ways to get some perspective and joy about her own kids. I hope my little intervention plan works. If it doesn't, I might enlist Claire's help. She won't mince words.

Speaking of Claire, she very kindly phoned last night to ask for Desirée's number. Harry told her about Phil and she was very concerned. Could it be I have misjudged her?

The three of us might go to the theatre this week after Mindfulness. Desirée will benefit greatly from some time out. I noticed today in the garden that she was quite abrupt at times. It's as if a wall of politeness that previously surrounded her has come down brick by brick leaving her exposed, teetering on the edge of a precipice of justifiably resentful and scathing directness. I am expecting any day an almighty outburst, a tsunami of emotion like nothing seen before. She's all controlled rage and fiery eyes right now. She said to me today:

"When someone betrays one's trust and deliberately puts their twisted needs ahead of their family, it leaves one angry." What an understatement.

Gracie is begging for another trip to Granny's. While I'm delighted that she enjoyed herself, I'm not planning on driving her back again just yet. We've a lot to do around the house and lots of plans for catching up with people over the coming weeks. Tomorrow we have a BBQ with Pharma Co colleagues at the country club. The children have a tennis activity on tap so the adults can be free to relax and imbibe. Not sure how Freddie will fare at a tennis session. I wanted him to start Toddler Tennis but I doubt he's ready for it. While he won't be the youngest he may well be the most disinterested and quite a disturbing influence. He'll probably horde balls and build forts rather than connect racket with ball. I have to admit I'm even looking forward to seeing Claire at the club tomorrow. I'd like to discuss her thoughts on parenting and careers again. She's very sharp, drives to the heart of the issue. I just hope there won't be a lot of gossip or murmurings about Phil there. Even with confidentiality agreements and so on the company is always astir with rumour and speculation. I know I need only call Harry or George's secretaries if I ever need to find anything out.

Wednesday, 16 September

Theatre trip was a success. Desirée's looking good. She seems to be working through her rage quietly and surely and benefitting from time away from Phil. She apparently took his hard drive and drove over it in the office issued BMW last night. She put the kids in the back and said Daddy needed some help destroying some silly old work stuff, then rolled over it several times. I didn't think she had that in her, to be honest. We went to Mummy's Word after the theatre, even though we could have stayed in the city and had a more grown up time. The reason was that the notice board there has an amazing plethora of material – classes, courses, workshops, galleries, spaces, discussion groups. I suspect there is a support network for wives of deviants, so I wanted Desirée to have the time and space to check it out without the pressure of going there on her own or in the morning when it's heaving with mummies and toddlers. 4pm is quiet time. All the usual patrons are in their after-school clubs and activities for at least another 30 minutes. Britta was doing an inventory of stock when we arrived and there was only one other customer. Britta was full of ideas for our kitchen and will post me some brochures she used when she redid the café.

Mind you, Claire made a great point. I've totally underestimated her value. She said:

"The decor is lovely *here* Verity, but do you want to walk into Mummy's Word every day when you wake up? You'll be redoing it in a year." Very true. I'm now in a bit of a quandary. Maybe I can ask Mrs G to meet with the architect with me.

Meanwhile I mulled over Freddie's party during my meditation and gratitude session. I began focussing more on what I'm thankful for a few months ago after a particularly fraught period when Freddie was not sleeping very well. The night nanny was not able to help very much, Sophie (who as Parent Know-it-all par Excellence had been a godsend when Gracie had sleep issues) had no ideas, and even the paediatrician could find nothing physically wrong with him. I put it down to stress – whether his own, mine or George's – I couldn't say. I still can't say for sure what was bothering him, but he seems pretty normal now. Anyway, suddenly one day he just slept through and has done ever since, apart from during the putty vomit debacle. After a week of unbroken sleep though, I began a gratitude list – sleep was at the top of it most days. I came across this gratitude thing at Mindfulness for Mothers. It's pretty good, if one remembers to do it. The challenge is making time for keeping a gratitude list and meditating given all that one has to take care of and worry about. Some weeks I use my library roster time as meditation time.

I thought library roster would uncover some gems in the world of children's literature. If anything it's revealed the dearth of taste prevalent among these overpaid, under-stimulated parents at Montessori. Most are happy with a "Mr Men" book in the library bag each Friday – less for them to do. One or two – usually the academic high achievers or the entrepreneurial mothers - send in a list of books they want their child to borrow. I usually throw in a couple of non-fiction books on things like rocks and jellyfish to mix it up a little. Having said that, most of the parents probably don't open the book bag and prefer to buy pristine, new books rather than rely on germy, shared library books. Not very eco-friendly.

So the party. Freddie wants real lambs and real calves, so I've been looking into renting a flat bed truck or a cattle van or whatever they're called and some livestock. One of Gracie's classmates lives on acreage and has chickens and dogs, but apparently that won't do for Freddie. My mother has kindly offered to drive up some creatures in her horse hauling thing, but I sort of hoped we could avoid inviting her. Now I'm in way too deep, and I still don't actually have any lambs. If I put it out there though, the universe will provide.

Sure enough – it does. I shall ask Maria to look into this for me. Goodness knows she does nothing all day.

I must shop for an outfit for Mrs G's party tomorrow. Normally I would mend and make do, but Sophie and family arrive from London in three weeks for the event and if there was ever a reason to splash out and make a huge effort, it was competing with her.

Monday, 21 September

George had a car accident today. He was returning from lunch across town and collided with a garbage truck doing an illegal right turn. He called me to come and get him from work this evening. The children were so excited to go out in their jamies to pick him up. His car is at the smash repairer, covered in pooey nappies and porridge slops – the truck had just done a pick up at a day-care centre near the docks. Since George was ostensibly driving for the purposes of work, the company will provide a replacement vehicle until the Lexus is fixed. George prefers the replacement vehicle, of course.

"You should have smashed it up worse then," I offered, helpfully. George was very cagey about who he was meeting for lunch just before the accident occurred. I'm a little concerned about that. He can be abrupt from time to time but never less than fully forthcoming about his work and friends. So his evasive answers to my innocent questions strike me as rather odd, if not downright suspicious.

I'll check our accounts tomorrow and see whether there's any unexplained expenditure. I thought some time ago that he was up to something with all of that preening and working out. I've been so distracted lately that he could be up to anything and I'd be the last to know. I'd better start paying him more attention.

I was with Desirée and Clothilde when George called this afternoon. All the children were swimming and having a wonderful time. Desirée and Phil have "separated" for the time being. He flew out to Latvia yesterday and she and the girls will stay here for the next two months until he can justify a trip back. At that time they will decide what to do. We didn't discuss it in any detail as we had to "do" the Yoga Babes gossip first. One of the instructors has started up an affair with one of the mums with children at Montessori, Louise. Fulvia is relatively new to Yoga Babes and quite something physically, but it didn't occur to me that she was a lesbian. Having said, that she is of Gen Y vintage and I daresay a stint as a lesbian is increasingly *de rigueur*, especially in the "alternative", green or non-corporate milieus.

Meanwhile, the tongues were wagging at school all last week, because it was almost assumed that Louise was gay and some of the parents had been laying bets as to who it might be that would finally out her. I blew $20 with my punt on the swimming coach. Tabitha was livid – she had $100 on Louise being straight and keen on Luscious Larry. But good luck to them – Fulvia and Louise, that is. Hopefully Louise will stop staring lasciviously at my legs at pickup. It's most disconcerting really. Clothilde thought it was very subtle and clever of Louise to target the legs – clearly not a breasts chick – considering most of us check out each other's legs and shoes any opportunity we get.

Interestingly, Desirée was almost wistful as we discussed it.

It got me thinking about the whole life-partner thing. What if George is gay and secretly seeing a man? What if *I* were to have gay tendencies? Who would I fancy? No one springs to mind. Or if George were to leave me for someone else? What would he go for? I'm going to meditate on this now – and say some prayers that George is not, in fact, gay.

Oh, blow, Beth's spa day is tomorrow. Must call Helen and remind her – she has a terrible memory for this sort of thing.

Wednesday, 23 September

The Spa day was wonderful. We tried a new place about 10 minutes from here called Spring to Mind Urban Day Spa and Retreat. It was amazing! I can hardly believe such a place exists. It's so much more than a spa and it would take weeks to experience all it has to offer. We barely scratched the surface. I did a cross-training class with their former SAS instructor. My legs are still aching from it. Then, to humour Helen who is anti-gym as a rule, I joined her in a class themed "Bo-i-nngg". I love their marketing blurb and class descriptions:

> Set to the upbeat and irresistible melodies of the Stock Aitken and Waterman stable of stars, this class has you bouncing (literally, on flouro hop balls) around our Sunshine Studio. When the going gets tough on the old thighs, you bounce right over to the super large trampolines and rediscover your youth.
>
> (Maximum weight restrictions apply).

Gosh, did we laugh!

After that we were ready for some treatments. Helen focussed on the pregnancy massage suite, while Clothilde embarked on an **Alpha Aqua Avalanche** –

> an intense and invigorating experience in which industrial strength hoses batter and blast you through three stages – the hit and miss, the power shower and the water slide to freedom.

I must tell Claire about this place! Meanwhile, Beth was relaxing and therapeutically detoxing in the Steam and Scream Room

> ..it also fights wrinkles, cellulite and fluid retention and surveys show that a 3 minute scream session and a cool glass of water achieves the same results as 20 minutes on the treadmill and a full body massage)...

and in "The Tears on my Pillow Room"

> ..a zen hideaway where you can relax and let it all out, knowing you will leave intact after a mini-facial and restorative head massage...

I spent the rest of the day in the **Deep Immersion Pool** -

> *an abyssal experience in a 15 metre deep diving pool. The challenge lies in resisting the ebbs and flows of the random currents and riptides (life jackets available on request...)*

and attending the aptly named **"Inner Child Workshop"** which uses *"a combination of toilet humour, play-dough and dressing up, (to help you) discover a simpler way of seeing things."*

This combination of pampering, challenge, sheer physical distraction and targeted play based coaching was absolutely transformative! I feel like a new person. I want to tell everyone about this place, but I also want to keep it just for me. I'll keep their brochure here in my journal to remind me of what I could be doing with my time instead of journaling all my problems.

George is still being evasive. I tried on my new party frock for him tonight – in fact I tried on three and paraded around our bedroom and sitting room for him, the children and Maria – getting their opinions on which one to keep for the party and which to return. I asked George to find out from Sophie what she plans to wear – would not like to be obviously upstaged by the prodigal daughter. Of course he's not called her or even mentioned it to his mother. *I* can hardly phone and waste their time with such matters. This is indicative of his whole attitude of late.

To get some sense of self back, in light of my feeling that George is preoccupied with something or even someone and distancing himself from me and the children, I agreed to run for secretary of the Montessori Parents' Association Committee next year, subject to my not being needed elsewhere – e.g. at Frobisher or on one of Mrs G's charities. I'm actually excited at the prospect of a more influential role in the PAMM and secretly hope that Wendy decides she's ready to let someone else run the show.

For now I'm delighted that Mrs G wants my help with the advertising material for her "Green Space" project. She is launching a sustainable –

absolutely no paper involved – ad campaign, to promote the greening up of more urban streetscapes. The basic plant-a-tree idea taken to extremes. I'm quite excited about the work and the scope it will give me to get acquainted with more environmental issues as well as greenies as I'm still attracted to the idea of becoming a hippie mum for a while. Dressing in floaty Irish linen smocks and eating lentils and sprouts and using only organic hair dye... Gracie looked most dubious when she saw one such smock yesterday.

"Are you having a baby Mummy or just doing more mosaics?" she asked.

Friday, 25 September

I'm in a zone of peace and child-like happiness following the bliss and detoxifying experience of our spa day. Beth went straight from the spa to the beach house with Yves. Her mother is with the children for three days. She certainly seemed very restored and relaxed when I spoke to her today. She sounded calm and contemplative, not concerned with calories, homework, shoes or makeup. It's as though the old Beth has returned. She's attributing her newfound perspective to the coaching session she had at Spring to Mind the other day. She said that unlike therapy where she feels under pressure to be a basket case and go over all of her childhood angst and issues *ad nauseum*, the coach encouraged her to focus solely on where she wants to go over the next three to six months and got her to brainstorm ways in which to achieve that. It would appear that, when asked straight out, Beth found herself answering that what she really wants to do is spend more time with her husband and less time worrying about her children and her friends. Hence this period away with Yves.

I'm really pleased for her and very relieved. I was beginning to live in mortal fear that she was actually losing it, spinning out of control over the boys' sandals last week, yelling at the nanny over an unironed pair of socks. If she but *knew* the shortcuts *we* take with the ironing!

The spa experience was perhaps not quite as positive for Helen, although she insists that it's actually for the best that she came with us. Following her too-active day there she had some false labor pains. We realized in hindsight that *Bo-oinng* may have been a little ambitious for her in her third trimester. She's so natural and unfussy that one forgets she's pregnant. She confesses that she too forgets. At least all that exertion has forced her to slow down and put her feet up. She has to take it easy until her placenta and baby settle down again.

Clothilde, as I write, is at a *"Le Petit..."* get together singing the praises of Spring to Mind and its founder Tess Wood. Before we know it those French ladies will be taking over the place. Mind you, Spring to Mind has a guilt free chocolate indulgence room so who could blame them. All those extraordinary ways to burn calories, I doubt I'd have guilt of any sort, ever, in that establishment. Those Femmes will probably "borrow" the best concepts and rebrand them in some terribly chic and exclusive way with sprigs of lavender and baguette strewn about and call it *"Le Printemps de(du?) bon conseil"* or some such romantic and enigmatic moniker.

Inspired by Beth's commitment to spending more time with Yves, I suggested to George that he and I meet up in the city on Monday for lunch and some shopping. He declined very quickly and fervently, pink faced:

"Oh Verity, some other day. Monday I've work commitments all afternoon. And the rest of the week is booked up too. Anyway, isn't Monday your yoga day? Or spina bifida? Or Parents for Peace?"

Work commitments – pah! I can tell something is up when George actually remembers what I do with my time? He's definitely up to something nefarious.

Note to self – follow George on Monday.

Monday, 28 September

Where to begin. After the wonderful day with the girls at Spring to Mind I resolved over the weekend, accessing my inner child to do so, to investigate, with humour and energy, the question of whether George is involved in anything devious or diabolical. I had plenty of time to ponder this on Saturday and Sunday as he was away in a Pharma Co Strategy pow-wow all weekend. Or so he said.

At first I relished the chance to set my mind at ease. First thing this morning I cancelled my 11 am appointment at the Reiki clinic and dedicated the next hour to the children and what to wear on my stake-out. I set out, after Maria arrived to take Freddie to the park and Football and Gracie to Montessori, to pick up a hire car, and headed downtown to start my surveillance outside George's building. I knew this would be the way to catch him out. The more I thought about his hasty and vehement refusal to meet me today, the more it seemed suspicious.

I managed to pass the morning fairly pleasantly (on the phone) as I watched the exit of Pharma Co HQ waiting for George to appear. I also had an eye on the car park exit, mindful that George was driving a replacement Audi Q5 (Deep Sea Blue Pearl Effect) on account of the pooey nappies still adorning his Lexus. I had a *long* chat with Emma, the First Lady of Ballet and Austin, Texas. She called to invite us to join her and three other Ballet families for Christmas in Colorado. They jet off to the ski fields for a week then head for the Californian sunshine – such as it is - in December. I fobbed her off saying George doesn't know yet what sort of vacation he wants. Clearly I've lost all aspiration this year with my simple little New Zealand winery plan. Apparently that's so dull as to resemble a retirees' spring break. My trek over the glacier and other highlights did not resonate at all with Emma.

"Gaad Verity, have you got a terminal illness? George can't be serious about this trip. Come snowboarding on the lip of the Grand Canyon, honey!" she screeched in my ear.

Could've sworn the Grand Canyon was in Arizona, not Colorado...

In any case, we don't have the money Emma and her crew have for private jets and midsummer ski trips, though I'm not telling her that, but even so, two weeks holed up with all those children would just about finish me off. As it was, I implied that we still had a fall back plan to meet up with Sophie and family in Val D'Isère – a complete white lie – yet another to keep track of; I need a spreadsheet for them all. Why am I such a sap?

I finally changed the subject and got her going on the topic of the upcoming ballet recital and lead roles, costumes and seating at the performance. God, I'm already dreading it. Not because Gracie isn't in the star role, despite being the prima ballerina for her age group, but because of those women *and* their mothers who will be there, dressed to the nines at if it were opening night at the Met. It's baby "Swan Lake" as well, with plenty of ugly ducklings in the chorus... and the balconies.

But back to the real business of the day. I had to move the car twice as the parking was restricted in Pharma Co's street, but I didn't miss George leaving. Rather, I was in pole position to catch sight of him at 12.20pm as he emerged on foot and hailed a cab in front of his building. Thank God I hired a small, zippy, nondescript car. Behind my sunglasses and under a floral scarf I was unrecognisable to George or any random Pharma Co staff passing, witnessing my illegal u-turn and then my stealthy but efficient tail of his taxi south to the upmarket shopping and restaurant area near the old docks – interestingly, not far from the scene of his accident! It wasn't hard to keep a couple of cars behind the taxi most of the way. And I kept an eye out for garbage trucks entering the thoroughfare too. The road ends at the docks so it soon became clear where we were headed. George had the taxi stop at a roundabout outside a small hotel and apartment development. I pulled into a loading zone while George paid the fare and alighted, heading into the Old Flour Mill Boutique Hotel.

There was nowhere to park – hence, the ever resourceful George knowing to take a taxi – so I flicked on the hazard lights, leaving the car right there in the loading zone, and scampered over to the entrance. I quickly took my bearings and skulked across the foyer. Luckily a restored flour mill is not exactly brightly lit so I managed to find a nook and some plants near the bank of elevators from which I could get my bearings. I lurked by the wall, pretending to check a text message. At this stage the adrenalin alone was fuelling my quest. I was sweaty palmed and almost shaking with anticipation; terrified of what I might find or of being discovered by George, or worse, a horde of Pharma Co staff at a corporate lunch or team building event. I didn't know what I was hoping or fearing more then – an innocent explanation or a drug deal going down in the Gents'. As for me, how would I explain my being there if caught? I was cursing Emma for wasting my time on the phone – precious time I should have spent concocting a cover story. But, let's face it, I'm good under pressure. It came to me right then as I gazed unseeingly at my phone. If cornered I would say I was meeting a sought after kitchen designer.

Thanks to Mindfulness I was able to take pause then. I breathed deeply for several seconds behind my now far too dark glasses, trusting that a plan of action would emerge from the shadows. And then I saw him, chatting to the waitress at the bar of the hotel restaurant. He was too far away to notice me – too far away for me to hear them. Damn that Male Psyche – should have done Lip Reading! I couldn't tell whether he was flirting or talking about the cost of pork bellies. Until it all became irrelevant, as I saw who he'd come there to meet. A very beautiful blonde woman dressed expensively and stylishly in a sleeveless red A-line dress entered from the courtyard beyond. She was both understated and eye-catching – like Betty Draper in *Mad Men*. She sashayed up to the bar, laid a manicured hand on his arm and smiled winningly. In itself this was not the death knell of my marriage, but his face upon turning to smile back at her was. He was radiant, excited and so pleased to see her.

"Who the hell is she?" I thought, my mind racing, as I watched her take an elegant perch on the stool beside him. Always quick witted when it counts, I struck upon the idea of asking the concierge who she was. Removing my glasses, but keeping the scarf (very Audrey Hepburn), I turned on my loafered heel and confidently strode to the concierge desk. I used my cover about the kitchen designer and came up with a story about meeting her here. Did the concierge know who that lady in red in the bar was, as I was due to meet a lady who said she would be wearing red? The gorgeous little boy (a little like what's his name from *High School Musical*) manning the desk replied naively that the lady in red was a communication consultant from out of town and to his knowledge was not a designer or architect. I said:

"Ooh. Are you sure her name is not Ms Grant?"

He replied that she's checked in as Rebecca Thompson of Thompson Communications.

Just then I had the sensation of being watched, of eyes burning into my back. Did George recognise the scarf or handbag from across the bar and the foyer? Had I blown my cover? I thanked the little boy, mumbling something about waiting outside for Ms Grant and scurried out before he or anyone else challenged my suspicious questions and incognito get up.

I nearly collapsed on that walk back to the car. A parking ticket guy was mere feet away from my windscreen, pen poised to write me a ticket. He saw my face, though, and hastily moved on. It was all I could do to find the ignition and reverse out of that ridiculous driveway. I somehow managed to drive back towards town, for several minutes my mind blank, completely blank.

Even now, hours later, I've not consciously thought through what this means or what to do next. Clearly it was the Old Flour Mill that he had been leaving when he had the run-in with the garbage truck last week. Another lunchtime rendez-vous? And was the garbage guy really executing an illegal turn or was George so unseated by time spent with Ms Thomspon that he could not safely drive back to the city without crashing the car? Despite all of which he is now conducting another "meeting" with Ms Thompson of Thompson Communications? She cannot go to the office to meet?

And yet after his crash, he called me to pick him up. Is that a good sign, or a bad sign? And this past weekend? A "tedious" strategy conference, or something more interesting involving "communications"? I'm in some automaton state like I was when Dad died. Only then I was a girl and I had to hold it all together for Mum until Felicity came home from work to share the load.

I'm completely at a loss. Who is Rebecca Thompson? What is George seeing her for? For how long has he been seeing her? Is she a consultant or a lover? What is a "communications" consultant anyway? What the hell am I meant to do with this knowledge? I've told no one. I must be in shock.

Thursday, 1 October

The past few days have been a blur. But I've survived.

I went to bed early the night of the Old Flour Mill Fiasco, leaving a note for George saying I had a migraine. I couldn't face him. He came home sometime between 9 and 10. Seriously. Tellingly, he never came to bed but slept on the sofa-bed in the study. He left me a note on his pillow the next morning, explaining, and apologising for not seeing the children. He left early for a breakfast meeting. Sure, sure, I thought: with Her. I resolved to come up with a really awful pseudonym for her – Mildred or Madge or Hussey. In another note – from me to Maria – I pleaded for a lie-in. She managed to get the children up and out before I stumbled to the shower. But what a shower! As the water pounded my weary neck and shoulders I formulated a plan. I would start an organised and strategic assault on Ms Thompson of Thompson Communications to unearth the truth of this "relationship". I had the big objective, the purpose – Get to the Truth.

But then I got confused. My Rational Self told me not to jump to conclusions before all the facts were known. My Primal Inner Woman told me to fight for my man. My (heaving and roiling) Gut told me it was innocent. My Better Self told me to ask him outright who she was. My Inner Child wanted to curl up in the corner of the shower and stay there for a very long time. My Former Self (ad exec) told me to look for the story, the spin and the angle and sell myself anew to win George back. The Mother in me said do what is best for the kids. My Future Self told me to fish or cut bait and to get a lawyer, pronto. I was conflicted, raw and confused. Finally, relying on some meditative breathing and an intense 30 minutes of Ashtanga yoga, followed by another shower, I knew what to do. Nothing – at least to start with and certainly as far as George would notice.

That's right. Nothing. I will pretend all is well, behave as normal, act nonchalant. I'll be like a duck – all calm and smooth and unruffled on the surface. Underneath I'll be kicking and pushing and pulling in the mire of the muddy waters.

So I began straight away. Now it's day 4 and so far, so good. So this journal entry will mark the beginning of a new phase in my life – Journal of a Lonely Housewife – or "How to make the best of your husband's mid-life crisis".

So you have just discovered an awful suspicion may be a brutal and heartbreaking reality. What to do. This is my guide to coping – for what it's worth...

Day 1 - Step 1

Go about your business as if nothing has happened. If you usually go to the gym – go. If you typically wash clothes - wash. If you're due to have your hair done – get it done. If you work – do not call in sick. Don't deviate from your regular pattern in any way, at least for the first half-day. It's crucial in order to convince yourself that you can cope, that you go about normal activities as you've always done. Quiet your racing thoughts and try to be in the moment. The benefits of this are three fold.

First, if you act normal, you will feel normal. If you feel normal you will think more calmly and rationally. So, at all costs, maintain your routine. Second, if everything *appears* as normal, people will not notice that your world has come to an end so you will not have to deal with unwelcome or intrusive questions from your yoga buddies, the salon, the boss/client or the physio, when you cancel out of the blue. Third, retaining a regimen ensures that you maintain some sort of control over your body/face/image/employability/laundry pile. At this stage knowing that you still look good, can function like a professional (if that's what you are) and that your house and persona are still as bright and shining as they were yesterday, buys you time and helps to keep all of your options open. Best not to let slide the hard-won gains at the gym (or on the career ladder) when you're at your most vulnerable to outside attack. In times of the greatest stress you need to be at your physical (or intellectual) prime.

Step 2

Do *not* confide in anyone else just yet. The tears on the nanny's shoulder will be tears in the lawyer's office faster than you can say "stupid whore" if you blurt your suspicions out to the wrong person. People aren't interested in saving your marriage, your face or your child support entitlements, but they'll become very interested in your appearance, your demeanour, your corner office, your children's behaviour and your husband, if it gives them some mileage or the first-knower-advantage at the charity lunch or around the water cooler at the office. If you don't want to be the topic of conversation in every book club, bridge club and golf club within 48 hours, then for goodness sake keep your own counsel.

Step 3

Start a list of what you need to do to ensure that you can follow Steps 1 and 2 for as long as possible while you amass the information and support you need to make an informed decision.

Step 4

If you haven't already done so, go shopping for something really beautiful. You may want something really practical too, like new locks, a sledgehammer or a disguise, but hold fire on these purchases til your emotions are more in check. In keeping with Steps 1 and 2, buying something lovely will not invite suspicion or curiosity, after all we all do this from time to time; it is expected. Indeed, right now you deserve it, but that is your little secret.

Step 5

Get lots of rest. Avoid stimulants and alcohol. Sleep as long and as deeply as you can. Tomorrow's a big day.

Day 2 - Step 6

It is now time to galvanise yourself ready for action. The action needs to be forthright and decisive. I don't mean get ready to make the bed or wash your face. I mean – call the bank and find out what's happening with the accounts. I mean – search your husband's pockets, listen in on his calls, follow him. Put in place the support and processes that you'll need if you are to properly undertake sustained and comprehensive surveillance (i.e. round the clock child care, a sick-note for the boss) or hire the most discreet and expensive operative to do it for you. I could recommend a few if needed (Google baby, Google). The key is to be *low* key. No histrionics, no tears if possible and lots of pragmatic common sense.

So, if the husband is planning a trip out of town this is where you need help to trail him. You want photos, audio, video. If he claims to be at the golf course, call the pro shop looking for him, using the name of one of his clients. If he says he's working late, hire a sitter and stake out his building. The aim is not to catch him in a lie so much as to ascertain what the hell he's really up to.

Keep in mind the fact that so far all that has happened is that he's been dissembling and evasive. You have evidence that he's met a woman; the evidence of an affair is purely circumstantial. It's possible nothing untoward is happening. Possible. And Yet.

For example, what if the suspected amour is in fact a style consultant hired by your husband's company to update his tired and boring image? What if she's his travel agent, retained to book that cruise he promised you when you got engaged? What if he's starting his own business and she's the accountant; he's not told you for fear you'll worry about a loss of income? There are many viable and innocent explanations.

But there are also many viable not so innocent ones too – so be canny and careful.

Day 3 - Step 7

You need to go into overdrive today with the maintenance of the facade of normalcy. Get stepping at the gym, take the front row at your course, speak up loads in book club, pick up the children from school, bake a cake for the teacher, stay back late and finish that memo ahead of time. Call your mother or mother-in-law for an innocent and idle catch up. This is called maintaining good will. You may need it later.

Step 8

Finally and perhaps most importantly, try to act natural around your husband. Be charming, be sweet, be perky and interested, unless to be so would tip him off. Don't try to trick him or defeat him or put one over him. Try to pretend that it's two weeks ago and all's fine (or fine-ish). Spend some relaxed time with him reminding yourself that he was, perhaps still is, someone you love and want to be with.

Day 4

Now that the dust has settled a little, get busy gathering information. No more hoping for the best or fearing the worst. Today you start the process of finding out the truth.

.....

That's as far as I've gotten, myself. Am now contemplating going into business as consultant to victims of infidelity...

Actually, I can't even follow the last few steps above: The 8 Step Programme for Losers in Love. Most of the steps are helpful but I'm not ready for the Truth. I'm going to cycle through days 1 and 2 (Steps 1-5) interspersed with manic keeping busy. What is the need for truth? Who's truth? Could I handle the truth?

No – I need an alternate programme of Denial which revolves around keeping occupied, giving my mind no chance to contemplate, lament or cogitate.

Accordingly, I'm planning to clean the pool tonight before edging the driveway, then I'll relax with something crisp and white with Clothilde. I made a fabulous pavlova for Mrs Melloy at Frobisher earlier. She was delighted and surprised, to say the least. I even achieved a school record - covering 139 books in the Montessori library - and welcomed Helen back to Duck Shop. She's bursting at the seams with child but couldn't bear to disappoint her children who want to see her behind the counter, nor to have to negotiate yet another week off with Wendy. Of course I *had* to help her. It wouldn't do those kids any good to see her waters break over their potato pancakes or jam pikelets. Might improve their flavour though.

Have signed up for another course at the discussion centre – a daytime one so as to be unlikely to run into the staff or students from Male Psyche – though now I'm wishing I'd stuck with Male Psyche. Surely they had a week covering fidelity, sex, commitment and lies! The course is candle making – it's only a two day thing – but it will keep me out of trouble and might even be relaxing. The children love my renewed focus and energy where they are concerned. 12 books at bedtime, an hour with each at the playground yesterday, new shoes for Gracie, tennis racket for Freddie and I finally arranged the lambs and ducks for his party in three weeks. I'm more excited about those lambs than pretty much anything else going on right now. Though a bit of me feels like the biblical shepherd searching for the one lost sheep... But ruminating is not useful!

So I moved swiftly on and found I had time and energy to whip up two new dresses for Gracie to go with the new shoes. I then rustled up three casseroles to store in the freezer. Today after an extra long session with Jorgé at the gym, I also squeezed in my swearing in as the new secretary of the Montessori Parents' Association and a long overdue coffee with Felicity. I even found that a long chat with Tedious Tabitha in which I learnt all about her bathroom tiles was a welcome distraction!

This is what I can only describe in my heightened self aware clarity, as a denial fuelled frenzy of activity. Fearing I may be about to enter a new stage of the process (I assume I'm grieving), given that anger and bargaining may lie ahead, I'm savouring this period of productivity. I feel so empowered by the current mania and heightened sense of normality that I almost wish I had been forced to stop taking George for granted a couple of years ago. Just think what I might have accomplished if I had suspected him of an affair sooner!

I told Felicity nothing. Just portrayed the usual happy families. I know she reports to Mum after she sees me so I can't afford to let down my guard at all. Mum would be all triumphant and give me her "I told you so" face and voice. That would definitely catapult me into the anger phase and I'm not ready to go there yet.

I'll see Beth tomorrow at a Green Mother's morning tea. Not sure whether to confide in her. I'm going to scooter on my new green eco scooter-mobile thingy. In keeping with my sage advice at Step 4 above, I bought this beautiful item yesterday. I am also planning to befriend Scooter Mom at Montessori – she's divorced and might be useful to know. I also bought new wellington boots, a charm bracelet, with a charm for each year I have known George and five new climbing roses to plant. I'm having such a good time.

Now sleep beckons me. I shall pretend that I want to snuggle up to George. Uurghhh.

Saturday, 3 October

Contrary to my own advice in Step 2 above, I confided in Beth. We were sipping green tea at the Green Mothers' Morning Tea, out of green cups in green wellies. It made a gorgeous photo for ECO-MUM magazine, on the shelves in all of the better newspaper shops next week. She was sympathetic but very quick to remind me that so far I only have suspicions and no proof of wrong-doing by George. Indeed, Beth came up with not less than seven alternative interpretations of the Old Flour Mill Fiasco, all of which cast George in a positive light. That said, he remains elusive and tight-lipped. I've drawn this to his attention, not in an accusatory way, but in a model wife way.

"Darling, you seem preoccupied lately. Is something wrong at work? Are you ok? Are you getting enough sleep?"

He dismissed my concerns somewhat impatiently and said that expectations at work are very high in light of events with Phil. He also implied that his mother was "giving him grief" about her party and generally "acting her age". In other words: "Stop nagging me, Verity".

Clearly this can't go on indefinitely, but with Beth championing him and my heart not ready to pinion him, I seem to have no choice but to bide my time. At the very least I need to wait til the end of the month; survive the visit from the prodigal daughter, get through Mrs G's party and give Freddie a wonderful third birthday. Eventually, I'll have to get to the bottom of this Rebecca mystery and find out exactly what's going on.

Right now I have to decide on a new kitchen theme and design, raise the children, and prepare mentally for the arrival of Sophie the Nazi, after I peruse the electronic proofs for Mrs G's green advertising campaign and bake several hundred meringues for the Montessori Cake Stall. I thought meringues would be easy – so few ingredients, fat free, one can use a blender, yummy spoon to lick, kids can help, leftovers can be given to Clothilde for *"Le Petit..."*.

Also if I have to bake, eat or see another gourmet patty cake, I will shove it into the face of the nearest gourmand mother. Who has time to decorate hundreds of these fat filled delights as beetles and butterflies, with little shiny baubles and flowers and God forbid, photographs? Who wants to eat a marzipan picture of their own child? They represent all that is wrong with modern motherhood; unoriginal, boring, inelegant, mutton dressed as lamb, fattening, cardboard tasting, frumpy and phoney.

I said this to Beth yesterday as she tucked into her third green cupcake – baked in silicon cup cake trays without paper wrappers - and she implored me again to "get a grip". It seems the mule is on the other foot, this time. Her coaching is ongoing and keeping her very much on her path of family time and relaxing with Yves. She's so transformed that she actually eats cup cakes now; two months ago she would have sold her children before touching one. Beth insists that as long as I'm in a state of manic productivity and possibly denial I might as well invest in a good dose of therapy to sort out the rest of my life, my past, my unresolved issues with my mother and of course the yet to manifest, dormant but lurking issues with my daughter.

Bugger off Beth! I know what I'm doing. My self-preservation instinct is governing my actions; it's giving me this energy, and the desperate need to avoid the truth. I'm not hurting anyone. I know in my heart that George is tired of me. I've nothing to say to him, I'm not young, interesting or successful. I'm just like an old half eaten, dried out cup cake on the edge of the table waiting for flies to come and poo on me, after they vomit on me.

I'm at a crossroads. Not just because my marriage may be over. *I* lack meaning. I am truly living without purpose. I'm like a boat cast adrift on the high seas, with neither rudder nor sail. All I have to guide me are the other lost boats and the manoeuvres their sailors make. While I scramble madly to follow the red, white and blue colours (US and French mummies) on the other boats – well yachts really - I go in circles much of the time or just bail water, trying to keep afloat. I have no compass of my own, and no skills in navigation.

What if I'm as hopeless as I feel? While Gracie is clearly advanced and gorgeous, these past few months with her have been a trial. Freddie seems in every way *normal* but what if he's just average? They're so young and I'm already burnt out. How am I supposed to raise them for the next 15 years? What if there is nothing I can do to make Freddie faster, brighter or cleverer than all the other little boys? What if he's not even particularly funny or eccentric? Not only will I have given up a good career to have this family, but I'll be stuck in a loveless marriage out of which I will never voluntarily emerge, given my hopeless lack of financial wherewithal - the alternative being to live with mother. It would kill us both. My children will be "from a broken home", blighted by innuendo, controversy and mediocrity. My friends will disown me. I'll have wasted the past 10 years. Even Desirée will recover from Phil's deviancy, but I'll be the sad, hopeless wreck that everyone knows couldn't even keep mild mannered George Fortescue. I feel like a character in an Edith Wharton novel.

Ok, maybe I'm being a bit melodramatic. Even if I believe the best of George, why is it that I can't seem to satisfy or interest him in any way? Whether it's my conversation, my cooking or my company – he is completely disinterested in me. Last night, my salmon *á la croute* was, he said, "reminiscent of college bubble and squeak", my post Flour Mill maintaining-the-facade haircut ($450) left him gasping and my suggestion that I start therapy so as to channel my inner child and thus free me to be a better wife and mother was met with an amused snicker and the remark:

"Verity, in a couple of months Freddie will be at nursery. Surely you can endure charity lunches, buying clothes and keeping the house til then."

As if that's *all* I do!

Then he added:

"If you want to be a better wife and mother, just stop trying so hard and start enjoying your life."

Mmm. I bet Rebecca the Hussey enjoys her life.

Monday, 5 October

Today was better. I'm looking at the current situation as a J curve. From here the only way is up. Green Day was perhaps the low point. But today I think I might have turned a corner. During breakfast – rushed coffee at the sink for George and whole wheat pancakes for the children – the phone rang. I answered it and spoke with the caller.

"Rebecca Thompson calling for George please."

Shit! "Certainly," I chimed, cheerful and chipper.

"George, it's Rebecca," I chirruped.

He looked at me with a vexed and confused look – or so it seemed - and took the phone into the hallway. I couldn't hear anything. The children were watching so I couldn't even leave my station by the stove, as Gracie would no doubt tell George:

"Mummy was not respecting your privacy Daddy." Damn.

I gritted my teeth and smiled at the kids as if beautiful blonde mistresses call family homes every day – nothing weird, wanton or sinister there.

Finally – it was actually only two minutes - though it was long enough for my life to flash before my eyes and my old room at Mum's to loom at me through the open kitchen window – George returned. He had the gall to ruffle Freddie's hair and squeeze Gracie's cheek, refill his mug and blithely sip his fresh cup of coffee.

"A colleague?" I asked, all innocent and interested, after a pregnant pause.

"A consultant," said George.

"Oh, who does she work for?"

"She runs her own business. She's done extremely well, actually. She's in communications."

Oh that old chestnut. "What does she do?"

"She manages messages and tailor makes images to enhance stock value and shareholder satisfaction."

"Fascinating." Yawn.

"I think so. But the Board have decided not to use her services so she was calling to say good-bye. She leaves town today."

"Shame."

Suddenly, from nowhere, Freddie threw a squidgy half-masticated pancake at George. Dough, syrup, blueberry and banana landed on the shoulder of his new Zegna suit and rolled with a plop, onto his shoes.

Pandemonium ensued. Maybe Freddie is not so average after all. At the very least he's highly intuitive. Consultant? Calling to say good-bye? Why did she have his home number? Where is she flying to? Is she coming back? The whole episode raised more questions than it answered. And unless he's a simpleton, George now knows I know something. Or perhaps he only suspects I suspect something.

Can I use this to my advantage? Yes – the power has clearly shifted in my direction. So things began to improve from that point on, despite my next chore – a trip to the dry cleaner's with that suit. From there I went to the airport to pick up Sophie, her grey husband Richard, and her two Mensa member children, Charlie and Claude (God forbid!).

Where was I going to find time to update Beth?

The rest of the day was given over to me feigning interest in Sophie's news from London, while the children caught up with each other in Mrs G's garden. Thankfully they all had a nap after lunch and Mrs G and I spent a good couple of hours going over her Green Space campaign that she'll launch on Friday. The project is ambitious, yet utterly compelling and sustainable. I'm delighted she's had a use for me. She's a visionary.

It's now very late. George fell asleep as soon as his head hit the pillow at 10pm. His sister exhausts him even more than she does me, and I had a day of her, not just dinner. She's mastered jet lag recovery and like some scientific miracle freak traveller is never fatigued.

Saturday, 10 October

Where have the last 5 days gone? I can barely lift my fingers to type. The week has been frenetic. Mrs G's party was a triumph. She's truly an icon. In every respect the affair was wonderful – elegant, joyous and memorable. Mrs G looked fantastic in a Dior gown of French navy in silk taffeta. I wore deep pink, not vermilion as Sophie called it, nor magenta as Richard insisted, but cerise. I glowed. In spite of all the stress and my overwhelmingly fraught time of late – I glowed.

Indeed, Mrs G's very sauve and charismatic bridge partner, Hugo, declared me "enchanting". Given he's only 55, I accepted this compliment graciously and saved the last dance for him.

George was very debonair in his dinner suit; his chest puffed out like a proud penguin coming of age. Sophie and Richard bored me senseless naming the colours of all the frocks in view all night. For intelligent people they are frightfully dull, but proof positive that there is someone for everyone. Remarkably they failed to describe Sophie's dress - a rather startling shade of yellow, dare I call it chartreuse. What had I been so worried about?

After an excruciating three days with Sophie buying all sorts of nonsense that she claims is better here than in London, I was so weary of hearing her voice and opinions that I almost overdosed on Nurofen before leaving for the party. I misread the instructions on the box – swearing off medicines a few years ago when several of the girls in the ante-natal class claimed to be addicted to herbal sleep potions or over the counter pain meds for the sciatica and neck aches - and I accidentally took four out of the blister pack rather than two, thinking it said four every two hours, rather than the converse.

George, needing some himself after a fraught week at work, grabbed the handful when I went to get some water and washed it down with whisky before I could stop him. Being a head honcho at Pharma Co he has no excuse for making that sort of mistake so I can only conclude it was deliberate and he's either drifting over the line into drug abuse or suicidal tendencies due to having spent too much concentrated time with his sister this week, or he's missing his consultant "friend" and can't go on without dulling the pain anyhow that he can. Now if he develops as ulcer, an addiction or suddenly drops dead, it will most definitely *not* be my fault. As if I didn't have enough on my plate to deal with. He seemed alright last night - and we were almost a fairy tale couple at the party - so perhaps an overdose of pain meds does him good. Certainly seems to keep Mia's mates at the yacht club in sparkling form.

Mrs G, never perturbed by the surroundings and ever prepared to speak her mind, said to me mid-party:

"What's been bothering George lately? Don't tell me it's just Sophie being here; he's been horrible for weeks. He's like his father was when he had his mid-life crisis. Is he coming home at night?" Speechless I gulped down my champagne and nodded vehemently.

"Yes, he's acting a little oddly but none of his routines have changed. He's just sullen and withdrawn."

"Might be his prostate," she confided turning on her rather lovely heel and linking her arm with Yves (where does one put the apostrophe there?!).

Yves and Beth are very committed to spending more time together and are getting on famously once more. Whether it was the spa day or the coaching or some other intervention, she seems to be back to normal; well beyond normal – actually happy. Never one to pay a compliment, Sophie made several snide remarks about Beth's appearance.

"Trust me Verity, I see it constantly in London, she's *on* something and that forehead's been filled." I swear she was adopted at birth.

Finally, as the festivities drew to a close, Mrs G launched, to the avid interest of immediate family and close friends and supporters (148 people) and at least 5 local journalists, her "Green Spaces" campaign. Thank goodness for outdoor garden theatres, eh? I was very proud of the campaign. It showcases the work of an amazing local topiarist and features a fragrant and inspiring maze, replete with fountain at its centre spurting recycled water.

The underpinning rationale for the project is that cities need more green spaces in the streetscape. Not parks, per se, but small outdoor green rooms – a herb garden here, a lavender patch there, a maze down that street, a hedgerow over there by that bus stop. Instead of signs and fences and bins and all the other bland manmade paraphernalia that clutter the pavements, we should be surrounded by little green substitutes. The guests at the party were rapturous, as only drunk masses can be. Buoyed by their enthusiasm and her own resolve, Mrs G takes her initiative to local government next week.

Sunday, 11 October

Today was rather quiet and anti-climactic after the hullabullo of the past week.

Defying all of our expectations, George woke early and went fishing with Harry. It feels as though he's been avoiding me all week – punishing me for existing. He's the master of passive aggressive right now. As though it took all he had to get through Friday night, he's now waging a cold war, full of stand offs and ambiguous gestures, reminiscent of secondary school. I have to admit I'm exhausted. I'm utterly at a loss as to what to do about him. Neither of us has broached the topic of Rebecca since that phone call on Monday. But he's different now - very diffident towards the children - which is troubling me as well as them. Even Maria, not the sharpest tool in the box, raised an eyebrow this morning in response to some offhand remark George made to Freddie. It's most disconcerting. At this rate I'll be at the child psychologist every week.

Meanwhile, since George is inaccessible, *I* spent the entire day with the children and now have worries about Gracie. She just doesn't seem ok. She counts everything. It's not normal to count steps, peas, Cheerios in her bowl, even cars passing ours in the street. I know she's gifted and talented but I think I'll have to take her back to the anxiety counsellor and have this checked. I've never heard of anyone counting everything, and keeping the number in her head too. So she remembers that yesterday she had 43 cheerios and today she had 49, yesterday she passed 9 silver cars, today she passed 15 white cars. Maybe she's autistic? Can one develop OCD from stress? I'll have to do some research tomorrow. This is all I need. George will *definitely* check out if she has a special need.

Desirée called late in the afternoon to hear how the party went and to commiserate on the fact Sophie is still blighting the landscape. It's one thing for me to moan about Sophie, but when others who haven't even met her weigh in, I can't help feeling I ought to defend her. Poor Desirée. She's a bundle of negative energy, struggling to find anything good to say about anyone these days. I thought she would thrive without Phil around, but she's lost and depressed. Not really the person I thought she was. I feel like telling her to man up and take some control back, but she doesn't seem open to any suggestions at all. I hate to be uncharitable but she's too negative, even for me, right now.

Tuesday, 13 October

Well, well, well. The counsellor thinks Gracie may be gifted with numbers. I couldn't tell him about George and the current tension in the house, but I alluded to some stress being a constant in our lives due to my husband's work, demands of family life and the schools admission process over past few months. He said that children often develop a special gift in times of lull or rest following periods of intense stress or occupation. Well done Verity, stressing her out so much really paid off!

He suggested that I start to channel her current interest into basic number facts and helping her consolidate her understanding of more advanced concepts. He also said she may need more artistic outlets. He gave me a list of things to look out for to reassure me that she's unlikely to have OCD. It was very encouraging – I think I could live with a savant like daughter, rather than a neurotic one. There are enough neuroses in the family already. He told me to keep it light and try to have some fun with her. So this afternoon we devised a bar chart so that she can pictorially represent the quantity of cars, cereal and stars and so on and minutes spent brushing her teeth each day.

Such was my relief that I called Beth to tell her all of this. She's such an old hand with counsellors and the manifestation of stress and even psychosis that I really needed her views. Beth's opinion is that Gracie is trying to control her environment and given she's super bright, she's not channeling her energy into eating disorders or tantrums, as most 5 year olds would, but counting everything around her. Beth thinks I need to capitalise on this while Sophie is here, thereby giving myself a much needed pick-me-up. She thinks it will do me good to feel superior to Sophie, or at the very least feel I can intimidate and compete with her. The truth is, gave up on that a long time ago. Beth suggested that a few pyrrhic victories with the least liked in-law will give me a huge boost in self esteem after such a harrowing time of late.

Beth has my interests at heart, I know but somehow I don't really have the appetite for a competition right now. I rang Mrs G to congratulate her on the success of her party and mentioned Gracie's newfound love of counting. I didn't make too much of it – felt silly even mentioning it. She may report it to Sophie. But is all seems petty and childish. I haven't the energy for overt gloating. In a pitched battle of the bright children, I think Sophie would win, anyway. Also, in light of Harriet's comments about George, I know that I'm perceived as competitive. Strategically, it would not be a good idea to rave on about Gracie's talents this week only for the rumours that George is sleeping around, to explode next week.

I tried to explain Gracie's situation to George over dinner. He actually looked interested in what I was saying by the end of the meal. At the start of my explanation of the "number thing" I could see he was trying very hard not to criticise my parenting skills. He looked implacable and even slightly annoyed. But the bar graph of Gracie's observations was a master stroke on my part. When he saw one that we did earlier, he was captivated. I think he might even have a glimmer of respect for my ingenuity where that was concerned.

I have generated a few graphs of my own.

Eg:

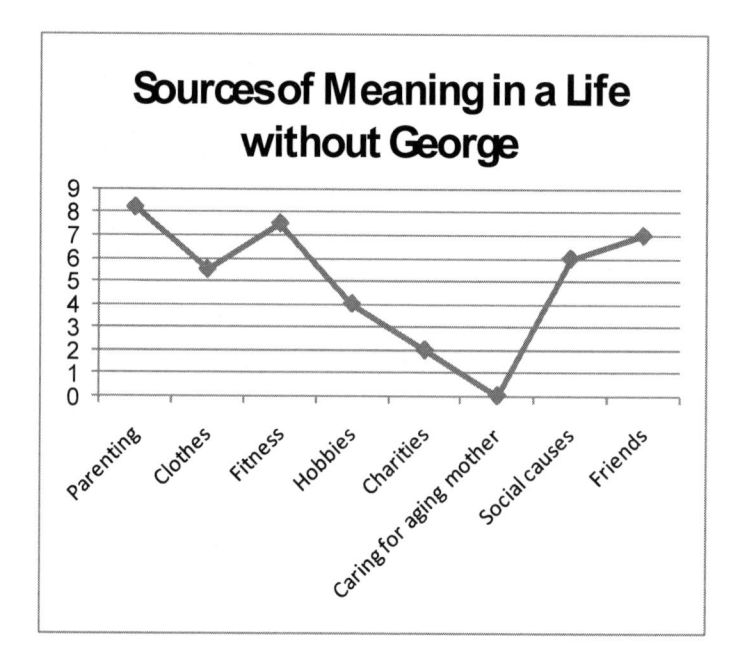

Sources of Meaning in a Life without George

(Line graph with y-axis 0–9 and x-axis categories: Parenting, Clothes, Fitness, Hobbies, Charities, Caring for aging mother, Social causes, Friends)

Or – How to Solve A Problem Like Rebecca...

[Rebecca] + [Me] ➡ [George]

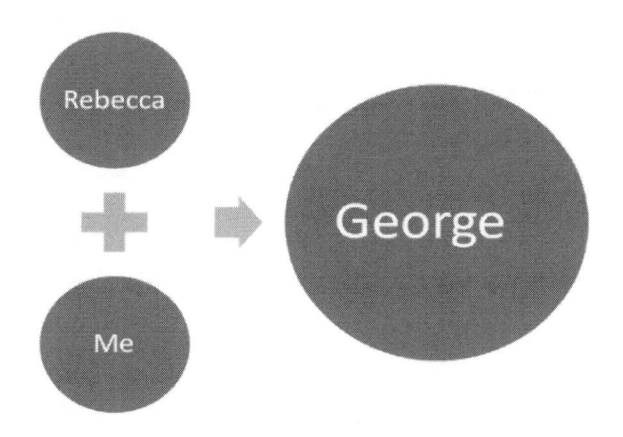

I also graphed my recent rankings of friends:

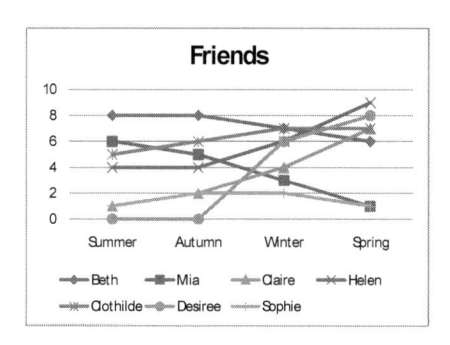

Friends
(line graph with x-axis: Summer, Autumn, Winter, Spring; y-axis: 0 to 10; series: Beth, Mia, Claire, Helen, Clothilde, Desiree, Sophie)

Oh George – what are you up to?!

Saturday, 17 October

The past few weeks have been immensely stressful and I've been so preoccupied with just keeping busy and doing things with the family that I've lost touch with most of my friends. Scared that I would have none left, I arranged a little soirée tonight. It was actually bizarre to have them all in one place. My line graph focused my mind somewhat on who and what I've been putting energy into this year, so in order to confirm my thinking or assuage my guilt or some other ulterior motive, like keep in their good books for the disaster that may be lurking in the not too distant future, I invited Cothilde, Beth, Mia (crazy, I know, but she phoned me to ask after Sophie and I felt cornered), Claire, Helen, Sophie (still here!), Desirée and sort of as an afterthought (but another inspired move as it turned out), Emma from ballet (of Austin, Texas).

When we had our spa day last month I noticed that Spring to Mind Spa hires out rooms to the public for events, lunches, launches etc. so I booked one of the terraces overlooking the garden. Being an urban hideaway it was conveniently located for all my guests and fabulously intimate as well. Beneath fairy lights and on a scrumptious jarrah wood veranda deck, I treated the girls to a Marlborough (so consistent of me) region wine selection and tapas. It was rather giggly in parts and very heated in others. The highlight was Sophie going head to head with Mia over discipline. I have to admit Sophie really floored Mia. Mia has no discipline – self or other – and really has no idea how to follow rules, so it was quite a sight to see her struggling to argue the point with Sophie; living proof that rigour brings results.

My mind was wandering off topic a little during this debate as I knew already who had won and I've heard a million times Mia's views on letting children be free (translated, this means pay someone to do all the mothering until they go off the rails and embarrass you). All the while Helen was shifting uncomfortably beside me. It seems she has some trapped wind at this stage of her confinement and between hers and Sophie's hot air I was a little uncomfortable. Desirée was giving me meaningful looks across the table. She was upwind of Helen so it could only have been about Sophie or Mia that she was catching my eye. But Clothilde did some French eye rolling and *"merding"* as well, and interjected from time to time with her opinions, so it was by no means a dull evening. I was grateful to have Emma there too. While virtually Texan royalty she is incredibly down to earth and jocular and really shook Mia up at one stage when she called her a "wild and crazy old trollop".

"I swear I've heard of you all over town Mia. The girls from Francesca's (hairdresser) are always talking about you. You go girl."

It was priceless.

Sophie, in her inimitable style, was just appalling. She's a boorish know-it-all, but even boorish know-it-alls cannot lay claim to expertise on every single topic. And yet, she thinks she knows more than Emma about Mexican immigration across the Texan border, more than Beth about real estate prices on the south coast and more than Clothilde about the ins and outs of membership of *"Le Petit..."*. As the hostess, it fell to me to distract her to let the others speak without interruption on more than one occasion. Exhausting. She and her prodigies leave in two days, thank God. Lucky Richard has had some peace since he went back to London straight after Mrs G's party. The only problem now is that Emma can be under no illusions about our real Christmas plans. Anyone could see that we wouldn't be rushing over to Val D'Isère to spend time with Sophie again so soon.

Nevertheless, I realised how lucky I am to have these women in my life, all different, all interesting, all doing their best (yes even Mia and Sophie in their own ways). Some of their anecdotes lightened my mood immensely – putting my worries about George into perspective. Emma had numerous tales of cads she dated in her younger years. Even

Sophie had some third hand stories of colleagues whose appalling antics shock and sicken her.

Anyway, Desirée called me today to say that Mia drove her home (drunk) and quizzed her about Phil, his whereabouts, whether they are together, whether he "is playing away", Whether she has enough help (as she thinks my girl – Maria - might be ready to move), whether she needs access to better schools.

Desirée claimed she was ready to join Phil in Latvia after 10 minutes alone in the car with her.

I am livid with Mia. She is *officially* blacklisted now as far as I'm concerned. It is all very well to pick on George, to make a move on Yves and to gossip about half the city, but purporting to offer *my nanny* to another mother is beyond the pale!

After hearing from Desirée, I played a game of cards with Gracie – she wants to learn poker, but I insisted it be cribbage first (Sophie's influence) – when Helen's husband rang to say the evening out with my friends was all Helen needed to precipitate labour and their fifth baby was born at 6 am this morning. No longer keen on the name Sophie, they have yet to agree on another. What wonderful news!

Damn – I forgot to call Felicity about Freddie's birthday. She was very snooty with me last week when I asked her to cater. Told me they don't do children's parties anymore. I know for a fact she did three ballet parties in the Autumn. One was Orphan Annie themed (easy to cater that one – or maybe I'm mixing up Annie with Oliver Twist). Another was all Seaside oriented – copying me no doubt from two years ago when I introduced these people to serving chips in paper cones. While the third was Alice in Wonderland. Felicity is mad if she thinks I don't know they do kids' parties. We were there! Gracie went as the Mad Hatter because I wouldn't let her upstage the birthday girl's Alice. At least 7 other mothers didn't have my compunctions, I noted. And I should also point out – to no one of course – that it was through me that Felicity met those Americans and rest of the pharma and ballet cliques who give her loads of business. I reckon she owes me at least one kiddie's party.

But no – she is standing firm. In fact, I haven't seen her so insistent in years. She says she has to draw a line at children's parties as it's nearly the silly season and she just has no more capacity. So either I find another caterer with 7 days to go, call off the event or do it myself. Beth says I should call Mum and get her onside to help. But Beth doesn't see the bigger picture. A perfect party is far less important than my integrity and saving face with my family.

I could do it myself. I undertook far more during my DIY-from-scratch phase, but right now I really don't feel up to it. It's not just shopping and arranging the menu, but the cleaning and decorating and catering for a host of farm creatures – the livestock I mean - not the guests. I cannot rely on George to help. Even with Maria and Carla's help it all seems just too much. I'm not the woman I was. A mere 2 years ago I would have jumped at the challenge, acquitted myself with pride and glory and been fending away accolades and offers of employment as party planner, decorator and chef. Now – I can't face it. George made a suggestion in his *drôle* fashion that since Freddie's first birthday was such a runaway success I could just do a repeat performance; even extend an olive branch to the Gordons and invite Fat Little Katie to come. Oh, I'm ruing my decision to host it at home. Why didn't I just book a track day or an aquarium trip or a night at the museum?

This is very difficult. Not only am I cross with Felicity and in a quandary as to how to sort this out, but I feel that I'm letting Freddie down terribly and perhaps, even worse, letting myself down. I know that I can't lay all of the blame at Felicity's door, tempting though it is. This past month has been so manic that I dropped the ball on the party front and just blithely assumed Felicity would be there for me. Live and learn.

I wonder if I could persuade Freddie to accept an alternative. Maybe we could take him for a picnic at the zoo – just us and one or two little friends, say Beth's boys. But that would invite problems as I would be disinviting thirty children and then rolling up to a commercial attraction with just four children. Someone would be sure to see us or hear about it – half the women I know have season tickets at the zoo.

I know, we could take him swimming with dolphins! As three is the minimum age for this he would be first cab off the rank among his peers. Gracie would love it and Mrs G would think me terribly eco-friendly. As much as I love her, I need to be cynical now and anything I can do to curry favour with her, I should do, just in case. One never knows...

We could make a weekend of it – at the dolphin place - and I could spend some quality time with George at last. And best of all, if I cancel the party I can blame Felicity, rather than my own lack of organisation and distractedness. Not only that, with the guilt it will occasion her when I prime Freddie to call his cousin and disinvite her and disappoint her (horsey little Jessica), I may get some help down the track. Frobisher parties are bound to be smart – Felicity will owe me a big one for Gracie's sixth birthday next year.

Wednesday, 21 October

Spent the day calling mothers of children I'd invited to the farm party to tell them it it's cancelled and chasing the animal guy to beg him not to bring the lambs. Freddie was very grown up and said he didn't mind cancelling the party. He minded losing the lambs though. The reason I gave to all those mothers was the truth. After a very busy few weeks for the family I realised I'd taken on too much and, given Freddie was indifferent, I felt it was best to cancel.

There were some rather stunned silences. It would seem that cancelling a party is just not done. And certainly not the way to reveal one has overcommitted. Far better to kill oneself providing the promised event and entertainment, than to disappoint 30 three year-olds. Of course, a legitimate excuse like a death in the immediate family, loss of job or house or serious, incapacitating and infectious illness would have been acceptable. I know what to do if this ever happens again. Next time I'll blame swine flu or an outbreak of bird flu amongst the rented flock of party ducks quacking away (still!) on the terrace. That will clear those women off. They'll thank me for cancelling.

One small mercy is that I didn't have to deal with Mia at all. It was most prescient of me to have not invited Toby. One less set of questions, recriminations and accusations to deal with. The only person who was reasonable was Hannah. She said she doesn't know how I manage to do a party for every birthday and that it's time to start looking after myself more.

Wonder what she knows...

Nevertheless, in spite of George's raised eyebrows when I told him the party was off, I'm basically impervious to the implied and explicit criticism from all my so called friends on this occasion. Galvanised to please myself and Freddie, I've booked three nights at the Golden Sands Holiday Resort and Spa and arranged three consecutive days of swimming with dolphins for the children. George was fine about it and even agreed this would be more enjoyable and memorable for Freddie. I doubt Freddie will remember beyond two years from now, but Gracie and I will.

The whole ridiculous situation has made me rethink my approach to parenting. Like so many women, I make decisions based on what I think people expect me to do. We compete to create the most amazing and over the top events for infants. We're not doing it for the children at all; at least not until they are six or seven and are at school and maybe compare themselves to others. Any younger and they have the attention span of a gnat and only limited capacity to enjoy a clown or a fairy or a mini-water park shipped into their garden for an afternoon. Somehow a baby brings with it a loss of the ability to make sensible decisions. The thinking is: I have enough money to hire a circus for the garden, Hollywood people do it, I have to upstage the last three events, therefore a circus it will be. God forbid I should do anything low key or age appropriate or (gasp!) - not hold a party. That would mean I'm a bad and lazy parent.

I'm really grateful to Felicity for being unavailable, to George for maybe having an affair, to Freddie for being so easy and straight forward, and to Hannah for her words of support.

If I'm completely honest I've rarely thought this hard about most of the things I've done as a parent. If in doubt, copy everyone else. If confused, do what the other mothers do. If there are options, choose the one that reflects best on me. Not very mature. But – no more. I've surprised myself this past week with how honest I can be with myself and how I'm not racked with guilt or self doubt about any of this. I think I'm ready to take some of the workshops at Spring to Mind Spa.

E.g. **Making time for me** - *harness your selfish whims and give them purposeful life.*

I'll still manipulate Felicity into helping me if Gracie wants a party next year. That's a different kettle of fish altogether. But I'll be sure to keep it simple, listen to what Gracie wants and only invite *her* friends, not mine.

Tuesday, 27 October

We've just returned from the beach. The dolphins were wonderful. Freddie was in heaven! George could only stay Saturday and Sunday so we travelled in two cars and the first dolphin experience was without Daddy. So be it. George was more communicative than he has been for ages. We took a walk on the beach on Saturday afternoon. While the children scampered along ahead of us he told me that he wants more time for himself. No kidding George!

He said he feels all he does is work and parent and neither gives him pleasure anymore. He says he's lost himself. Crikey – you're not the only one mate! Intriguing. Not sure what this all means yet. I was a little too stunned to answer him. I was half expecting him to announce he's leaving me for a communication consultant, but that revelation never came. The conversation just ended and we walked in silence the rest of the way back. The big question as to whether Rebecca has a part in this "I'm lost and not enjoying my life (with you and our children)" dilemma is still unanswered. What is her role? Is this just a pretext? Is he in denial that he is in love with her? Will she help him find himself? I'm kicking myself for not asking questions on the weekend - not for his sake – for mine. I'm never lost for words normally. What was I thinking? That less is more all of a sudden?

I'm still processing all of this. I suppose it's a breakthrough – he's told me something anyway – which is a start. I just don't know what role we have in the life of someone who's lost, tired and fed up. Is that just a long winded self protective confabulation to avoid admitting he is seeing someone else? Beth is adamant that George isn't having an affair. She thinks it's an early midlife crisis, as Mrs G suggested. Is that better? I might have a chance of holding onto him through an affair, but

139

a mid-life crisis could end anywhere. Why must he be so earnest? Why can't he just buy a new car like everyone else? Or do what all the other 40 something men do after they buy the new car; take a boys trip trekking in Patagonia or up Mt Kilimanjaro.

Meanwhile, Felicity isn't talking to me. The ballet mums have been gossiping about how she would not cater Freddie's party. Kate asked Felicity outright why she wouldn't do it. I gather the words used were:

"But you catered Betty-Jo's "Alice" party! And not your own nephew? Are you and Verity estranged? Is it a jealousy thing? Has it always been tenuous?"

Mum actually rang and told me to stop badmouthing Felicity. I denied all knowledge. I went out of my way to take responsibility for the cancellation and never mentioned her at all in any of those phonecalls. I'm livid that these women have nothing better to do than invent dramas and speculate about my family business. I rang Felicity and explained that I'd made no such allegations and that people will always say what they think or suspect – just ignore it. I told her I had plenty of my own reasons for cancelling and was pleased we did the dolphins instead. If anything, she did me a favour. She didn't believe me. She said:

"Well where would else would your druggie buddy Kate hear such a thing if not from you?" She's such a prima donna – and getting Mum involved is just adolescent – worse, pre-pubescent. Man, get over yourself, Felicity.

....

As if that weren't enough to contend with, Christmas Play roles were handed out at Montessori today. Gracie, despite leaving at the end of this term, was given a dud role. Or perhaps it's because she's leaving! She's the Christmas sprite (not sure where the sprite comes into the donkey and stable scene) – in fact, one of *three* Christmas sprites – but the other two are fat and dumpy, so we can more or less regard her as the dancing star. Maybe the parents of the other sprites will have the good judgement to keep them home on the day of the concert. I'm going to be selfish this year – look after myself, I should say - and do nothing to help at school. I singlehandedly made 23 costumes last year – not quite over the do-it-from-scratch-thing at that time! Well and truly woken up now. And besides, as secretary of the Parents' Association next year no one will remember that I didn't pull my weight this time.

I now have to focus on the Christmas holidays and how to spend them. George has more than six weeks leave accrued; ample time for a solo or boys' trekking holiday as well as a quality family vacation. I need him to say what he wants to do. Though I dread being alone with him and am dividing my time between avoiding him and being Pollyanna-esque around him, we need proper time together.

Friday, 30 October

The children asked if we would go trick or treating tomorrow. I banned all contact with the neighbours apart from Clothilde following last year's Halloween debacle. Gracie ate some liquorice from the Prices two doors down and had a diarrheic gastric bug for the next week. One glance at the state of their garden tells me that the place must be infested with insects and vermin. It's overgrown and reeks of rotting undergrowth. Last year it was George, in an attempt to be the fun and merry parent, who took them around the street knocking on doors for food – so crass. I said that we do not do Halloween and they needed to go to bed. But George insisted they needed to have the experience. I stood on the doorstep like a crazy woman from some deep South tragedy ringing my hands and recounting the tale of the child who had his throat and oesophagus cut by razor blades in the mints all those years ago, but he ignored me with that flippant little wave he gives me when he thinks I'm being neurotic. Well, five days of illness and a filling in Gracie's tooth at the age of 5 should ensure we stay in with our doors bolted tight this year. Clothilde may pop in with Emmanuelle for some marshmallows just to be sociable, but that's all.

George will not be home in any case. Pharma Co, being US owned is having a Halloween party for staff and families. I begged off. The children don't need the sugar and I don't need the pressure to appear happy little wifey number one. I'm sure people there know we are having problems. The place leaks like an old tent in the rain. Moreover, I'm not going out alone with George again until *he* suggests the outing and doesn't invite children to come along too.

I'm almost ready to move out of denial into anger. I can't go on pretending anymore that he's just busy. He's patently unhappy. *And* I saw him with Rebecca the Harlot. And he looked happy with her. It's time to accept the new reality. He's over being a Pharma Co guy and tired of being a parent. I've not asked him his state of mind about being *married*. Would rather not hazard a guess. Maybe if I had let him buy the mini-Cayenne for Freddie this might have been avoided...

So, am I grieving anymore? Longing for the good old days when George and I would sit for hours in his parents garden chatting and making plans for the future, or even the not so old days when we would just seek each other out to discuss our day, the children or the news? Yes. But I'm no longer in denial, that's for sure. I'm not sure that I'm angry and I don't think I'm about to start bargaining. Rather, I think I'm in whingey acceptance mode out of sheer mental and emotional exhaustion. What alternative is there?

I can only stay calm and hope for the best and keep the children from being upset by the situation. Maybe I'm a robot, or hard hearted. I haven't cried since the day after I saw him at the Flour Mill hotel.

Perhaps my subconscious prepared me for losing George then. And anyway, it could be a lot worse. He's not abusing me or fighting with me. I've not heard any horrid rumours about other women. He's not a porn addict. Is he? Assuming what he said at the beach is true then there is no one else. But I don't know what to think. If only he would talk to me.

Monday, 2 November

Went to mass yesterday with Helen. It was her first trip out with her gorgeous little baby, Eloise. I wanted to go for Dad's anniversary. He would have so loved having grandchildren. It's unimaginable some days to think of how much of my life he's not been here for. He was such a force for good and so light-hearted. Despite Mum's controlling ways, he always kept things real and simple. I miss him still. I wonder what he would make of us all now. All our lives, our problems, our issues, our petty peeves. He would dismiss them with a cursory wave and little joke and a suggestion that we "take a little walk to clear out heads". He took a lot of little walks when Mum was hounding Felicity to study and cut her hair and put on tights and tidy her room. In some ways he's so much better off where he is... I just wish I could see him again, occasionally. He would know what to do.

Right now I can honestly say that I have no idea where George is. He texted me earlier to say he would be delayed and to eat without him. Then another text arrived just now saying not to wait up. He could be anywhere. He could be aboard a jet. A Pharma Co jet or a small chartered thing that allows him to liaise in person with beautiful communication consultants around the globe. He could be in some hotel room with Rebecca, or maybe even in another city with her. Whoever invented the text message has a lot to answer for.

This is the third night in the past week that he has played this little trick. The children have barely seen him since the dolphin trip. I think I need to confront him: face up to this reality once and for all.

I'll have a little swim to clear my head – can't go far with the children asleep here and no other adults in the house. Maybe I should; maybe if I disappeared for a night he might realise he's avoiding his responsibilities and come home. He thinks I'm a sap, sitting here with my sad little journal in the dark, nothing to do, no one to see, waiting on his texts.

Friday, 6 November

George finally came home before I was asleep. In fact he broke his routine and actually read the children a bedtime story. I feel as if I have been in some sort of suspended animation this past couple of weeks. I'm going through the motions with everyone. I can summon up some energy for the children; indeed they are my one joy and solace. Mrs G rang me yesterday saying she had not heard from me and was everything alright. I let down my guard and told her I have no idea what is going on with George. She offered to come over, but it all seemed too melodramatic. I'm more numb than sad, to be frank. I think my mind has slowly and unconsciously adjusted to the fact that he's virtually gone. Slowly but surely he's moving on, out of reach.

Mrs G said she suspected some sort of trouble in the lead up to her party, but didn't want to alarm or upset me. She said his father went AWOL for a good year when George was in the States doing his internship, so she always feared it might reoccur. Something to do with an overdeveloped yet admirable sense of responsibility for the troubles of the world. Problem is Mr G did not have two young children at home when he went "AWOL". Also George and his father are different people and problems don't "reoccur" across a generation. This is a new situation. What exactly does she think she's telling me? And where does an over-developed sense of responsibility come into the equation if he can't even drive his daughter to school or kick a ball with his son without feeling burdened and miserable?

I must confront him. This is no way to live.

Bugger. I just remembered. The Montessori school fête is tomorrow. President Wendy has left me seven messages today checking that I am prepared to man the slip 'n' slide!

Saturday, 7 November

Bloody Montessori. Sunburnt, knackered, pissed off. Just right for a chat with George!

Tuesday, 10 November

I see above what I wrote just four days ago. I must be clairvoyant. Or perhaps I put it out there and the universe sent it to me. George is moving out next weekend. He needs to find himself and he's using the opportunity of a special project in Hong Kong for Pharma Co as his means to do so. I hope he succeeds. Seems to me that a "special project" might take up all of his capacity and he'll come back even further from himself than he is now, if he comes back at all. It's all so sudden. He keeps saying we're not separating; it's merely a career enhancing step that will buy us all some time and space. How fortuitous.

How did this happen? I've been going over it in my head all day. Maria kept Freddie busy in the pool and garden while I had a manic spring cleaning episode in the house. The kitchen is gleaming – just in time for the builders. It seems ridiculous to be redoing the kitchen while my husband is leaving me. Helen says to pretend he's going off to war. Life goes on.

Would he have taken this opportunity in Hong Kong if I'd not confronted him Saturday night? Expecting yet more obfuscation and denial and a good dose of passive aggressive drawer slamming – very difficult with the state-of-the-art drawer quieteners - I was taken aback with what ensued. It was right after I last wrote in my journal. He was meticulously folding up his clothes – for the hamper - and arranging his shoes in the wardrobe – as if it mattered where he put his shoes. I was sitting up in bed with the kitchen design magazine open beside me and my laptop secreted in the bedside table drawer (having just finished my latest rant).

"George," I said, almost calmly, "I've tried to give you some space lately. I want to be patient and accommodating, but we both know you're unhappy. You said you feel lost but I don't understand; I don't know what's wrong." He looked away, pulling off his socks and balling them up together. He took aim for the hamper; missed.

I continued: "I know it isn't work that's keeping you out all hours of the night. I know that you're up to something that you feel you can't talk to me about. I've gone over every possibility in my mind - over and over. You've no idea what I am coming up with to explain all of this. Insider trading? An addiction? An affair? A disease? A newfound love of ten pin bowling? A sideline selling drugs? No matter what it is, I think you owe me the truth. I'm still your wife and still the mother of your children. Please, tell me what's going on?"

George sat down at the end of the bed. A good sign, I thought. Then he buried he head in his hands and sighed deeply. Not such a good sign.

"Verity, you're right. I owe you an explanation. I appreciate the space and that you're not pushing me to talk. I'm grateful. The truth is more or less what I told you at the beach. I just can't see clearly. I feel hollow. I feel old. I've no idea what I want anymore. And I'm sorry. I can't really explain it."

He reached for my hand then and rubbed it like he used to. "I'm not doing anything illegal. I'm not selling drugs – or taking drugs." Phew, my visions of a deal going wrong under the railway tracks and Mia's dealer giving everyone up at the local copshop, started to recede.

"Well where are you every night?" I asked incredulously.

George looked sheepish. He stood up and began rearranging the books by his bed. National Geographic now at the bottom.

"At Mum's – though she doesn't know it. I let myself into the garden and sit there thinking." No, she certainly doesn't know it! I thought to myself.

"Oh George – what's the problem exactly? When did this start?" I started to feel genuinely concerned. He seemed to be in earnest. While George is a wonderful person, acting, like physical coordination isn't one of talents. His despondency was clearly genuine. I was also starting to feel a little relieved that it wasn't me, per se, to blame.

"It's been coming on for months, perhaps years. Maybe since Freddie was born. I was denying it for a long time, but this thing with Phil really brought home to me what an intricate web of lies and dissemblance we create. The guy is twisted and lost; a fraud. I can't bear to think of hurting you and the kids, like that, but I feel like a fraud too. I'm living a lie and I don't know how else to live." He flopped down on his pillows beside me and reached out to me again. I took his hand, thinking "Oh God, he's gay."

"Are you...?" I couldn't give voice to the words. I held his hand and looked out the window. The trees were moving in the breeze outside. It was a lovely spring night, blustery and cool with the scent of wet earth in the air. George read my mind.

"No – don't go there. It's not porn and I'm not gay. It's nothing like that." He paused, staring at my magazine as if the answers lay there amidst the glossy pictures of tiles and paint swatches.

I kept very still. God knows *I* can find meaning in those magazines. If George needed to take his time, I would let him.

"It's a profound sense of loss and sadness. I can work and forget it while I have something to keep my mind occupied with, but the minute I stop, I'm overcome with a sense of futility. Basically, I think I'm a high functioning depressive."

I looked at him with amazement. Where did George learn terms like "high-functioning" and "depressive"? Had he been listening after all when I was talking about my friends over the past 5 years? It made me pause. Perhaps Rebecca was a therapist and George was in fact already having counselling. I needed to tread carefully. He was finally talking to me and I didn't want to shut him down and push him into the arms of a beautiful blonde source of solace and understanding. Moreover, this was my chance to prove to him that I'm as evolved and compassionate as she. Also, after the silence and avoidance, it felt good to hear him self-diagnosing like that. As if he still had some control. I smiled gently and said:

"What can we do? Have you seen anyone? A therapist a counsellor, a priest? We can get you some help to work out what to do, to talk this through properly. You can get medication. This is fixable. It's not even that uncommon."

George let go of my hand and pulled away, sitting up and facing the window.

"I'm talking to someone. It's too early to say where this may take me, but it's helping a bit. But I don't want meds. I'm not sick. I just want to find the right answer." He turned back to me. His face was pale. He'd lost weight. I hadn't noticed before. He looked young and old at the same time. Worn out.

"The truth is Verity: I love you and the children, but I feel trapped. I have no sense of self. I am *your* husband, I am an executive at *Pharma Co*. I am a *father*. But who the hell am I?"

"*I* know who you are. Ask *me* George! Don't shut me out – I can tell you." I knew I was begging. I didn't know what else to say. And yet part of me hoped he wouldn't ask. I knew clearly in that instant that I had no idea who George is now. I don't know him anymore. And I think he saw that too. I lost him a long time ago, gradually, but surely.

He was getting impatient now. He stood up and began pacing back and forward by the window.

"No Verity," he said slowly, as if I were Freddie doing something ridiculous like pouring milk onto his laptop.

"The point is I have to find this out for myself. I have to do this work on my own, and I have to feel like this for as long as it takes, for as long as I need, to enable me to recover. Which I will."

"Ok George." I was feeling pretty overwhelmed by this stage. It seemed too late to be talking at all. I knew he was planning to move out. I could see it in his eyes. I was torn between bottom lining things and just putting a pause on the conversation so I could process it, so that he would not take any more steps. I wanted to freeze the whole thing there and go and get some air. But I saw the risk that pausing might entail. Getting him to open up again would be a challenge. So I opted to bottom line things.

"So, where to from here? How can I help?"

He came over to me and sat down on the edge of the bed, pushing my kitchen design magazine to the floor and kicking it under the drawers in frustration.

"You can't. Not directly. I need time and space and no pressure. Can you give me that?"

I hesitated there, but not fatally or for long.

"Yes, anything, whatever you need. But George, don't lie to me. Tell me what you can, what you know. Be as clear as you can be with me. Please don't avoid me, please don't lie to me." I started to cry then.

"That's just it Verity. I don't want be dishonest or unreachable. I just don't have the capacity to share this. It's all I can do to get up and go to the office. Some days I can't face the children, or Harry or the usual crowd at brunch or school, or my mother, or the monthly social club, or tennis. Today – at school – was hell." He was staring into space now, no doubt lost in the crowd at the Montessori event wishing himself under a bus somewhere. I knew the feeling...

"I can make it to the gym because at least there no one needs me. I put in the earbuds and I'm alone, left to myself, anonymous. I'm sorry Verity. I know this is hard for you. I feel bad about it. But I can't let feeling bad for you get in my way. I'm grappling with a lot of stuff and I can't be here for you, or anyone. I need you to try to understand and to just let me be." So many words from silent George – and they made sense. I wiped my eyes and stood, walking across the room to the window.

I had to say something. I had to let him off the hook. This was not the time to analyse or question. He was asking me to give unconditional support. I felt the breeze on my arms and saw the leaves shifting and sighing in moonlight. Below in the garden the water in the pool shimmered. I thought of all the lives going on beyond our garden, of how small we are and of my father and his wisdom, patience and love. I felt very alone. Yet I found some words:

"George, this makes sense at lots of levels and yet it's completely surreal too. You're the rock, everyone relies on you. I can see that it's not easy to tell me this, to even face it yourself. I imagine you feel guilt about failing us and that, on top of everything else, makes all of this even worse for you. I get it George. I didn't think I would, or could, but I do."

I left the window and went to him then.

"I love you George. I feel for you. I want to help. I want to sort this out. I want to save you. But I know I can't do any of that." He shook his head, confirming this.

"I'll give you time and space. All you need. We're not going anywhere and we'll love you through this."

Just don't leave us, don't hurt yourself, don't give up, don't lose hope, I secretly prayed.

We hugged then. I held on tight and he kissed my eyes where the tears had been. But after a while he said he needed some air. He found those shoes and left me where I stood.

The next day, Sunday, we talked some more while the children were swimming before breakfast. But he had nothing much to add. He wasn't really present and he clearly needed to get away. He was dressed for the gym. I was wise enough to know that pushing him would not change anything – maybe even drive him back to Mrs G's shrubbery.

Gracie asked me why Daddy would not play with her. I told her he was tired and needed some rest.

"He wants to take a nap then," she said in my mother's tone of voice.

Indeed.

George came home from the gym and read to the children while I went for a run by the river, blasting Missy Higgins into my ears, switching off my mind. Later we went to a weird yoga party at Louise's – the mother from school who hooked up with Fulvia from Yoga Babes. It was all very strange. I didn't think we were that friendly but Gracie plays with little Sarah, so we were all invited. I guess it was a "coming out" party. George stared into space for most of the afternoon or pretended to be on the phone. I wanted to tell him to leave but I couldn't quite do it – bring myself to send him away. No one bothered with us apart from Louise and Fulvia. The yoga mums that I like were nowhere to be seen and the other guests were intense whole foods and lentils people chatting about politics and asylum seekers. We were the only family from school to be invited, though Hard-Done-By Harriet was there, looking aggrieved as usual, wearing skinny jeans and shoulder pads. Freddie weed in the veggie garden when he couldn't find me to tell me he needed to use the bathroom. George was about 3 metres away at the time and missed the whole thing. No one noticed.

I was starting to feel a little manic yesterday from the exhaustion brought on by three sleepless nights. I was scrubbing the terrace on hands and knees – good old fashioned elbow grease being more therapeutic than delegating the task – when George called to tell me that he wants to take on a project in Hong Kong. It would be very autonomous, give him a fresh perspective and less responsibility and some geographical distance from all that he feels hemmed in by here. Goodness knows where I've found the self esteem not to take this personally.

"Ok George, sounds like a plan." I replied gallantly, as if he'd just suggested sushi for dinner. I hung up and cried into my toxic soap suds.

He leaves Sunday – 5 days.

Wednesday, 11 November

Auspicious day. Remembering those who fought and died for us puts things in perspective.

Four days til George leaves. We're not making too much fuss about his going in front of the children. We told them that Daddy needs to do some travel for work. He'll go to a new office for a while and he has to take the plane there because it's in China. They were pretty interested in China so we looked at pictures on the internet of Hong Kong and the Great Wall. Freddie seems to be quite excited about the whole thing so far. He made a Great Wall with his Duplo, so that must be a good sign. It's quite an imposing edifice; life-like in its proportions and scale, if more colourful and straighter. Gracie, always very empathetic, said "poor Mummy". But I'm trying to be stoic and keep things light and breezy; to not let on to them that this is serious.

I've not deviated much from our normal routines this week. George is still going to the office in town, so there seemed no point in upsetting the apple cart at home. I saw Jorgé today after a Step class. I thought I was fit, but there's a woman in Step who leaves me for dead, almost literally. She arrives with her two small sons who she drops at the crèche each day before commencing an almost obscene stretching session. She takes a position right in the middle of the stretching area, hogging the mirror and the mats so that only four people can fit alongside her, rather than the usual 9. Even so, another half a dozen sad and pudgy men usually start milling around when she turns up. I was in the lift with her today on the way into the gym and her baby who must be about 9 months, was grabbing her breast the entire trip. At no point did she move his fingers or change his position on her hip. It was gross. I can only assume she couldn't feel it.

After stretching she humiliated the entire Step class as she pranced around, barely perspiring, springing up and over at least four risers, abs of steel braced, impervious to the exertion and her sharp featured little face grinning at her gal pal next to her.

No wonder I felt ill afterwards. I was sweating so profusely this morning that Karen, the instructor, gave me several pointed looks when asking the class as a whole: "Are you doing fine?" and "Is it all good?" and "How's the heart rate?" I never have trouble finishing a class; indeed usually I do two back-to-back, but I'm starting to lose it. It was all I could do not to slink out part way through. It occurred to me to feign an episode of some sort rather than lose face with the gym bunny set, but that would have been hard to justify given I was meeting Jorgé straight after Step. I hate having gripes about the gym. It will be my lifeline with George gone. I guess the learning is to stay away from group exercise til this George thing settles down, or if I do a class, to take a position near the door.

My personal training session was incredible, though. Despite thinking I was about to collapse during the boxing set, I managed to push through my pain barrier and reach an incredible high – a rush of endorphins to compensate for the struggle earlier. Indeed Jorgé was rather battered and bruised after the combat element of the session. It was his fault though. He told me:

"Visualise ze enemy, Verity. Punch your nemesis". This got me rather fired up and I focussed on an image of the Uber Fit and Busty Step Diva. When I had pulverised her muscle bound neck and face, I visualised George sitting in his mother's shrubbery texting me.

Jorgé was up in arms.

"Verity, take it easy. You vill injure yourself. Vat is zis all about – so much anger today?!"

If I can channel the anger optimally then the current stress may help me get fitter rather than develop a cortisol gut. Yvette told me once that cortisol released in times of stress makes us fat. She was lithe until she lost her mother in the middle of a huge pitch. She suddenly developed a massively fat stomach – more a beer belly really - and had to buy new work suits. It was unbelievable how quickly she changed and she put it down to stress. A year later she was trim and svelte once more. What could be worse than George coming back to find me fat and hangdog?

I daresay pregnant would be worse...

I also need to keep in mind the visualisation techniques Jorgé uses to win marathons. Visualise George sorting himself out. Visualise George coming home tanned and slim and happy.

Friday, 13 November

Only two days left.

Went to see Helen today and cuddled baby Eloise. They're doing so well. Helen is inspiring with her can-do attitude and cheerfulness. She says it's baby hormones and being cosseted in a nest of love right now, but she's always like that. Perhaps another baby would be a good thing for me, after all. Ingle mother to 2 – single mother to 3 – same difference... Maybe I'll run it by Beth and Desirée. Having said that, Desirée is driving me crazy at the moment. Phil and she have decided to reunite and return to Boston. He's miserable in Latvia and apparently the time away has cured him of his fetishes. Perhaps too many buxom Latvians in the flesh, an undoable job and lots of snow and local vodka mixed with other homemade spirits will cure one of one's perverse tendencies.

I said she must insist he continues with the therapy in any case. It's only been a few weeks. No one changes that quickly, even in Latvia. He's winning her back with his nerdy charm and she's being a sucker just because she's lonely. So much for her resolve and anger and feelings of being irreparably betrayed. I think George is right – many people are living a lie. She would rather be with Mr Mediocre who can earn good money than stand firm for herself and her daughters. One day those angelic girls will ask her why Daddy went away that time and she will lie to them to protect him and herself from their vitriol, amusement and disregard.

I told Beth the whole sorry tale – Phil that is. What else could I do? George won't talk about it anymore, and since Phil is leaving the company with a tidy packet of cash, I think all confidentiality deals must now be off the table. Beth suggested that I give Desirée some latitude and not be judgemental. Easy for Beth to say. She wasn't privy to the embittered ranting 2 months ago. Well, admittedly, she didn't really rant. But the principle seems to have been forgotten. I just can't feel any sympathy for her. If she takes him back and he messes up again who will be interested in supporting her and giving her comfort or advice? Is she a masochist? Beth thinks Desirée must have worked it through and come to her own peace and that we should stand by her. She also said that it's better for the world that Phil be married to Desirée than single and searching. I agree with that at least. If I take the bigger view of it, I think Desirée is the only person who could suffer him, so perhaps it's for the best.

But it leaves me feeling disappointed. I feel as though there's no one on this earth that I truly trust and believe in. Everyone is flawed and everyone is doing what they want or need to do and I don't really feel connected to any of them. Not even Beth. If it weren't for Gracie and Freddie I would pack my bags and go to Italy for a year.

In fact it's high time *I* threw my hands up in the air and decided I feel lost and bereft of meaning. Maybe *I* should spend months finding myself. I reckon I would uncover some decent insights in the Uffizi or the Vatican Museums or the ruins of Pompeii, and perhaps a few pearls of wisdom could be found in Antarctica or the Caribbean. When will it be feasible for *me* to have a sabbatical from the real world of responsibility and worry and standards and take off to find out who I really am?

Kicking myself that George thought of this first.

Sunday, 15 November

He's gone.

We met Harry and Wilbur this morning at the country club for brunch. Harry's usual jocularity was a welcome relief from staring at George in silence, the air thick with all of the unsaid things I cannot or will not express, but which I want him to know. I barely tasted the food – award winning eggs! As the day went on, my resentment subsided leaving me with an ominous sense of doom. George suspended his membership at the club indefinitely. What a relief. One less place to have to tell lies. Hannah, who has been amazingly supportive, came to the airport and offered to come back with me to the house afterwards so that we could talk. It was very kind of her because I didn't feel like putting on a brave face for the kids all afternoon. Tim and the boys amused them for me beautifully and Maria came after dinner and put them to bed.

As if it weren't bad enough to have lost George I see that I have several missed calls from my mother to deal with. Mrs G didn't come to say goodbye because she's in Seattle at an environmental conference, but she sent a text wishing me the best. I bet Mrs G rang Mum and told her something is going on with George. I'll need a stiff drink before I return her calls.

Sunday, 22 November

The past week has been a flurry of activity. I didn't want the children to feel bereft with Daddy gone so we've done a myriad of new and exciting things to distract them from his absence. Maria and I lugged home a pottery wheel and bags of clay and paints on Monday and have set up a little art studio in the new summer house. It's still raw lumber luckily. Gracie was so excited at the prospect of turning it into a dedicated messy zone that I agreed willingly and put the painter and decorator off. We have made some amazing pieces. I'm starting to think we could do something with bronze.

Tuesday we had a day of baking. The kitchen is on its last legs and will soon be a thing of the past – builders arrive in two weeks. I found some that will work over Christmas while we're away and they'll create a new room. The architect (ended up going with the firm that did Beth's Room of Her Own) will project manage the process for me, though I need to scout around for lots of handles and taps and all the other little bits and pieces we need. I'll do that this week with Gracie. She might enjoy being a big girl and helping me with that project. I decided to go with Scandinavian minimalist after all. I don't think I'll spend that much time at "Mummy's Word" anymore so I'm unlikely to grow tired of it. It all seems a little futile and ridiculous to get a new kitchen and lose a husband, but George persuaded me to go ahead. Guilt in action, perhaps.

Wednesday I sent Gracie back to school. She needed to return to her normal routine and see her friends. She missed at least four activities due to the "Daddy's gone, let's kick up our heels" lackadaisical attitude on Monday and Tuesday. But Wednesday was back to normal with an intense and excruciating two hours of after-school activities – the first hour being dress rehearsal for the Montessori Christmas play, and the second being ballet recital rehearsal. Gracie is the only one in her troupe with any talent or coordination. I know that as her mother I am meant to think that – but it's objectively true. I'm withdrawing her next term if they don't put her in a class with some kids who can actually plié. It's all political at that ballet school. If you don't suck up to the right mothers and staff or make the biggest donations your kid is persona non grata in spite of talent, poise or looks.

Take Emma's Honour as a case in point. To call her plump is an understatement – not that I am fat-ist – really – but she's actually clumsy and inept and throws the other, more able children off their timing, not to mention their balance. Yet she's the star of every recital. Even Gracie is starting to notice how unfair the allocation of roles is and how hopeless most of them are. I had to avoid Emma like crazy, kidding I was on the phone or helping Helen (she had four of the five kids with her), because I've not yet worked out my lie about what we're doing at Christmas. Suffice to say it will *not* be skiing in Colorado *en famille*. The cost of my avoiding Emma was steep, however, as Georgia, another mother, from California, told me I was looking haggard and would be very welcome at her Dermal Fill Drinks next Wednesday night. Gosh - so tempting! But, alas, I think I might be regrouting the mosaics in the guest loo all next week.

Thursday we had orientation day for Freddie at Montessori. What a joke. A bunch of three year olds, half of them asleep in their strollers and left at the school office while their too eager parents asked too eager questions, the other half (most being carried) shown around the school they know like the back of their hands having spent most of their toddlerhood there with their older siblings. I was sorely in need of some alcoholic lubrication after that, so I called in reinforcements in the form of Colthilde and Beth. After the kids went to bed I told them what has transpired with George and they let me have a bit of a self indulgent tear or two over the Verdelho. Clothilde is no stranger to husband issues and was quite phlegmatic about it all.

"Do not worry, Cherie, he will return to you. Just stay beautiful and don't obsess about it – it will give you wrinkles." Beth was a little more analytical, as is her style. She loves George but thinks this recent turn of events is a little sappy. Her advice is to milk it.

"Why stop at the kitchen, dahling? Do the whole house."

I've finally spoken with Desireé. I've no interest in telling her the truth about George. However, in speaking with her I developed a plausible cover story for the whole George moving away thing. She fell for it hook, line and sinker and she's no dummy, so now I feel confident I have a version of events that I can roll out for public consumption, namely, George has been given the opportunity of a life time to run a new project; we'll manage without him so that he can foster his career and have some exposure in Asia and China.

Given what Phil put her through, and how she's taken him back, I don't trust Desirée's judgement as I once did. Ergo, not sharing my business with her. I've couched my opinion about her decision in non-committal terms but she knows I think she's making a mistake.

There but for the grace of God go I. If I don't manage this thing, that is. My biggest fear is that I somehow leave myself exposed and vulnerable or worse, put myself out there to wind up looking ridiculous when all of the George mess is sorted, or even now, while he works out who he is and what he wants. I *feel* ridiculous in this situation. Why would people not get a huge kick out of discussing and analysing it? It's interesting, after all. *I* would find it hard not to talk about it if it were happening to someone that I knew. If George comes back sorted and clear, then I will be in a position of much power and owed a good deal of credit (from him); none of which needs to be discussed by anyone else. Less said, soonest mended. Gossip and discussion will undermine my resolve to support George, destroy my faith in him and even reach the children's ears. People won't understand my motivations in letting this happen and explaining it will unsettle my tenuous sense of equanimity about the whole bloody thing. Some people will even blame me or second guess the veracity of the whole midlife crisis story.

At the end of the day it's not as though George did anything wrong. I can't kick him out for cheating or stealing, being a porn addict or bashing me. He's been a complete and utter gentleman, albeit a selfish one. The situation is hard, inconvenient, worrying and uncertain. I may lose him. I may become a statistic, just another victim of a selfish husband. In light of that, it's too raw and I'm too exposed to put the truth out there. I can't comprehend a life without him based on a conscious choice to stay away from us. And if he does make that choice, having no one else to blame.

Anyway, enough of this.

There are a million things to do. Ruminating on this is not productive.

I must arrange for the garden to be replanted for the summer and organise our Christmas holiday. George thinks he'll join us but, once home, doesn't want to travel. Not even to New Zealand. He won't consider Easter Island, either. I doubt that either of us could face the usual crowd and social whirl at the beach so it looks like we'll have to find a new beach or country retreat to escape to. I just dread it being all heavy and morose with George putting a sombre pall over everything.

Damn, I still haven't spoken to Mum. She left a pointed message today. She definitely knows something is wrong. She said she rang Mrs G for news since I hadn't phoned her back. Now I have to deal with her as well as everything else.

Thursday, 26 November

Having an absent husband sure is a wonderful way to create time and space. His going away to find himself really forces me to look hard at myself too. Who would have thought so many benefits would flow so quickly? For example, after several weeks of skipping tennis I now find I'm really missing it. Since we no longer have membership at the club I'm in the rather pitiful position of wanting something I can't have. It's been quite some time since I've felt this way and I actually find it rather humbling and therapeutic. This is how most people live. I'm feeling a sort of virtue in being self sacrificing and somehow bonded with the rest of humanity. I'm going to miss out on a lot more, by choice, from now on. Perhaps through deprivation I'll find what I truly value.

In fact I've discovered that I rather enjoy my own company. I always did as a girl and after Felicity left I was happy enough to be alone, but through my working career and since having children I've rarely spent time alone. I was struck by George saying how much he savoured his gym time. I always saw the gym and yoga as primarily exercise arenas with competitive and social benefits. A glance around the class in yoga spurs me to lunge deeper and strain to have the best and lowest warrior two. The very idea of listening to music was previously foreign to me. But George may be onto something. I'm thinking that many activities are in fact better pursued solo. For example, rock climbing. I've found a wall and I intend to become proficient. I had some time to kill today while Freddie napped so I took out George's old golf clubs and putted some balls around the terrace. I figure that I may as well develop a few strings to my bow now that I'm facing single life once more.

I was busy sorting out kitchen cupboards Monday and Tuesday, after a trip to the garden centre. There's a rather lovely young fellow outside planting perennials and pruning the hedge around the pool. I know that

I'm coping very well by the sheer fact that I'm not out there playing up to him, nor micromanaging his every move. Speaking of which, Claire wants us to come over this weekend for a garden party. She never entertains, as far as I know. Actually, she may frequently entertain and just not invite us. Anyway, she's extending a thin and bony hand of friendship so I shouldn't be churlish.

Basically, I'm not nearly as bitter and twisted as I thought I might be this week. This is quite a nice change and a change is as good as a holiday. It's only day 11 of life without George, but the time is going by reasonably well. His mother has called three times. Her heart's in the right place but it feels a little officious. Do I seem so hopeless? Mum certainly thinks I am.

I finally called her back on Monday between a trip to the garden centre and a spring clean of the loft. She was evidently relieved to hear from me. Felicity was down at the property over the weekend and they were fearing The Worst. Not sure what "The Worst" entails, mind you, given the scant details Mrs G seems to have given Mum. I played a very straight bat and a very close hand – mixing my metaphors but it seems to be an apt description for how I dealt with her.

"No, Mum, I don't need you to come up and I don't need to come down to you. We're fine. We're too busy with all of our activities and routines to miss George."

Jabber, jabber, jabber.

"I think it's for the best. The children are happiest in their own home with their mother. Anyway, George wants time and space and this project accommodates him very well and keeps his options at work open too."

Blah, blah, blah.

"I think it's known as a major depressive episode, Mum."

Interrogate, interrogate, interrogate.

"I can't second guess him. Why would he lie? It seems it's been brewing for a while. If I worry about every woman he knows I'll go bonkers. We can't have the sole carer going bonkers can we?"

Natter, natter, natter.

"Well, Mum, he can ask for help if he needs it. He knows I'm here for him. If he wants me to go to Hong Kong I will. Right now he wants to be on his own."

Harangue, harangue, harangue.

"Well I happen to think it was not avoidable. Depression rarely is."

Pick, pick, pick.

"If it should come to that you can recommend a lawyer for me. I doubt George would screw me over Mum. Shall we try to keep positive for now?"

Diatribe, diatribe, diatribe.

"I don't remember you telling me so Mum. Maybe I'd stopped listening by then."

Lecture, lecture. Lecture.

"Actually I have to go now. Freddie has fallen into the pool. Thanks for your concern."

I took Desirée for dinner last night to say farewell and good luck. Her girls came to play yesterday after school which brought it home to us all that they really are leaving. While I think she's being precipitate in taking Phil back, I know she just wants to keep the family together and ensure the girls have a father in their lives. I hope I have the same option.

Sunday, 29 November

Our afternoon at Harry and Claire's could have been very pleasant. There were a few other families there, many of them familiar to me or even acquaintances from Pharma Co and the various children's activities we all frequent. Unfortunately, Kate the Hypochondriac was there. It's bizarre how she turns up everywhere we go. Am I the only one who finds her unbearable? Avoiding her took most of my creative and physical energy. It occurred to me to start outdoing her with more and worse conditions, but I couldn't be bothered. I think yesterday was what they call in the separation business – "a bad day". Having held up very well for two weeks, the wheels began to come off yesterday when Maria called in sick. The children are starting to miss George and ask questions. "Where is he? Why is he there? When will he come back? Why can't we go too?"

I ran out of excuses for him by lunch time and bundled them into the car and drove to duck ponds at the university with old bread from the freezer – sour dough, mega expensive – that I had to cull in order to make room for the new casseroles and banana bread I made last week. I should have bought a new freezer, but I've not decided on appliances for the kitchen yet.

Feeling like a weird old bag lady with my sacks of bread and the birds surrounding us, we passed some time. If I can keep coming up with interesting ways to break up the day with the children we might just get through this challenging time, ostensibly unscathed. The bickering between Gracie and Freddie is starting to wear me down, though. Maria can't manage them at all when they go for each other. I'm drawing on skills that have lain dormant for years – since I was a newbie in the ad business and was working with hostile and competitive interns - to wrestle them apart and find new and interesting distractions around the home. It's such a shame that almost all of Gracie's activities have wound down for the summer holidays, apart from ballet and swimming. She needs to relearn how to amuse herself. Sorely tempted to book one or both of them into Tweenie Holiday Camp.

George is in touch every other day – so far that seems to be enough. He's sympathetic towards me and seems to be managing with the new team and life in a serviced apartment. He's tight lipped about his other concerns though. He suggested that I get more help. Oh what a conquering hero.

Now I have to come up with an excuse for next weekend. Three or four of the wives who were at Claire's invited me to join them on a sailing boat for drinks next Sunday at the yacht club. We've studiously avoided the yacht club for years. It's full of people like Francine and Mia and it's not my cup of tea at all. Indeed, I'm surprised Claire would be bothered with some of these women. They're all thin and wear too much jewellery, so maybe that's the attraction. I was noncommittal when they asked me whether I could make it, but now that I contemplate an afternoon aboard a boat with them and more like them, I start to get the heebie-jeebies. My third worst nightmare is being stuck on a boat with people I don't like. Second worst is fancy dress parties. Absolute worst is raising the children badly and having them hate me when they grow up.

I wonder if I could persuade Beth and Yves to come as well.

The thing is that word has spread like wild fire that George is away on an exciting project. A part of me suspects that people are looking for some insider information with which to make stock picks across the pharmaceuticals industry as the year closes out badly for their portfolios. But all of a sudden I've been inundated with invitations to events and galas and lunches. All in the next fortnight and all with people I could do without having to explain things to. Either they see me as the poor abandoned wifey who needs to be taken out and distracted or they really *do* think I can help them somehow. Truthfully, while I feel reasonably robust about the whole George situation, I'm not interested in going out all the time and meeting a million new people, or seeing a million old familiar ones. My main concern is ensuring that the children are ok. My gadding about all the time isn't going to be good for them. I don't want them screwed up later with abandonment issues.

Funnily enough I'm enjoying them more now that the buck stops with me. I feel as if they're mine alone and I have to be good to and for them. Drinking all night with Emma and Kate doesn't offer much appeal compared to going to bed early with a good book.

In fact I shall be very glad this week to steer clear of almost all of this silly season hullaballoo and focus on Gracie's break up from Montessori and her ballet concert, Freddie's swimming and golf and the kitchen and garden. I need to speak with Maria about her attitude to the gardener as well. A thorny issue. Finally, I must decide on a Christmas plan.

Friday, 4 December

Terrible day and night with horrific migraine and nausea. Visual disturbances began at yoga. Luckily got through the warrior poses quite easily as my legs sorely need some attention before swimsuit season hits at full throttle. But during corpse pose the blotches before my left eye were so intense I couldn't see Fulvia, not that I had my eyes open. There was an intense ringing in my ears as well such that I began to wonder if I was having an aneurism. I asked Fulvia to help me to the change room where I called Beth out from her hairdresser's appointment to take me home. Really grateful I managed to get through the entire session before my collapse. I hate to think that my yoga credibility could have been undermined by physical ailment. The car is still in the lot at Yoga Babes. The scuttlebutt will be about me, rather than Fulvia, next week.

Beth called Dr Jeanette Rowe, her sister-in-law and physician to all the movers and shakers, who I've never managed to see, when my own GP refused to make a house call. Apparently I'm not his favourite patient. How is it that these people have such fragile egos? It was months ago that I asked him whether he had heard of the male pattern baldness cure. I wasn't suggesting he needed to cure his baldness, I just assumed a bald man would be interested.

Apparently in addition to the migraine and nausea, I have elevated blood pressure. I'm to have complete rest for the next three days til it normalises. Dr Rowe told me to go back to my GP then and get blood pressure medication if it was still elevated. I don't think I can go back to my GP so I was scouring the yellow pages online, through my right eye, for blood pressure equipment suppliers. Maria, with alarming bossiness, ordered me to turn the computer off and get back into bed.

My head was exploding so I did as I was told. I'll worry about doctors on Monday. I can always walk into the Emergency Room if I have to. I should report my GP. Surely it's unethical to refuse to see a patient.

Just stirred from a deep slumber to write this entry. I'm in no state to go to the Montessori play tonight. Gracie will never forgive me. I rang Helen to see whether she thought I had the influence to get the play shifted to another night. She laughed and laughed.

"Verity, have you lost it entirely?! NO way will they move the play for you. Go to bed and get some rest. You saw the rehearsals. You're lucky to have an excuse to stay away!"

Maria will have to go and video the whole thing.

Aaahhh.

Tuesday, 8 December

The migraine was a shocker. Beth had plans for the weekend so while I slept most of Friday, in between delirium and falling over and being chased back to bed by Maria, Beth called Mum. I woke at around 8 pm that night to find her reading to the children in the guest room, having sent Maria home. Mum, Maria and the children went to the school concert together earlier. It all went well apart from a cow falling over, three stars collapsing in tears at the sight of the cow tripping and one of the sprites bursting out of her too small leotard. Sounds like a surreal and nightmarish "Hey diddle diddle..." And yes, as expected, Gracie was the star sprite!

The children were delighted to have Mum to themselves. She brought her lap top and entertained them with pictures of her horses and ducks. When I finally staggered out of bed and followed the voices to find them snuggled up together on the sofa they shooed me away. Mum looked very comfortable and wouldn't hear any suggestion that she head home.

"I'm staying for the children, not for you. Anyway I have meetings on Monday so you're doing me a favour." As I still felt drugged and exhausted and was nursing a chronic headache, I would have agreed to almost anyone insisting on staying at that point. I slept most of the weekend. Maria came and went and Mum brought me tea and soup. The children came in every couple of hours to tell me how much fun they were having with Granny and Maria. George rang several times – I only remember one - to check on me and had "good chats" with Mum.

By yesterday I was feeling a lot better. I managed to eat breakfast with the children and wave Mum off to her meetings. I then rediscovered the merits of day time TV. It was the first time since Freddie was born that I sat still in one place alone in my own house and put my feet up. It was actually serendipitous that Dr Phil was discussing incompatibility in marriage and how we cannot fix anyone but ourselves. Too true, Phil, too true. I spent some time with Mum last night. It was surprisingly comfortable. She didn't lecture me or advise me. We just chatted about the children and Mrs G, the farm and her meetings yesterday, my friends and the state of the nation. Apart from one comment to the effect that it was good to speak with George, we avoided that issue altogether. It was as if she was someone else's mother. Perhaps I was still delirious.

Mum left early this morning. One of her horses is racing tomorrow in a regional meeting and she asked me to come and watch it. I declined – I'm not ready to see her again so soon. Don't want to risk bursting the little bubble of niceness we enjoyed last night. I felt bad though in the way one does when one knows one is being mean spirited and cutting off one's nose to spite one's face, and agreed to stay for Christmas. She caught me at my most vulnerable; what could I do? The children were begging me to say yes and George had already agreed it with her over the phone on Sunday. Gracious, what is going on? I get sick and 72 hours later I'm reconciling with Mum and she and George are having "good chats"!

Saturday, 12 December

The kitchen renovation has begun. We're eating microwaveable dinners, salad and toast til New Year. I went back to the gym Thursday. I've sworn off classes for a while – the last thing I need is to see Busty Diva from Step. I had a pretty light workout with Jorgé. He said Felicity called him on Wednesday. She was supposedly pricing his packages – fitness training, that is – but ended up quizzing him about me and my situation. Jorgé, since he knows nothing, said:

"Vot situation?" She played coy and said:

"Verity's fitness regime," but Jorgé is not as dumb as he looks and he knew that something else was going on.

So I had to tell him that George is working abroad and since Felicity is still sulking at me over the ballet mums and Freddie's party she's not privy to the details so assumes there's more to the story. She's so transparent. Why doesn't she just call me and ask me herself? Or more interestingly, call Mum? For that matter it doesn't say a lot for me that she thinks Jorgé would know the juicy details of my marital strife, nor does it say much for Jorgé that she expects him to share those details with her! At least she's not called my friends – to my knowledge. Bugger. I'll bet she *has* called them. Only most don't know anything to tell. Clothilde would never say anything!

The whole episode is bizarre. I can only surmise that she's upset over Mum's kindness towards me last weekend. But why should Felicity care?

Oooh. I get it. Because Mum came to town and stayed with me and must have confirmed that George is away, but evidently not much more than that. Perhaps I've misjudged Mum.

It's almost too much to contemplate. I'll need to meditate on this. Last weekend could have been a blip – an anachronistic exception that proves the rule about her – but the very fact that Felicity is not getting the gossip about me suggests that Mum is being loyal and supportive, rather than critical and divisive as I would have expected. Or - maybe Felicity has herself fallen out with Mum over something and now feels ostracised; out of the loop. A very strange sensation no doubt for the Golden Haired Daughter. Whatever, even at face value, Mum was very good to me last weekend and neither said, nor did, anything to upset or annoy me in any way. We were both on our best behaviour.

It occurs to me now as I reflect on this, that perhaps Mum is not my problem. Could be that Felicity is the fly in the ointment. After all, Mum and I got on incredibly well during the years Felicity was away... I shall have to workshop this with Beth I think.

I've been keeping an eye on the Turf pages in the paper for Mum's horses and I even made a special trip to the betting shop today to back one of her 3 years olds. I outlaid $10 on it for each of the children. They are now $80 richer. I had forgotten how enjoyable horse racing can be. Or at least the winning money part of it. I went off the whole thing after Dad died. Racing had been his passion, and his canny investments in race winning horses and quality stables earnt him enough money to make his studfarm retirement dream a reality. Until the cancer was discovered. But then it was Mum who nurtured the hope, cheering him as he suffered and faded before our eyes, with talk of where to buy land and who to partner with. Beguiling talk that we all knew would never become a reality. Until suddenly, after all those years she went out and did it and built remarkable stables of which he would be so proud.

I was supportive of the idea; thrilled when she "got back in the saddle". I always hoped it would be a success and sustain and interest her for many years. Yet it's done so much more – she's absolutely thriving and enjoying great accolades in the racing fraternity. It would be wonderful to be part of it - if one actually liked horses and had nothing else to occupy oneself with. But I never wanted to breed thoroughbreds. She always knew that, but when George and I got engaged she seemed to panic and offered me a full time role as her partner, which I declined as diplomatically and gently as I could. She then seemed to push me aside, inviting Felicity to share in the project. Felicity was newly-wed and focused completely on building her business and credibility across the city. She never said "no", just "not yet". Then before long, she was pregnant, which got her off the hook.

It was tense and rocky with Mum then for a while. I know she was hurt and felt abandoned by us both but I think I suffered the brunt of her resentment, as usual. It could not have come as a surprise that I wasn't interested in breeding horses. And it was plain the first time she met George that he was not exactly an equestrian. To my credit I never gave her any hope; was never less than completely honest with her. While she said she understood, her overall attitude towards me suggests that she's never really forgiven me. For a while we barely spoke. Then when Gracie was born she made an effort and we saw her more, but it's never been relaxed or easy.

In contrast, Felicity has managed to keep out of the firing line entirely – self-made entrepreneurial dynamo, prodigal daughter, potential partner. She lets Mum tell her how to do things (then does whatever she wants behind her back) and lets her think she might take over the farm one day. She's no more suited to a horse business than I am; she's just better at deception. Or as she puts it – she wants Mum to feel respected and loved. Pity she didn't come up with that notion when Mum was grieving for Dad and worried sick about her being overseas by herself. The bottom line is – Felicity is Mum's prodigy and knows how to manage Mum. While I, on the other hand, am a constant reminder of what happens when you drop the ball. Plus, I have no interest in duplicity or "management" of my own mother.

The upshot is that for the past 6 years I've felt criticised. She judges my choices, poo-poos my interests and thinks I sold out when I gave up work. How exactly I sold out I can't see. I worked hard and was a good and dutiful daughter. I met a nice, suitable fellow who also worked hard and was a dutiful son. We married and started to raise our family. My husband supported me when I was working and fostering a career and he understood and supported my choice to give it up. There was no sell out. I did what millions of women do. Focus on their own family and try their best to make a success of it. I don't owe her an explanation for why

I chose to stay in advertising or later to stay at home with my children. I didn't break a promise or abandon her, I merely got on with my life. As Felicity had done before me! The difference was that I did it when she was on solid ground and without blind-sighting her.

The infuriating thing is that there's never been any acknowledgement that I was the one with her, holding her hand through those long lonely nights of guilt that she'd outlived Dad and remorse that she'd never really appreciated him while he'd been alive. While Felicity lived the life of Riley and, like most of my friends then, went travelling, I was taking care of Mum, counselling her, talking her through her decisions, going with her to see banks and financiers, and applying only for jobs that would keep me close to her. Never letting myself want anything more or different.

To be honest, I don't blame Mum for wanting a business partner. But the rest? Given that she can't acknowledge my role in her survival and that she hates the fact she needed me so much, I really do resent that I'm not free to just be myself and please myself. And I find it fascinating that I have been pushed to the outer extremities of the family – or perhaps I voluntarily put myself there to avoid scrutiny. Also fascinating that there's no acknowledgement that Dad never chose to die. Poor Dad. Robbed of his dream but leaving Mum the wherewithal to have a second chance at life.

While I'm thinking about it, it seems the only real recognition given was to Felicity, for coming home. Big deal. At the hardest point she went away to look after herself, to pursue her own dreams, to find her own way. Instead of just rejoicing in the return of Felicity and enjoying the opportunities and the potential of her business, Mum had to go one step further and resent me for finally admitting that I had dreams and aspirations beyond her and what she could provide for me.

I don't regret that I moved away then or took a better job that gave me international exposure. Nor that I married George and refused time and time again to get involved in her business. I don't regret that Felicity's been Mum's confidante these past 10 years. My only regret is that I've never told her how I feel. I've silently sucked it up for the sake of the kids and the "family". Grinned and borne the long lunches, the endless tours of the paddocks and the showing off of new stalls and irrigation systems – all so that they could know their grandmother and so that she could have a role in their lives. All the while enduring the caustic remarks about that "puerile" career and "workaholic lifestyle" that made me feel so "valid", until suddenly I left advertising and she was all concerned that I was "cutting off my options", rendering myself unemployable, joining the scrap heap of former bright stars turned layabout yummy mummies with nothing to do but preen and worry and obsess about their diets. Oh there's not much Mum won't offer her opinion on.

So it's been a long time since we spent any good time together. Felicity was allowed, indeed encouraged to choose a career of her own, start a business and a family – she could do no wrong once she came home. She came good in the end and she built her business through tenacity and drive and passion and diligence – all the qualities Mum values and instilled in her. It's as though Felicity is an extension of Mum, a living manifestation of her success as a parent. And as if I'm such a bitter disappointment.

Perhaps she wants me to need her. Perhaps now that George is temporarily out of the picture she wants to assert a role for herself. She surely doesn't want me to have a part in the farm now, but she wants me to depend on her or to seek out her counsel. In spite of all she has done for herself since Dad died, her own self-worth depends on us needing her, being in her thrall, dancing attendance on her, being wrapped up in her life and having her wrapped up in ours. She could just about accept that I had found a partner in George, but if he's not around – well – bonus! Would she prefer that I collapse into her arms than survive and be strong and self-sufficient? It's not healthy. Indeed, it's perverse.

And I guess I know where it all comes from. She carries monumental shame that it was me alone who was there for her when Dad died – the lesser child. She's burdened with the fact that for the first time in her life she was vulnerable and beaten and it was me, not even her favourite, who stood by her and kept her going and saved her from herself. She hates that. Nothing she or I do or say now will ever change the fact that Felicity and Dad let her down. But facing that is beyond her. What do I care? She owes me nothing. I want nothing. She has a good life full of meaning and engagement. I take no credit for that. I only did what Dad would have wanted of me. The rest is all by dint of her own hard work and commitment. All I want is for her to let go of the past, accept that she is human and let me be.

I tried to explain this to her once, but she laughed me off. She was embarrassed, even humiliated, that I understood it all. She thought, or hoped, that I was too young to know what was going on. But we both know she wouldn't have gone on if I'd not been there. She was too proud to call on her own friends or family. I alone saw her, lived with her, and comforted her. It was what it was. But I'm not like her. I'm my father's daughter. Whatever happens with George I won't need to be saved. I won't need to be propped up, or protected. She can't play *those* roles. She can't rescue me in order to free herself of me.

It is what it is.

Wednesday, 16 December

I have started to notice a worrying trend among the women of my acquaintance. While they are basically concerned and intrigued by the fact that George is away now for weeks on end, they're starting to withdraw from social contact with me. For a few days I thought I was imagining things. I'd been ill, hunkered down with the children. But now, what was once the busiest time of the year is extremely quiet. For three days running I've had no engagements whatsoever, which is unprecedented.

I thought it was uncanny last week when none of the yoga girls invited me to come to coffee with them. I assumed it was not happening due to school holidays or Christmas shopping commitments and didn't really think about it when they ignored my cheery "Anyone for coffee?" as we rolled up our mats. I even fleetingly worried that my corpse like state on the day of the migraine had scared them away, but then I saw Louise later that day at the tile shop and she said she was so delighted to be included in the exclusive coffee circle for once – why hadn't I been there? At first I thought perhaps they'd had a change of heart after I left or maybe it was a different group from my regular crew. But Louise rattled off the names of the usual suspects, who met for two hours at the usual venue at the usual time. Luckily, I didn't stumble in there on my own. I wanted to give them the benefit of the doubt so channelled positive interpretations of it for a couple of days and had more or less forgotten about it until the weekend – the quietest one in living memory!

I previously declined an invitation to yet another kiddies' party that was held on Saturday. The invitation came about two weeks ago, in a bottle – message in a bottle! – completely over the top. I immediately called the mother – it was bloody Francine – pleading a prior engagement.

The venue was the yacht club (again!) and since I've no desire to set foot there I was delighted to beg off. At the time I felt more than vindicated doing so as well.

For a start, the invitation came late. I know that Beth received her bottle for Zach at least a week before mine arrived. If my mother taught me anything it's that pride goes before a fall and I'm not so desperate as to accept late invitations offered willy nilly as an afterthought, to bolster numbers or as a form of charity. Second, the whole message in the bottle was so overdone for a four year old's party as to be just *naff*, as Sophie would say. Finally, while I can endure, even quite like *some* of the likely guests – playgroup crew - the thought of being condescended to by Mia and Francine on board a yacht nearly did me in. Not only is being on a boat, in a dock, with kids, my idea of hell on earth – Jimmy Choos sticking in the grooves of the deck, botoxed cheeks and foreheads glistening at me in the sun, screaming children, weeing in a bucket, if at all, banging my head on beams and masts and flapping sails – but the whole palaver is a huge whopping lawsuit waiting to happen.

As it turned out there was no prior or later engagement on Saturday *or* Sunday. The weekend was completely unsocial. I saw no one apart from Clothilde. We kept ourselves busy enough on Saturday with swimming and shopping and a visit to the museum, but the usual 4 or 5 texts from various girls from ballet, school or play group never arrived. I even checked my phone and broadband services. I didn't even hear from Beth which is quite unprecedented. On Sunday we took a drive to the hills and paddled in a little rock pool George and I discovered years ago – only because I had to get them out of the house and take my mind of the solitude.

So I'm watching this space to see what, if anything, is really going on. One weekend isn't fatal, after all. It may be a coincidence that everyone was too busy to get in touch for the past week. Moreover, some people *do* play the old "it's your turn to call" game so it might just be poor diary management on my part. Maybe I've burnt some bridges refusing so many invitations these past few weeks - beggars can't be choosers, after all. But by the same token I sense that being sans husband is neither trendy nor worthy of attention. While I stood by Desirée after Phil left, it seems that not too many people are similarly inclined. For a start, the story that George is having a lark of a time in HK gives no one any currency or influence (unlike the truth of course). Second, who wants a solo woman and kids lurking around one on the weekend when husbands are home seeking attention and QFT (Quality Family Time), especially in the run-up to Christmas? Single mothers dressed up with no place to go are not high on the invite list of the women I know. Of course the other possible interpretation is that I am simply not that well liked and people only keep me around because of George. Humbling. Still, I had better get used to it.

Saturday, 19 December

Despite pretending to be reconciled to a lonely life with few friends, I could not face another weekend of social ostracism, so I invited several families over for tea and swimming today. Carla baked loads during the week at her house – the kitchen being a bomb site - so we had ample refreshments – just a paucity of guests. Only Beth, Helen and Hannah could come and they all came without husbands and half their children. It would appear that I've moved firmly out of the role of sought after and into the role of outcast. I even had Maria stay late last night so that I could go to the movies – by myself. Friday night alone in the movies. How the mighty are fallen.

Having no mates and so much extra time on my hands has forced me to focus more on what I want to do with myself. Perhaps it's not a bad thing to have few friends. I've finished the garden ahead of schedule.

I've all the bits and pieces I need for the kitchen, the builders are ahead of their timetable and the children are ready for school in January – uniforms pressed, books bought and bags labeled and packed. I almost don't need Maria during the day, apart from when I'm at the gym, or a class. I joined a small tennis club nearby and have been enjoying a game every other day with Luscious Larry from school. Freddie and Gracie play too and are enjoying spending time with Larry's kids.

I can't believe George has only been away a month. The time has both dragged and flown. The children seem to be coping very well with his absence, though we're now counting the sleeps til we see him. I just hope we don't built it up and find it all terribly disappointing. The children probably won't notice George's state of mind in any case, as we decamp to Mum's the day after his return. She has a couple of brand new foals and a new pool. Felicity and family will also be there from Christmas Eve. Felicity doesn't do Christmas catering after the 24th and Alan closes his surgery until 4 January. Happy families.

I went through my phone directory tonight and found that the only person I felt like speaking with was Yvette in Paris. We had a wonderful, though moving, conversation. She's dealing with her daughter's issues with the cutting and has been seeing someone herself concerning eating issues. When I first met her at the agency 14 years ago, we were the best of friends. We stayed close for several years even though she moved to Europe. She was very hard working, but also fun loving. She partied hard and could out-manoeuvre, out-strategise and out-campaign anyone. She was destined to make a lot of money, run her own business and be one of those people that have articles written about them in the pages of the local weekly glossy. What I never knew though, during all the years we've been friends, is that she has suffered from an eating disorder since she was 14. How could I never have seen it? She insists she knew and mastered every means of concealment, and that almost no one knows, even now. But man, I never had the slightest inkling and I had a bulimic sister and pretended to have an eating disorder myself!

The situation with her daughter has forced her to look at her own issues and she's now three months into an intense programme designed specifically to deal with eating disorders in high-achieving women. They say she failed to make the appropriate separation from her mother as a young child and never came to terms with her father's role in the family. As a result she began using food as a form of control and power in her revenge laden plans to torment and punish her mother. This began as early as kindergarten, but only became truly self destructive during the laxative and over exercising years in the ad agency. There I was, trying to keep up with her on the treadmills, never realising that I was racing against a psychological disorder beyond all of our comprehension. Now her metabolism is completely shot and it's a miracle she ever conceived, but by golly she looks good in those figure hugging skirts she wears. Anyway, she has to learn all over again how to eat. She's begun what will be a long and difficult journey with a psychotherapist and a family counsellor.

It sure puts my problems into perspective. It's also a salient reminder of the fragility of one's self esteem and the constant issues that may confront one's children. I'll be hyper alert to the skipped meals, the flushed veggies, the after dinner toilet dashes, the uneaten lunches in the lunch box and the breath of the bulimic. I can't imagine Freddie would use food as a means of control, though - having said that - his propensity to eat all manner of indigestible and inedible substances is concerning.

Note to self – arrange to see the counsellor again and discuss potential damage to kids with this absent George situation.

Tuesday, 22 December

We leave for the farm tomorrow. George arrived this morning. We had a good day. He was pretty cheerful. It didn't feel forced. The children really enjoyed having him home and after my initial trepidation wore off, sometime during his tour of the half finished kitchen and over a skinny soy latte made by the new deluxe café sized espresso machine, I began to relax and savour his being home. He's now asleep, having worn himself out in the pool all afternoon with the children. He promised to talk to me on the drive to the farm while the children are glued to their DVD screens.

After several days without any contact from my circle of friends, these past couple have seen my inbox crammed full with an influx of Christmas greetings, end of year update messages and links to Facebook photo galleries and invitations to follow various blogs. Perhaps I was not being abandoned to a life of ignominy and isolation as a pseudo single-mother, after all. Rather, all of my acquaintances were so preoccupied drafting their Christmas missives and annual updates and uploading their classy studio shots of themselves and their families looking natural *á la plage, en plein air, en famille* etc, etc, that they just didn't have time for me. I feel very guilty for thinking ill of them and must do a belated annual update and Christmas message of my own.

Who's on the distribution list, though? Is 189 too many? I can't decide whether to include the following:

Mrs Melloy at Frobisher.

Admissions team at Hillmere – never hurts to have them realise what they passed over.

Hard-Done-By Harriet.

Trudie – lost her address and don't want to make her regret leaving us to get married.

Former clients.

Felicity – never quite know the etiquette with these things as regards family.

Mum – expect it will backfire.

Crazy Price Family of Halloween Gastric Poisoning debacle, up the road.

Here goes:

Draft One.

Another year passes blissfully for the George, Verity, Gracie and Freddie Fortescue of Frangipani Grove.

George continues his climb up the corporate ladder at Pharma Co; his lofty appointment in March to head Southern Hemisphere Strategy and Business Development was surpassed only by his most recent coup – Special Project Coordinator, China and Asia/Pacific. George has made time to rediscover his love of all things physical this year. Embracing a healthy and outdoors lifestyle, most weekends see him active in his or his mother's gardens, cycling or competing in triathlons. Perhaps a trek along the Great Wall of China or a little bit of base camp climbing in Nepal lies ahead? Could things get any better?

Gracie enjoyed her second year at Mortimer Montessori and once again led the cast in several of the school and her extra-curricular performances. Her pliés and arabesques, her poise and her flair for the dramatic continue to woo the crowds of admiring parents and teachers, while her fellow students gape aspiringly at her athletic skill, gymnast's style and angelic singing voice. At risk of becoming too big a fish in her local ponds Gracie has gained admission to Frobisher Academy. Gracie is sure to thrive in such a richly stimulating environment where her copious talents can be developed and her true potential met. Gracie has discovered this year the joys of reading and has a voracious appetite for all things literary, French and chic. It's even been suggested that she market her gorgeous style in a mother and daughter clothes range. Thankfully, Mummy can sew!

Engineer in the making, Freddie, has come into his own this year – embracing the joys of sand play, putty and clay. His pottery creations are remarkably accomplished. His exuberance and joy in all he surveys and attempts is inspirational. Freddie has reached and surpassed all of his milestones with finesse and aplomb. His engaging and hilarious take on life keeps all in his acquaintance amused. Frank Lloyd Wright meets Picasso meets Bob Hope?

Verity has had a wonderful year too. Her busy schedule of Montessori engagements (and appointment as Secretary of the Parents' Association), social and health oriented pursuits has abated only enough to permit of the redevelopment of the family kitchen, a complete garden overhaul and the building of a bespoke summer house. The odd flirtation with a return to business either as a style entrepreneur or as a doyenne in the making in the eco-movement has kept things interesting. Embracing the challenges of part-time sole parenting to support George in his wonderful career moves across Asia, Verity has discovered an even greater capacity for child-rearing, friendship and mindfulness. As Freddie nears school age Verity finds herself exploring new and unchartered territory. Watch this space in the year to come!

.....

Beth is probably the only person who will really see through all that hyperbole and she wouldn't judge me. Surely. Or tell anyone the truth.

I'll sleep on it. Mustn't be precipitate – once sent there's no take back.

Wednesday, 23 December

Delete that crap above asap!

Saturday, 26 December

Whew, I have come up for air after a frenetic time over the past four days. Christmas is all about family and we've certainly fulfilled that requirement this year. Even Mrs G came down on Christmas Eve laden with gifts and treats for all of us. Surprisingly there was very little tension. Mother's on her very best behaviour; no doubt inspired by Mrs G.

I seem to have mended fences with Felicity, which is to say she's no longer sulking at me and seems very relaxed and congenial. I secretly suspect she might be pregnant. Normally she dominates proceedings in the kitchen, sampling everything, directing us all to do her bidding. This time she's been very low key and almost uninvolved in preparing the meals. She claims to be trying a diet that restricts alcohol and sugar. Either she's preggers or she's trying to chivvy Alan into shedding a few pounds. No small feat. He's gigantic. Too many "Felicitations" left overs, not enough exercise and too many lunches wooing wealthy women and vain CEOs.

I shouldn't pick on him. There was never a sweeter fellow, and it's certainly been good for George to have another man here to talk with and have a (furtive) drink with.

Mother has been amazingly gracious. I'm on tenterhooks for fear that she may suddenly just lose it after so many days of being non-critical and actually keeping her ideas about myriad topics such as schooling, parenting, careers and holidays to herself. Felicity confided that she suspects Mother has a love interest. A trainer from the south who was here the day we arrived. The one I met back in September when Gracie stayed over. Mmm. Could explain her gentler tone and happier demeanour these past few weeks.

Gracie's equestrian skills have progressed apace since we arrived. In just three days she's started trotting and insists she no longer needs to be led around the paddock by an adult. Thank goodness Mum and George are keen to encourage this interest and are keeping an eye on her. I find the whole thing quite nerve racking. She's so little astride those big ponies and I have grave fears she'll come off and wind up a paraplegic. It's almost too much to bear. Thank God Freddie is scared of the horses. Apart from small fluffy creatures like lambs and ducks and kittens, he's pretty indifferent to animals. Further vindicating my decision to cancel his farm party, I might add. Best of all, his violent streak with bugs seems to be a thing of the past.

Freddie enjoys the clay and modelling toys that Mrs G brought for him. He's very engaged with creating cities and airports and putting Chinese walls, as he calls them, around them. Something good has come of George's absence...

Meanwhile George seems almost relaxed. Putting aside the uncertainty surrounding his movements and options after May, he's better than I expected. He's trying hard to be fun and easy going. He's not exactly his old self – whoever that was given we may not have seen him since Freddie was born(!) - but he's certainly putting on a good show for everyone. We discussed his current thinking on the journey down and while taking a walk on Christmas Eve. He needs more time but he's convinced he wants to leave Pharma Co – go out on his own. I suggested a sabbatical, some travelling. But he says he needs a permanent break with big pharmaceuticals and to explore new careers altogether. He says he has to "give something back". He was brutally honest. He wants to be with us, but he can't live as we've been living.

Then he said I have to tell him what I want, what's non-negotiable. I have to work out whether he's who I want and if so, to what extent I'll be part of a George that isn't an executive for Pharma Co.

What the...

Where do I start?

Sorry George – can I have about 9 months to think it over! Oh – or three years feeling lost first!

How am I meant to answer this - in a vacuum - as a hypothetical? It's ridiculous. I'm not the one having the crisis! He buggers off to China and leaves us to get on with things without him. We do so - just coming to grips with this pattern of life - and now he's changing the terms again. We're all on tenterhooks here, waiting for George to drop a bomb or swoop in and save the day. Which is *exactly* the role and the pressure he's tired of and is running away from. Well, guess what George: in the real world that pressure is called responsibility and no one goes through life avoiding it. No idea what to say to him. I almost wish he'd not come back. Doing it for the kids... And what if this whole leaving pharmaceuticals idea is just a phase; a kneejerk reaction to having some time and space - or a test? What if he winds up changing nothing? I can't be brought into a decision at the 11th hour, without any involvement along the way. We're due to talk again after the children go to bed – he wants my answer!

Great – bring it on.

.....

I finally got some gumption – several glasses of white wine fortifying me, of course. The children were asleep and the rest of the clan had retired so we sat on the back deck to resume the Conversation. I was supposed to have an answer to the Big Question - do I want George without his job. I finally said:

"George, the way I see it, this isn't my decision to make. Either you come back here and sort this out with my help as a partner, or go, be by yourself and sort it out on your own as you said you would. But you can't have your cake and eat it too. This is your problem. You need to work out what you want. What I want doesn't matter. Do what you need to do."

He was a little taken aback but pretended to be fine with that answer. He did the little hair ruffling thing he used to do when we first met and he was anxious or nervous. I felt oddly calm. I could hear the waves on the shore all the way across the paddock. Soothing.

I was on a roll now.

"It's not up to me George. You can't ask me to choose what sort of person I want. Isn't this the whole issue – that you are lost pleasing everyone else, living a lie. Have you forgotten why you moved to Hong Kong? I'm not going to make you choose the door behind which lies another 15 years of misery. I'm not taking responsibility for it. Get help, resign; but it's your problem. I told you weeks ago. I'm here and I'll still be here when you work out what you want."

He was visibly shaken now. He said nothing for a while. In fact he appeared to go into a funk. I was tired of it. Tired out by him and his issues and his sad, depressed, nervous *crap*. I almost asked him whether that Rebecca Cow was still in the picture, but I held back. For the first time in months I felt like I had the upper hand, was on the moral high ground. Hauling her into the frame would have reduced the whole issue to a tawdry little viper's nest of extra-marital doubt. So I left him on the deck and went up to bed. After a while he appeared in the bedroom and finally, out came the *real* bombshell.

There it was – laid out for me. George's little "dream plan" – to make up for his time at Pharma Co. I wonder when it would have been revealed if I had given a different sort of response on the deck; if I'd said: "If you leave big business and stop making huge money I'll divorce you." I'll never know now. Anyway, he says he needs to make good for his years in Pharma Co and the only way he can think to do that is to stay in Asia and help them build hospitals and local medical centres, to work with their NGOs and scientists to develop inexpensive competitor medicines to those peddled by Big Pharma.

And end up dead, taken out by some pharma hit man with a grudge.

Man, what happened to a nice peaceful Boxing Day? He's now sleeping the sleep of the innocent while I sit here typing, processing this news. I said to him:

"Ok George. That's an option, sure. Let's not discount *all* the others. Can we agree that you'll consider other things too? Perhaps there are less extreme paths you can take that'll still fulfil the need to give something back." Like donating to a good cause, I thought to myself. Or spending more time at home.

He said he'd keep all options open.

He's going to finish the project in Hong Kong in May, then resign. He wants to make the most of this thinking and alone time and come up with a viable and sustainable alternative plan for himself. And us? I asked. He said yes – but that's my call when he has his new plan. He then fell into bed, his back to me. Like I'm the bad guy in this scenario!

I would love to work this out for him - take away the angst - but at the same time I consciously don't want any part in it. What does all this mean? How is going to live out the "dream plan"? Is he serious? Is this just talk, musings, a backlash?

Very modern, I must say. Very un-George.

So where am *I* now - four hours later, sipping cold tea and creating new furrows and wrinkles in my brow? All I know is that I'd better find a few plans of my own to focus on in case his idea of a new career involves me serving soup in orphanages in China.

I won't get in his way if this is what he wants, but I know my own limitations and needs. If he plans to live in a developing country and "give back" then he'll have to do it on his own. Call me selfish, but my life plan does not involve malaria, AIDS work or proximity to communicable diseases. Nor, to be brutal, does it involve living as an expatriate amongst a dislocated white elite. Give me my own bed – empty but comfortable - any day, over adventure, mosquitoes, foreign languages, runny tummy and knocking back mojitos with bored, sweaty, ruddy faced post-colonial expats. Hand on heart – I'm no use to anyone if I'm hot, grimy or more than a kilometre from a soy skinny latte, a gym or a day spa. I'm not cut out for trekking, back packing, camping, roughing it, chancing it or trying it out.

No way, not me, not gonna happen.

So now, as I sit here in Mum's kitchen, smelling the aroma of my first pot of coffee for the day, watching the first light of another glorious summer's day creep over the trees outside, I feel happy and clear. I actually feel compelled, indeed, inspired, to engage with my own needs and ambitions, whatever they may be.

And that's the point!

I need a compelling and let's face it, equally high-minded pursuit to occupy me. He can save the world, one polio victim at a time – fine. But I'm not leaving my house without a fight. I won't emigrate, go loco or otherwise give up my new kitchen, summerhouse and hard won gains at Frobisher that easily.

Get over yourself George. Charity begins at home.

I know I sound like a cow. A part of me wants to be sympathetic and be seen to be caring, to follow George to the end of the earth. But frankly, he needs to grow up. Who jumps off the corporate ladder at his level of seniority, with a family to support, to join a commune? Ok. So he never said he was doing that. But it's patently obvious that he's trying to be the hero he claims he can't be anymore. Instead of answering to 10 or 12 people he plans to save a few thousand. He's completely overcompensating. What an ego. As if *he* were responsible for the damage caused by the pharmaceuticals industry! Mighty George will single-handedly save the third world after half a millennia of exploitation and pillage at the hands of the West. Not only that, while doing so he can make it up to his father – a little too late, to my way of thinking - for "selling out" in the first place. His words, not mine. Oh and be the talk of the town and most admired before 40 blah, blah, blah.

He'll get it out of his system in any case; feel virtuous and wind up on the scrap heap of society, blogging about it. He can't undo the mess in the developing world by making some self sacrificial statement at the expense of his wife and children, not to mention his own status and self-esteem. What happened to the racehorses, the sailing boats, the chalet in France? He's kidding himself if he thinks he'll be happy without his Brioni suits and his big fat plush car, his corner office, his tidy house and garden and immaculate and fetching family.

Ok – so what's the plan Verity?

The sleep deprived, raw but viable, plan, is to play my cards close to my chest. No giveaway sighs or eye rolls. No. Just sweetness and light; very supportive and calm. Secretly I'll be frantically finding something to do that will save me from having to relocate to some godforsaken hole of a country where no one speaks English and no one serves Campari, let alone knows how to spell it and the best school's are full of anachronisms from the fifties dating from before the colonial structures came down and communism moved in. God forbid. The only blessing is that George has five more months of corporate shenanigans ahead, plus his notice period – a year! That gives me ample time to find a job/business/purpose outside the home to compete with the starving and ill millions who need George. Oh, in fact there's another blessing. Given he's so incredibly private and precious right now, no one will be privy to these plans. Managing the information flow, creating the spin and sheltering from the fall out, need not yet concern me!

Thursday, 31 December

Well here I am – back home. All is peaceful and calm. The children loved their time at Mum's. We were all sad to say good-bye. It was quite a tearful leave-taking, surprisingly. Freddie and Gracie are now playing with their new toys in their own house and spending lots of time in the garden. The kitchen is looking great. The builders worked right up to Christmas and were back in on the 27th and all is very smart and clean and elegant. I daren't even use the stove lest I mess it all up. It was wonderful to see Clothilde again and to speak with Beth this evening. Beth and the family are still away at the beach; by all accounts not the place to be this year given the economic malaise. Yves and Beth have been the only diners in some of the restaurants some nights, God forbid. I tried to sound interested but for once I speak the truth when I say – I really do have more on my mind.

My plan is to get on with things with a smile and a spring in my step. George leaves tonight. It's not New Year in China, so he has to get back to the team. We're maintaining another very pleasant and arm's length stand off right now. Try as I have, I can't really get excited about him or his problems. I've been supportive and I'll stand by him, but I can't hang on his every word, pretending he's some captivating entertainer or a prophet of hope. He's just a man, doing his best. And his best might not be right for me. It's time for me to look after myself and the children now, and if that means keeping him at a distance, protecting myself from disappointment, then so be it. This was the risk we took when he signed on for the midlife crisis. It will be sad to wave George off this evening, but I won't fall apart. I won't lose it in front of the children. We'll make the most of this and one day George will wake up and see that he can't actually change the world one malaria tablet at a time. He'll accept that his calling is not in remote Asian villages and he'll come back to find us happy and whole. Maybe we'll be happy to have him back.

Farewell George – have a great time working out what to do with *your* life.

.....

He called from the airport a couple of hours ago to say goodbye again. He chose that moment to tell me – Gracie begging to say goodbye once more and Freddie screaming for help to get out of the tub – that he's going to be working with a consultant called Rebecca (der!) who's joined the Project in HK (he thinks he's mentioned her to me!) and that he thinks she may be able to help him unpack some of the issues surrounding his next steps. Now he tells me! Oh and he loves me. Right. Bloody fantastic. I feel so pleased that Rebecca will help George "unpack" some of the issues. Better be *all* she bloody unpacks. Shithead George. I wonder if Rebecca wants to do soup kitchen chic with George while he figures it all out. See you when I see you George.

Honestly. See – my instinct was right all along. Bloody Rebecca is in the midst of this. Grow up George and stop beings so sanctimonious. "Unpack some issues!" - Good Lord.

.....

I'm so cross. If I even bother to begin a rant here about this I may never stop. So I won't waste the time or energy.

Instead, given it's 9 pm on New Year's Eve - children asleep, exhausted – I will make some resolutions.

1. Get busy and engaged with anything that can objectively be regarded as compelling enough to mean that I never have to leave this house and traipse after George i.e. not sewing new curtains or Roman blinds, nor spring cleaning and not going back to uni.
2. Involve the children in meaningful and productive activities to fast track their development and ensure they are fully engaged with life here. The more deeply entrenched they are in their academic and extra-curricular pursuits, the harder it will be to argue that life abroad will be better for them than staying here (assuming George even wants us in this New Life).
3. Come up with some new ideas for Montessori fundraising – maybe a talent show will grab them, or a Readathon. Become indispensible.
4. Introduce Gracie to fractions. If maths is her strength, build on it.
5. Start redecorating the children's bedrooms.
6. Find new friends – lots of them.
7. Found a charity. Not sure what for but it has to help someone as needy as George's desperate diseased millions.

Wednesday, 6 January

I brought the children back down to Mum's yesterday. Maria joined us this morning. She was missing us too much to have another week off. Our time here over Christmas was so wonderful and we were beginning to feel quite lonely and spent at home, so it was obvious we had to return. The children were a little lost after George left us and while I had energy to start with, I soon ran out of steam; my resolutions abandoned somewhat. I need a good kick along and no one can do that better than my mother. I surprised myself, eagerly acquiescing to her suggestion that we return for the rest of the month. With everyone from town still away – after all it's only the Epiphany today – we're not missing anything by coming back to the farm. Indeed being a little out of reach might do my ailing social status some good. It was like a homecoming to return to the fresh air, leafy glades and the long summer country evenings. My slide into self-pity completely abated as we arrived to be met by Mum's open arms and jugs of fresh juice and freshly picked berries.

Somehow I'm more productive here. Probably the fact that Mum never sits still, but hustles and bustles me into activity. I spent this morning weaving a shaker style rug for the summer house. I told Mum I was feeling a little despondent this morning. I was lulled into reverie by the *Little House on the Prairie* style atmosphere of mother and daughter bonding over the handicrafts, and confided all the details of what is really going on with George. She was very supportive and made no comment about George per se. She stopped her own weaving while I was telling my tale and began arranging flowers. I wonder if she intended to be acting so therapeutically. The scents and colours were very soothing to me in that moment. Holding up a long stem of bougainvillea, she said:

"You need to find your own thing Verity. Just as you showed me after Dad died. You need a purpose. Of course the children are your purpose, but you have more to give. One day the children will leave you, and even before they do, you'll realise they need to make their own way. You need your own thing to take you through that time and beyond."

I knew this was true; I didn't know she knew it though. It was exactly what I had felt when I kept working after Gracie was born. I'd lost sight of it in the euphoria of motherhood and DIY, home-making and being a wife to George and, compared to the days at the agency when I was always entertaining or travelling or preparing a pitch, having so much time to myself.

"I know Mum. I forgot that for a while. But I know it and it will be even more apparent when Freddie starts Nursery in three weeks. But even so, the terrible part of all this is the low grade sense of panic just below the surface that I feel all the time. It's as if this whole thing with George is completely out of my control. I've never really felt that before, or if I have, it's only been about things that don't matter so much to me."

She mopped some spilt water off the granite work top.

"But control's only an illusion Verity. You taught me that all those years ago. I'd never accepted what your father had always known and what you also seemed to get – we can only control ourselves and even then... Anything else is a myth. It's taken me years to make peace with that. Even now I struggle. You at least don't have to undo 50 years of habit and fear. You just have to let go a little bit and accept that it will all work out for the best. You've always been brave and charted your own course. You'll get through this."

I was very touched that I was getting so much credit. I had a lot to think about.

.....

Mum is *right*. I realise that so much of what I've enjoyed and cultivated over the past few years has been based in an obsession with certainty and control. Even the DIY stuff was probably ultimately about a need to control my home environment, that, and a desire to show off and seem so accomplished,, over-compensating for giving up paid work. Not that I did not enjoy every moment of it. But tellingly, when I lost control of everything at Freddie's terrible party I stopped the doing-it-from-scratch domestic goddess mania – almost cold-turkey. I felt defeated and exhausted despite the fact that for 18 months I'd been so productive and engaged. And then almost like a zephyr rising from the ashes I transformed into a new zen-like creature who cared little for such matters anymore and began my obsession with fitness and yoga. As if the fact that I was doing yoga and Pilates and meditation meant I was a superior and calmer being. All that energy previously expended on mosaics and weaving, painting and planting, was transferred into hours at the gym, in the park with the trainer and online surfing for health tips. And then these past few months I guess I transferred the obsession for control onto Gracie. Her schedule, her school, her friends, her activities, her nanny, her clothes.

So, could it be that the last 4 years has all been about keeping control. Do I ever just relax and go with the flow? In yoga? No way – what keeps me going is the thrill of competing with my personal best from the previous week. In the garden? Hardly – that's about control, and showing off too. What a revelation! And yet, I've persuaded myself that I'm so easy going. Fascinating.

Wow, this time with Mum proves invaluable yet again. And the thing that's amazing is that she's quoting me back to me. I apparently knew that there was no such thing as control when I was 23! What happened to me?

I think I need a good session of hard labour to get my thinking straight; let go of this control thing and find a valid calling! I'll go and muck out some stalls – can't control animal poo - while the children swim with Maria.

.....

So I was pitch forking hay in the stable all afternoon, a lather of sweat and just longing for the children's bedtime; curling up with my book in the luxurious window seat of Mum's guest suite and relaxing, a soft evening breeze playing over my blistered hands, when my phone rang. The children had hidden it amongst the bales of straw. Like the proverbial needle, it took some finding. I pressed the answer button without looking at the caller's name on the screen, half expecting to hear from George. It was Mia. It's been weeks since I saw or spoke to Mia, so I was a little surprised to be receiving a call from her mid-holiday.

"Dahhling! How are you? You must be done in. You'll never guess who Francine ran into in Honkers. None other than George and his blonde lady friend. Rebecca, Becca? Gorgeous. Betty Draper look-alike eh? No wonder you've been so out of reach. Mystery solved. Why didn't you say – you sly dog. You must be livid. Do you want me to come over? Does Beth know? Is it on FB? I'm calling her now."

I hung up.

I had a moment of clarity then. I saw myself as if from a great height, ankle deep in horse shit and straw, sweat saturating my shirt, dirt all over my face, stinking like a jackeroo in a muster, wracked with sobs and I stopped myself mid-heave, thinking:

"Bitch. I don't care what she thinks."

And,

"Never let a good crisis go to waste."

I don't know where that thought came from. I hadn't realised I was in a crisis. Mia's assumptions about Rebecca and my feelings, her expectations and judgement thrown at me so insensitively in those 40 seconds could have catapulted me into a near breakdown.

But they didn't. Maybe Mindfulness for Mothers was paying off at last. Or perhaps my awareness of Mia's limitations was now yielding fruit. Or maybe deep down I was already prepared for this type of call – indeed had been since that first afternoon of insight after the Flour Mill Fiasco.

Mia has no idea how I feel. About this or *anything*! I didn't set out, when I chose to marry George, to better my lot in life, to feather my nest or to gain access to money, status or a new social set. I wasn't hoping to inherit someone's country pile or New York loft or to secure a villa in Tuscany in the property settlement. I expected to be married forever. I anticipated long years of dotage with George, travelling, reading, playing cards, enjoying our family. And yet here I am, on the brink of an entirely unforeseen precipice, over which lies goodness knows what future, all because George has lost his way. I'm teetering on the brink due to a depressed and unreachable husband in crisis. To say I feel a little bit resentful is to put it lightly. But I can't hate him or deny him the time and opportunity to work himself out - after all that is what for better and worse really means. If it were just George I had to worry about I could wait a long time.

But it's not. The children matter more than anything. What's in their best interest is the key. And all those books and courses have taught me one thing – happy mother, happy home.

Of course word will spread. Of course they'll be talking at "Mummy's Word" and "*Le Petit...*" and at pick-up. And they'll assume the worst. They'll nominate a spokesperson and she will call to offer faux sympathy and to extract more details. They'll greet me with their plumped lips, dry brown faces and eager white smiles searching for signs of my collapse. It will be all over the internet by now thanks to Mia. Twittering? Squawking, like a craven crow on a wire. Go - feel superior, enjoy my misfortune, rub my face in it.

So from that great height looking down on myself, just then confronted by a tearful Freddie who had a splinter in his foot, it became clear. I knew with the certainty I had not felt since my father died and Felicity left us, that it was time to stop feeling sorry for myself and start facing up to some things; no more self pity and negativity. Look for the good in this situation, the opportunity it presents. I'll look back on this time as the making of me. I'll be damned if I give Mia and her coven the satisfaction of anything less.

Not only will I show them that everything about the situation is to my advantage, I'll believe it too. That's what I did with Mum all those years ago; looked on the bright side, became Pollyanna, learnt and grew. This very morning Mum told me it had been the right thing to do. But now I'm ready to do it again. And better still – I'm now skilled in the art of crafting a tale to go with it. All those years in advertising, spinning a yarn, creating an image, crafting a story (about deodorant or mayonnaise, or gloss paint) will come into their own. I've a special gift for finding the good in anything – some call it denial – but I can package things nicely and sell it to people who neither want nor need it. This will be my best work yet.

So now, sitting here on the window seat, the twilight sky with the first twinkling stars just outside, the children asleep next door, washed and glowing with the exertion and joy of their summer day, I feel lucky. I have the opportunity of a life time to find what I want for myself and my children and no one to answer to while I do so. I can see a story board for this in my head: a halcyon and rosy life where Daddy calls and emails, maybe even Skypes from sunny hotel rooms in exotic and sultry climes, while the children climb trees and swing in hammocks, roll in verdant grass and splash in crystal streams. In this picture the birds always sing and I'm fresh and cool, sipping something icy and virtuous and feeling calm and rested and cherished.

And guess what, Betty Draper – you wooden yet icy blonde – you are not part of that picture!

Bloody elbow eczema is back, dammit.

Saturday, 9 January

For a couple of days I've mulled things over in my mind. The day after Mia's call, I heard from an anxious and concerned Beth, eagerly trying to assess my state of mind and reaction to Mia's "bombshell". Mia apparently wasted no time spreading the word of my marital woes. After all, it was her monthly "book club" meeting the night she called me. One could hardly expect her to bottle it up in a forum like that. Eight captivated, poorly read and under-stimulated, slightly drunk, if not high, dahlings hanging on her every word! This was how Beth related it to me in any case. Beth and various members of Mia's nest of vipers were quite enthralled by the severely exaggerated tales of Curious George (as Mia has now nicknamed him) and the luscious Betty/Beccy. So no - not much discussion of the book – my life is more compelling than their choice of over-sexed tripe masquerading as self help literature.

Beth – who claimed to have returned from the beach to see her doctor – serendipitously turned up to book club. For the life of me I can't see why she would make book club at Mia's a priority after the Yves-Opera-in-Venice debacle, but that's Beth – forgiving to a fault. She apparently attempted to moderate the discussion and to interject with a more balanced version of events, assuming that was the right thing to do. She soon realised she was on a hiding to nothing and left with a demure:

"Mia, I don't think this story is quite accurate and does a huge injustice to all the parties, especially Verity. It also doesn't reflect well on you to be delighting in telling it to this extent."

The rest of the girls were less concerned with my state of mind, than Beth, bless her. Their Schadenfreude was sickening, even to Beth, who usually has a very high tolerance threshold when it comes to gratuitous gossip and salacious slander about people she *doesn't* know.

In summary, Mia has single-handedly undermined all my shenanigans before Christmas. I either look like a complete liar and fraud or a big idiot, prepared to believe any lie told her by her husband. Thank God I didn't send that End of Year greeting! George's "wanton" ways and my complete inability to deal with it will have the tongues wagging for weeks.

I long ago made my peace with how little real feeling I had for Mia as a friend, but even so, to milk this misunderstood and unfortunate situation for her own social gain – at a book club no less - is just pathetic. Why am I surprised?

I decided to laugh. What else could I do? Go rushing back to do damage control with these people whose views I disdain at the best of times? I managed to convince Beth - and myself - that I'm impervious. This conversation with Beth buoyed my spirits significantly. She was very supportive and not the least bit judgmental of my trust in George. Because despite all of that innuendo I still believe that he's only seeking to find answers, not having an affair. Maybe I'm delusional, but I know the essence of George hasn't changed. He wouldn't be so cruel, selfish and short-sighted as to lie and obfuscate about this in the way Mia assumes.

And to be honest, a mere affair would be something of a relief after all of this anxiety about identify, "giving back" and purpose.

Anyway, I feel ennobled by the puerile game playing that Beth described and even emboldened. So much so that I took the first opportunity to share all the sordid details with Mum. It was actually very therapeutic to divulge the big mess to a live person. She laughed at the thought of the ladies in the edge of their seats, books abandoned in their designer handbags. She told me she has a lot of respect for how well I'm handling everything, how supportive I am of George and what a strong role model I am to the children.

Perhaps inspired by this, I'm gradually coming to the realisation that I've been mistaken about Mum for some time. I've been harbouring ill-conceived grudges against her for years. Has she been secretly championing me all this time? Is this why Felicity makes churlish remarks about me being the favourite child? For years I was convinced Mum didn't approve of me and yet, based on the all the evidence from the past several weeks, she seems genuinely proud of me, even admiring, and just wants a friendship with me. I've thought of little else this past day and while the control freak in me hates to be wrong, I have to concede I've done her a huge disservice.

I've attributed to her all sorts of negativity and criticism that she never intended at all. I've demonised her these past few years when really all she wanted was to offer advice and support. Where I heard criticism I can now see that she was only pointing out potential blind spots or trying to help me see the bigger picture. I'm *devouring* humble pie, right now! Naturally, I've not told Mum that I feel culpable in our difficult relationship to date – not in so many words. I'm trying to show her through my actions that I'm ready to make a clean breast of it and rebuild our relationship. Her own demeanour and conduct is saying pretty much the same thing. Very proud lot, we are.

The only outstanding issue is just how I feel about Felicity. If I'm forgiving Mum, or more accurately, letting go of the past and reassessing her, then perhaps I should reassess my relationship with Felicity too. Not that I held any substantive animosity towards her. We get on pretty well apart from her occasional sulks. No worse than many sisters. No, it's more that in coming to a better understanding of Mum, I'm seeing that Felicity has played a large part in driving a wedge between us while all the time being as sweet as pie in her dealings with us, as individuals. Don't know what to do with this newfound awareness. Perhaps nothing. I guess it's understandable after being the sole object of Mum's interest for years that she would feel threatened by me. I'll keep an eye on things with her. No doubt once she returns to her routines in the city this week and realises that we're back here with Mum til term resumes, she'll start to panic that she's been left out of something. I resolve to be impervious to that too.

The children are having a wonderful time, barely missing George at all. Gracie is riding like a professional now (another potential source of grief and envy for Felicity) and even Freddie is now prepared to sit on a pony. We spent yesterday afternoon at the beach across the paddock, to their delight. We dug holes and tunnels and made walls just as we did in August. And I burnt just as many, if not more, calories, free from inhibitions, on that beautiful deserted shore. How different from our trip in August. What a different time that was. My goodness.

I'm feeling almost restored to my old self. Not my anxious mid-term, mid-application to schools, migraine inducing normal, but my old do-it-from-scratch-domestic-queen self who was always cheerful and full of energy. I'm ready to think about how best to channel this energy and zest so as to build a viable and sustainable "life". I remain convinced that I'll not thrive overseas, ministering to sick orphans and propping up George's fragile self image. Rather, I'm drawing on Mum's perception of me and focussing on my positive attributes. And I'm remembering how Mrs G does just that; plays to her strengths and pleases herself in all her pursuits.

Here goes:

Verity's strengths and interests

Strengths	Interests
Tenacity	Fitness
Energy	People
Pragmatism	Local causes

Positivity	Reading
Creativity	Children
Friendliness	Wellbeing
Having Ideas	Decorating
Honesty	Gardening
Marketing	Green issues
Thoroughness	Chocolate

So where does that take me?

Obviously, I need to see Beth's coach! But in the meantime, something to do with raising awareness of fitness and green issues as they pertain to children's health and happiness at a very local level? Mmm. Hitting a bit of a wall there. Might need to meditate for a few days... or call in Mrs G to help me take this to the next stage - to focus on what I love and am good at and find a calling of my own. No excuses. Freddie will be at Montessori every day and Maria can earn her way around the house for a change.

Sunday, 17 January

Well, well, well. This week has proven to me that if you walk the walk and talk the talk you become a different person. Amazing. I've neglected my dear old journal in the rush and fever of dreaming and creating something new for myself and now I feel that I have to get it all down while it's fresh in my mind.

First, the children are just angels. They are getting along so beautifully. Gracie is reading in her hammock by the stream every day without me pushing her. Freddie's painting every morning and right now he's making a mini-city with all of his construction equipment, diggers and cars. He's in Heaven. They've made friends with the grandchildren of one of Mum's preferred trainers. Let's be honest – her new beau – who has been here almost daily these past 10 days. His son's children are staying with him for two weeks while their parents travel in Africa.

Doug, the trainer, is a charming fellow, quite earnest to start with, but then as he warms up and gets familiar, terribly funny and easy going. He comes from a long line of horse trainers, was widowed 6 years ago and works with his two sons. He's known Mum about two years but only recently, at the urging of his sons breached Mum's defences. I'm delighted. He seems to be wonderful for her. Indeed he reminds me of Dad in some ways, though he's more of a chatter-box, not as cerebral; but he's an animal lover and a genius with the horses. Felicity was here Friday and yesterday and described him as Mum's very own Redford (*The Horse Whisperer*). He's very good for and with Mum - he makes her seem younger and more vital. And they complement each other very well. He understands her business, its pressures and demands and she his, and they share a passion that frankly, the rest of us don't, which is creating champion horses. The fact they have clicked and share this means Mum is quickly letting go of her obsession about one of us coming into the farm with her. She realises that it can't be forced.

For the first time since she moved here, she's happy for us to just enjoy the farm as a wonderful respite from the city, free from the expectation we love it as much and in the same ways as she does. And she is so much happier as a result. Who knows, maybe one of the children will want to take it on in a few years, but for now, this is feeling like the closest things to happy families since Dad was diagnosed with cancer. And even then, despite Dad's calming presence, it was not all beer and skittles. After all, back then Mum was a maniac; variously hounding Felicity, doing her good works, forcing Dad to exercise and generally being neurotic all over the place.

I was right about Felicity. As I expected, she was jealous and annoyed to learn, after calling me last week, that we're ensconced here Chez Mother for another 2 weeks. Hence, her visit this weekend, I suspect. Fearful her place between us was no longer available, she came to butt herself in and try to upset our equilibrium. To her credit, she's taken the temperature of things pretty quickly and sees that nothing she could say or do will upset our little apple cart here, not least since Doug and the children are virtually staying too. To create a row or to even be snide about Mum and me getting along so well now, would only have revealed her nasty side and left everyone in no doubt as to who had caused or exacerbated the pre-existing tension in the first place.

So, disaster averted there. Felicity seems to be reconciled to letting Mum and me just get along, and indeed she cannot really want to waste her time worrying about it given that she is indeed preggers, finally! Baby is due in May – thereby ensuring she won't be able to cater Gracie's 6th Birthday party in April, after all. Never mind, might be able to do it myself.

But enough of all of that. The best part of the past week is that I had a massive breakthrough in working out what I want to do. Using the ruse that she *had* to meet Doug and share in our little sojourn here, I persuaded Mrs G to visit us at the farm. Lucky for me it's January – her only quiet month, in truth – and down she came, delighted to be invited, thrilled to meet Doug and as always, more than happy to spend time with Gracie and Freddie and Mum.

Selfishly, once the greetings and catch ups were out of the way, I lured her off to town ostensibly to go antiquing, but in fact to download my half baked ideas and get her input. As always she was superb, cutting right to the heart of the issue, understanding intuitively my urgent need to create a compelling calling for myself in light of the uncertainty surrounding George and his plans and in view of the fact that right now I don't want to be available to anyone in my social circle.

Mrs G is incredibly wise. She says she hasn't had a "meaningful conversation" with George about his issues, so she's quick to point out that her views were not necessarily true – just the private musings of a too old and too wise mother. But she really has a gift. Even if she's completely wrong she's so persuasive and charming that one wants to believe everything she says. I was hanging on her every word.

Basically, she thinks George is trying to make amends to his father for pursuing a career that he thinks his father didn't respect. Mrs G says George has lost all perspective because he failed to deal adequately with the fact that he was unprepared for his father's death and had never resolved this unspoken tension between them about why he wasn't doing more for the world.

Mrs G was at pains to assure me that Mr G never felt that way about George's career. He certainly didn't disapprove of his choices. Rather, he was proud of George, the way he lived and his values. The part of him that chided George about big pharma was a contrivance – a tease - perhaps to hide the complete love and devotion he really felt for George. And perhaps a challenge, a gauntlet thrown down, a suggestion that George never forget how lucky he was and never forget that he could give more to the community when the time was right.

I'm very relieved to have gained so much insight and background on the whole issue. It begins to make a lot more sense that George is so hell bent on this soup kitchen/save the world thing if he has this sense of failing his Dad on his shoulders. I know how hard it was for me to live with the idea of Mum's disapproval – but she's alive. And, let's face it, I'm a lot better at dealing with people's opinions than George. Poor

George. Not only does he feel he let his father down by working for Pharma Co, but he seems to need to persuade himself he's a worthwhile human being as well. Who would have thought anyone could be so screwed up about what they perceive their parent thinks of them? At least at the zenith of my troubles with Mum I was not taking off to far flung climes in search of myself. But then, his Dad is gone and reconciliation isn't possible.

Naturally, I suggested to Mrs G that we call George and set him straight, but she insisted we let things play our as they will. If and when he speaks to her about it she'll tell him what she told me, but for now she believes he needs to get this out of his system. Selfishly, and in the interests of Gracie and Freddie having their father around I said perhaps we could drop a few hints anyway, but Mrs G is adamant that everything will work out for the best. She's very much of the view that if George does not confront these demons now we'll be headed for a worse catastrophe later. Now, he's relatively young and well-placed to capitalise on his position and experience. If he stays where he is and drifts on in this state of misery and yearning for another few years it'll be too late to change track. His employers will have let him go in disgust, his kids will hate him and even I would have tired of his morose self-pity. She's right.

It was a strange day – I set out with her to share my plans and I emerged from the "Three Cypresses Bakery" feeling positively charitable about George, the world and everyone in it. It seemed almost inappropriate to talk about myself after all of that, but I felt I ought to make hay while the sun was shining. We stopped off on the way back to the farm for a stroll on the beach. Even with her linen trousers rolled to her knee she looked elegant.

I told her where I am with my plans to run a business, namely, something involving children, fitness and happiness. She was all over it! We brainstormed it for 30 minutes and I dusted off the sand and climbed into the Audi with a virtual draft business plan scribbled on the back of the "Coastal Antique Directory"! Mrs G has challenged me to get the plan formalised before I head back to town and then email it to her. If she likes it she will come in as an investor and stump up any capital I might need for the set up.

I'm just so excited. A part of me feels incredibly disloyal to George though. I'm on the cusp of something that could be amazing and have come to it out of a desire to avoid being with him. It seems wrong, yet it's so right. I'm just trying to be with it right now and let it all sink in. Tomorrow I'll start mapping out the ideas and researching the various services I want to offer. Amazing, amazing day.

Thursday, 21 January

I've been hopelessly distracted from kids and Mum these past few days. I'm hunkered down under the tree in the hammock - after doing my beach workout each morning at 5am – working on my business idea. Thank goodness the children are so happy with Doug's grandkids - they hardly notice, or miss me, and Mum has been superb. It seems that she and I have so much more in common now that I'm trying to build something; she'll do almost anything to accommodate me. She even suggested I leave the children and go home to the city to be completely distraction free. I was touched, but declined. I feel so connected to this positive time and place here and now that I don't want to break the spell and leave until I'm sure I've nutted everything out. It's as though a dam has burst and every last bit of my creative and visionary abilities – lying underutilised for years - have come roiling through the floodgates and over the broken walls of my former boxed in self. I hardly know myself. I catch my reflection in the French doors and see myself smiling all the time. It's uncanny.

I told George a little bit about it last night. I couldn't conceal it any longer – I had to share my excitement. He seemed genuinely pleased for me; interested, albeit briefly, as we only spoke for a short time, but not at all bothered or resentful which I had feared he might be.

Have heard from no one in town apart from Clothilde – by text. They're home from France and she ran into Hard-Done-By-Harriet at the hairdresser telling her stylist – hardly a style if you ask me – about her "friend" who has dropped off the face of the earth due to the ignominy of an unfaithful husband. The stylist said that no one cares these days and that the friend – me – has probably moved on and shacked up with a "new fella"! I can't say I really needed to hear it – but it was a bit funny. A "new fella?" If only. Thanks very much girls, for all of your support, attention, love and care. I suppose I should be proud that it's my "desperate situation" that has distracted Harriet from herself for a few minutes. The entire neighbourhood and the crew she calls friends should be thanking me for providing such a rich topic of gossip and such a rare excuse for Harriet to feel something close to superiority. Well done me.

Tuesday, 26 January

I emailed my plan for the business to Mrs G today. Now I'm relaxing and revelling in the thought of what I might be launching myself into. It's so exciting. I feel like I just lost 3 kilos, ran a beachside leg of a triathlon and won and received a fabulous handbag made exclusively for me by Hermes – the "Veritas" (deep cerise pink, elegant, elite and unattainable - and did I say - only one made)! My goodness. All these years convincing myself that wife and mother was enough. Sure, it's *enough*, but it's time for me to do some other things too.

I'm beside myself with anticipation and energy and so grateful to George for having his crisis and forcing this upon me. Imagine if he'd not lost his way. I'd be sitting in my air-conditioned, new and sparkling kitchen noticing hand marks on the stainless steel matt fridge and counting calories in the children's lunch boxes, before planning the next overhaul of the garden, my wardrobe and my hair, all the while embittered about Mum, Mia and Wendy. Now – in my lonely abandonment I have a higher purpose than my appearance. Indeed, with this smile plastered on my face, freckles on my nose, unpainted toe nails, massive calluses from stable duty and my uniform of shapeless smock dresses all month, I'm unrecognisable. The icing on the cake would be if Francine and Mia drove up now in Mia's top down swanker car looking for me.

The kids must think I'm putting on an act or some brave jolly face to distract them from the fact that in three days we'll be back in town, sans Daddy, and a mere four days away from school starting. New schools, new friends and no doubt, new neurotic parents to meet and avoid. God – what a bring-me-down!

Friday, 29 January

It was a happy yet poignant departure from the farm today. Mum begins a very busy season now and will be run off her feet over the coming weeks. She seems to face the prospect with relish though, which I ascribe to Doug. We'll go back every three or four weeks to help her out and to enjoy more of the wonderful respite we've enjoyed there over the past month. It's been a balm. Two months ago I could never have imagined longing to be at Mum's every weekend.

It felt good to be home this afternoon. The garden looks so lush and beautiful thanks to the crew from Clothilde's gardening firm who looked after it during my absence. The summer house is going to come into its own for the rest of the season as the children want to recreate the ambiance at the farm. We'll not be investing in hay or dung just yet, but I think more hammocks and swimming can be arranged.

There was a letter from Desirée waiting for me on our return. I was so delighted to see it – until I got half way through and her news gave way to concerned platitudes.

She wrote that she and Phil had a change of heart on returning to Boston. It was too hard to go on as if nothing had happened. They could not pick up their lives there and decided he would go back to Latvia – he persuaded Pharma Co to give him one last chance. She and the girls are basing themselves in Stockholm – a scenic cruise across the Baltic from Phil. I can imagine all the poor cold Eastern European girls are just beside themselves with Phil in their midst. Desirée assures me he is in "rehab" for his porn addiction. Sure, sure. Rehab in Latvia? Oh well. It's not my problem and whatever happens, she'll get through it. She's very forgiving and compassionate. I could learn a thing or two from her. Maybe I'll visit them in Sweden some time.

Page 2 was a whole bunch of mis-conceived crap about me and George based on – wait – Beth. That's right. Dear old life-long friend Beth saw fit over Christmas to pop my news in her first ever Christmas card to *my* friend who she was jealous of just three months ago. Now that Desirée is gone, is a "victim" and an object of her pity – not that Beth is even meant to know about Phil - and now that his family is in exile in frozen Nordic climes – Beth feels she can reach out and spread my news to her.

Pathetic. Why do people need to talk about me at all? They were not so enthralled by my every thought, movement or gesture two years ago when I was the hottest home-maker this side of the Pacific! Oh no.

Good old kick 'em when they're down has been motivating this little postal catch up.

Just bloody great – Desirée can now feel superior, married to that insipid, spineless pervert and condescend to advise me to stand by my man and be true to myself and at least six other self-help addict adages of no application to my situation. Why? Because Beth could not even convey the truth about me and George. In some hopeless attempt to find me a friend – knowing full well how abandoned I was feeling around Christmas – she has to implore Desirée for some attention. Am I so desperate? All this charity! Desirée clearly thinks, or has been led to suppose, based on her letter, that George was sidelined and sent to China as punishment for the Phil debacle – not unlike Phil's forced removal. Desirée now feels superior since she has come through the "same" thing and thinks we're estranged as husband and wife because I can't cope without him. Good God! I could just about throw up all over my new floor. Self-righteous, ignorant, holier than thou... crap!

If Beth gave a damn she would pick up the phone and ask me if she can help, visit, take the kids for a play, suggest an outing or just talk to me. Rather than find out the truth of how I really am or feel, she thinks she's helping by broadcasting lies to my extended circle. She can't tell them the truth because she has no vocabulary for anything beyond a man devoted to her and her children, dedicating his life to her. That's fine – but even Yves with his wonderful veiny arms and gorgeous eyes is a simpering fool. If he ever had to work a day in his life, and if he hadn't fled his ruined first marriage in France, he might find that in the real world women like Beth are a dime a dozen. Closeted in his fool's paradise he seems to think she's a catch. Well, compared to Mia she's a catch. And yes, she has been a great friend to me for years but now – when things might be tough for me - she remains so completely self absorbed as to be borderline narcissistic. I had been blaming Mia and Harriet for spreading all the rumours and feeding the gossip mill and in fact if Desirée's letter is to be believed, it's Beth who has to take credit for it.

Her card to Desirée said that she's "trying to be there for Verity despite being shut out and pushed away. "Verity is angry and self-loathing and is not yet taking steps to cope or address these feelings. Their marriage has no hope if she continues like this."

BULLSHIT Girlfriend.

I know I'm being intolerant and intolerable, but I reckon I have at least 5 years of pent up frustration mounting up inside my head. I need a bloody good purge. Tomorrow I'm going to Spring to Mind Spa and getting some Hot Stone Therapy.

Great end to our wonderful holiday.

I just rang Mum – I was so annoyed with Beth that I couldn't sleep. Mum laughed at me and told me to get some perspective. She's right. Bugger these women. I need to focus on my plans and settling the children into school next week. I need to plot my own course for now. Mum made a very good point saying:

"If I've learned one thing from my business life it's that you can't soar like an eagle if you're cooped up with turkeys."

Saturday, 30 January

Heeding Mum's advice, focusing on letting all of that gossip wash past me I had an amazing experience at the Spring to Mind Spa. I detoxed in the Scream and Steam room, pelted hot stones at the idea of my female friends and swam and swam like a fish for two hours in the wave pool. I'm getting membership so that I can use their coaching packages and workshops at a discount. What a service!

After my rejuvenating morning the children and I spent the afternoon in the garden with Felicity and one of her catering friends and the children. It was very energising. We read the newspaper and chatted about restaurants and the challenges of surviving in the food industry. I learnt a lot about marketing and playing to one's strengths as I listened to Felicity and Jane reflect on their businesses and the importance of networking, knowing when to delegate, when to ask for help and when to retain control. I was longing to run upstairs and amend my business plan. I'm still eagerly awaiting Mrs G's input on it. We have agreed to speak next weekend, so this week is all about the children.

Loving the kitchen. We Skyped George and showed him how fabulous it is. He seemed relaxed and pleased to hear from us. He thought the kids seemed older and very calm and easy going. Not one row over the computer during the entire call.

George is flying in on Tuesday. He wants to be here to take the children to school with me on Wednesday. I was very surprised and actually pleased about this. He seems to be stepping up for the children. They're thrilled of course.

Gracie was so excited she took almost an hour to fall asleep tonight. She's missing Mum and the horses and Doug and she's a little anxious about Frobisher too. We'll have to keep it pretty low key til she settles in. I had an email from slimy Desperate Housewife Jeff from Montessori this morning – just picked it up. His daughter Emile was on the waiting list at Frobisher for months and he just heard that she has a place. He wants to discuss car pooling. God forbid. I thought we were rid of each other!

Wednesday, 3 February

A very tiring but wonderful day. The children love their schools. Freddie went off so meekly, without a whimper, like a lamb to the slaughterhouse, completely unaware that life as he knows it is forever over. Gracie on the other hand was almost hyper – she was so excited about her first day at Frobisher and Daddy being home in its honour. We had no choice but to be swept along in the general merriment and anticipation. And it did not disappoint. Both children were in bed soon after 6, such was the stimulation and exhaustion of the day. Their teachers say they had great days and have made friends already. Gracie had Emile shadowing her all day, which I dare say is a mixed blessing – better the devil you know. Freddie knew half the children from play group and from several of Gracie's activities over the past couple of years – siblings – so he too had no fear or anxiety about leaving us at the door and taking his place on the carpet.

Admittedly he was only there three hours and was picked up by George at noon – early pickup for the first couple of weeks - and taken off for a walk in the park and some Daddy time at the Porsche showroom downtown. George is quite besotted with them (the kids) – making up for the past month. He seems quite a different person, in fact. Maybe it's me though. I'll find out soon enough, no doubt, as he's here a full week.

Friday, 5 February

Had lunch with George and Mrs G today at her house. It was delightful of course, not least because we shooed George out into the garden with Freddie and later Gracie, and spent most of the afternoon discussing my plans. Meanwhile, over lunch George volunteered that he has been getting help from an executive coach (not Rebecca but a "Franz"!) and has gained clarity on a lot of his troubles and knows that much of the issue lies in the wish to lead a more meaningful life. Ironically, "meaning" apparently means more family time, more time for interests and less at work, more time focussed on the things that give him pleasure and which he is good at and pursuing work and interests that are purposeful and not purely oriented towards making money. He thought this was a bombshell and he clearly dropped it in his mother's company in order to protect himself from what he feared would be a backlash from me.

Well, no such backlash ensued and we had a very warm and encouraging dialogue about what jolly good sense that all made. Mrs G even said she knew he would find the way. Now that the hard work has been done all he needs to do is find a way to monetise the idea so as to afford the school fees. We all laughed, somewhat nervously, at that. The upshot is that George is planning to keep on seeing his coach – indeed, we have the gorgeous Rebecca to thank for putting him onto this chap she has used – and he hopes to have some ideas within the next month or two. I asked, tentatively – also sheltering behind Mrs G, I admit – whether the soup kitchen idea was likely to make the shortlist. Mrs G stifled a giggle and George looked at me quizzically.

"What soup kitchen idea?"

"I thought you wanted to make drugs freely available through developing Asia and hand them out in soup kitchens," I replied innocently, munching my pomegranate slaw.

"I don't think I said anything about soup kitchens V," he said patronisingly.

I let it go. Don't want to put ideas into his head, just happy his coach has helped take a few out.

Anyway, I'm not really worried. He seems so much happier - lighter and easy going. The children are loving having him back and I too find him not the least boorish or hard to speak to – a transformation, indeed. I plan to enjoy him while he's in this optimistic frame of mind and keep hoping I can cement my own plans before he comes up with anything too crazy or disease ridden.

Mrs G was very reassuring and said she suspects it will all blow over and he'll take a nice safe salaried role in an NGO with charitable purposes such as assisting with debt relief or AIDS prevention or something related to pharmaceuticals and he'll spend more time on the golf course. She's convinced he is, at heart, conservative and cautious; far less adventurous than Sophie. God forbid we call her "adventurous" – a real Nancy Drew meets Amelia Lockhart. She thinks that while he has definite issues about finding meaning in his work, she doubts it will involve long term separation from us or his friends, given what he said today. He does seem to have matured – become less extreme.

I didn't mention the possibility that he might just want to start a new family. Find some nice compliant girl with no baggage...

Enough worst case scenario, Verity!

I have an action plan to be getting on with and a proposal to put to the bank for capital for my venture. I also need to find a space in which to run it. I need to think about advertising, marketing, press, printing, websites, administration, finance, staff, Facebook pages, goodness knows what else. So terribly excited.

I told George the basics tonight. He was very impressed. He really had no idea I was this serious and driven and seems genuinely startled. I also told him how well things are going with Mum and even Felicity. He wants to take credit for that – no way George – this is not your doing at all!

Tuesday, 9 February

George headed back to HK this morning. The children had a little bit of a teary breakfast time after he left at the crack of dawn. Not even three extra frothy hot chocolates with marshmallows from the new Nespresso (sent the café size machine back) could really compensate for his absence. The house feels all empty and echoey now that he's gone and the children are at school. I don't even have Maria for company – she's helping Helen now three mornings a week. Carla's in the garden sweeping but she's not the best of company when George leaves. She misses him and blames me. Good heavens – who else needs to be managed through this whole thing?

Beth's no longer speaking to me apparently. Helen told me as much yesterday at drop-off. Beth thinks I'm driving George away, that I'm ignoring her and am too proud to let my friends help me. I'm a little at a loss to know what to do with her. I was away for a month on holiday – looking after myself and my children. We then returned to our schools and lives and suddenly I'm her worst enemy for not telling her my woes. Well, gosh why don't I just make some up and Twitter them to everyone so they can retweet them all over the planet? Seriously, what happened to "live and let live"? When did my marital problems become cause for everyone to feel neglected? I'm not whining or complaining, seeking solace or sympathy – hell, I'm trying to make the best of this. Why do I have to share? It's *my* life.

I look back over the past couple of months and realise I've completely lost touch with my friends. I've nothing to say to them. I want to talk to Mum and Felicity every couple of days and Clothilde and Helen – loyal and low-key and constant – they expect nothing from me. Clothilde is just sweet and even-keeled. Helen is wonderful – so much time and so intelligent and supportive, no agenda apart from being a fantastic person, free from guile and disingenuousness, relaxed and centred and caring.

But Beth, Mia, Emma? Kate? Even Desirée?

I'm truly an island unto myself.

That said, the yoga mums seemed pleased to have me back today. However, the joy at my presence was short lived when I hinted that I have plans to start my own business. God forbid that anyone should break out of the group think and do something original. Shopping for yoga kit at a new store is about as game as they get. For yoga people they are bloody militaristic about women self actualising. Breathe Verity, breathe. Suffice to say the instinct to keep my business to myself is well founded. The barrage of criticism was too much to take. The skinny wizened looking woman whose name is something like Penny or Polly or Henni or some such thing said:

"Business means no more yoga, no more asanas and no more coffees after, you know. You won't last a week."

They all nodded in agreement as they slurped their decaf non-fat soy whatevers. I hope they all get soy problems – mind you over-consuming the stuff can cause fertility problems and most of them are over the child bearing stage anyway...

The lesson for me is that beggars can't be choosers. I spent years shunning real women and cultivating fair-weather friends with bigger problems than mine. It's my own fault for being so flaky. No one really "gets" me, or wants to know who I am or what matters to me. It's pretty revealing when my oldest friend won't return my calls and is more interested in moaning about me and my so-called problems than actually hearing how I'm dealing with them.

Ooh, maybe that's the point! I'm not supposed to be dealing with them at all, at least not on my own. I'm meant to be a whimpering, simpering mess, crying over my manicure and dermal fill rather than getting back out there making something of myself.

Perhaps I'll find a kindred spirit at Frobisher soon enough. One or two mums seem pleasant at the drop-off each morning. Luscious Larry is still a familiar face when I collect Feddie from Montessori, though I doubt I will find time to fit in our tennis sessions this term. Thank goodness Maria is doing Freddie's pickup every other day (walking in and bringing him to the car where I wait, that is) – the whole Montessori fish bowl is just not my thing now, especially since today I resigned from the Parents' Association, blaming George and our crazy separate lives. Everyone seemed relieved but in a week or two there's bound to be a backlash when no one else volunteers to work with Wendy.

Can't be worried.

The most important thing is the children. They are happy, calm and relaxed. All is going well at school. We've scaled back the activities now – just violin and ballet for Gracie. I encouraged her to drop the ballet but they finally moved her up a class so she is not prepared to give up the hard won gains. I am cynical enough to think that her admission to Frobisher may account for the advancement too. Success breeds success even at 5. Freddie is continuing with toddler tennis. He's amazed us all with a love for the game. It has inspired him to master the TV remote and he can be found surfing the channels in search of Federer. Fingers crossed that we continue as we have begun the year.

Tuesday, 16 February

I'm aghast that a whole week has passed since I last wrote in my journal. I took the bull by the horns and joined a new yoga studio last

Thursday. The straw that broke the camel's back came on Wednesday when I ran into Harriet at the organic market. She sat me down and berated me for 20 minutes about her problems (the usual stuff, bullies at school, mother-in-law, not sleeping) and then drew a small breath to set in on mine – as she has heard them retold, thanks to the yoga ladies. According to them, I'm a mess, have let myself go completely and am running myself ragged trying to find an income because George is such a bastard and has cut me off. Supposedly I'm too proud to get a decent lawyer to fight him for proper child maintenance.

I actually burst out laughing at that and jumped up in delight, tripping over a display of eco-friendly toilet cleaner.

"I have to go Harriet! Too much to do – meetings, you know. Thanks for the chat!" I rushed outside, barely containing my joy at leaving Harriet to pick up the tab for my Diet Coke and endamame (since I drink cow's milk I run little risk of soy overload) and explain the spilt and rolling mess of loo-cleanser to the approaching security guy.

It was with much anticipation and excitement that I surfed the net via my new and groovy smart phone looking for an alternative yoga club. In fact, after a good look, I realized that the Spring to Mind Spa offers all varieties of yoga as well as various fitness classes at excellent times and often back to back so as to be complementary. A fresh approach to total body conditioning. Best of all, due to the coaching and self-help ethos that Spring to Mind espouses there is very little chance that I will see anyone I know there. Most people I know prefer to *talk* about change and growth rather than actually *achieve* any. I've signed up for some group workshops next week. I'll start with "*Get Out of Your Way*" and follow up with "*Visibility and Presence*". Might suggest a workshop on Mindful Management of Troublesome Relationships...

Friday, 19 February

Finally, after weeks of silence, Beth dropped by today.

I was just home from a meeting at the bank with Mrs G (my guarantor!), making a cappu and preparing a to-do list when I heard the knock at the door. I was expecting Clothilde for lunch and assumed she was back early from her daughter's class trip, so when I opened the door to see Beth standing there all tanned and blonde I did a double take.

"Clo-Beth – is that you?" I cried.

"Verity. How are you? Sorry to stop by without calling. Have you got time for a chat?"

"Of course. Come in. How are *you*?"

We kept up the overdue pleasantries for a few minutes while I made her a coffee and she admired the kitchen – white and minimalist with *Tiffany Blue* and stainless steel accents! We took our coffee outside – better vantage point from which to show off the garden.

After a good 15 minutes of back and forth small talk that went in one ear and out the other she finally got to the point, a brown hand placed lightly on my arm and her long hair flicked back over her shoulder so as to see me better.

"Are you sure you're alright, V? I've been hearing all sorts of things, some of them very worrying. I know you've called me and I've been meaning to call back, but you've no idea how busy I've been. You must forgive me for neglecting you. It's just been crazy settling the boys into their new schools. Yves' ex has been plaguing us with threats and Mum has down-sized; I've not had a moment to draw breath since Christmas." She looked as me beseechingly, reminding me of how she used to look at uni when she wanted a copy of my lecture notes.

Frankly, my mind was elsewhere. I was admiring the garden as she talked and was reflecting on the last time she had been there. I couldn't get over the fact that she hadn't asked directly what was happening with George and me. I was not inclined to help her out.

"You know, Beth, I can honestly say, I've never been better. Of course I forgive you. Don't worry about it."

She didn't seem to know what to say to that so we sat there smiling at each other for a few beats until she said:

"Are you still journaling? I stopped a while back. It wasn't helping. I couldn't work out what I was meant to be doing or where it was meant to take me. I think I'm better suited to traditional talking therapies. How about you?"

Oh crap, I thought. If I admit this journal has been a godsend then she'll know I was on the verge. If I lie then I'm no different from how I was this time last year – and if there is one thing she needs to know – I am very different from that. Shit.

"Beth, I think journaling is useful if one suits *oneself* as to how to do it. By definition it's quite personal, so being told how to do it sort of defeats the purpose. But sure, writing can be therapeutic, as can talking. But there is no single "right" way to help oneself. Don't we all just do our best with what we have. And sometimes we don't realise what we have til crunch time comes. More coffee?"

"Euurhh, no, I'm fine." She was looking less beseeching; more befuddled.

"What are you saying, Verity?"

"Nothing really. I think we both know that the past few months have been trying. We can gloss over it and pretend we're fine or we can be honest. I guess I'm trying to be honest." Now she looked scared. So I went on:

"Beth. I've had to face a few challenges lately, as you know. But I'm actually doing fine. A lot of good things have come out of this period with George away and I'm not spinning this or pretending to you. I'm not in denial. George is working things out. I'm hopeful we'll be back together before long but it won't kill me if we're not. We'll manage. You see, I've let go of a lot of things that were in my way, holding me back, and somewhere along the way I saw that trying to control everything would eventually kill me. In coming to that realisation I actually found there were some things I wanted to do for myself. So – yes – honestly, I'm good. I wish I'd needed you or trusted you, but I didn't and that's ok too." I shrugged and patted her hand. "It's ok."

She looked relieved then. I was ready to move on so I took her cup and went inside. She followed soon after, her heels clacking on my new floor and we hugged. She said things about how relieved she was to see me doing well and not depressed or fat. She said she likes my new haircut and promised to call more and to invite me to the yacht club regatta for St Patrick's Day. Oh yay!

So that was that. I guess it's good that she came around. Not sure when I'll see her again though, as I seem to have plans in March. Oh well - that's ok.

Meanwhile, the bank called not long after, approving my loan. It's not a huge amount, but it's a big deal for me with no income of my own yet, apart from the equity Mrs G is putting in.

Felicity is coming for dinner tonight, to collect some baby clothes of Freddie's – scan shows she's expecting a boy! Then we'll go over my business plan and discuss a possible role for her in the venture. So excited.

Monday, 1 March

My poor journal – abandoned and cast aside. Sorry Inner Child Journal/Lonely Housewive's Diary!

Very good week since I last wrote. I'm getting to a class at Spring to Mind Spa almost every day and seeing Jorgé there too. I asked the manager at Spring to Mind whether I could bring my own trainer and she was delighted to oblige. In fact they've offered him some studio classes too, so everyone's happy. His classes are fabulous!

The children are thriving. Gracie loves school and wakes at 6 every day to get ready all by herself. She's made friends with some lovely little girls and is keen to have them for a garden party next month for her birthday. Felicity offered to make sandwiches and cakes but Gracie and I won't hear of it. Felicity must put her feet up and chill out. Freddie's also doing well at Montessori. Parents are invited to help out on Fridays and seeing him in the classroom interacting with the children is a delight. He's hilarious and very sweet!

George is coming home for a week from next weekend, which is lovely. We're all counting the sleeps. The plan is to take the children out of school for a day and drive down the coast via Mum's. I was at Mum's all of this past weekend with the children and Mrs G. I thought I might scope out the real estate situation in the area – a weekender might be worth considering now - but just relaxing and talking with Mum took up all our time. I've seen a few potential sites for my business here in town and have put in a couple of offers – just tentative really, low-balling – to test the water. It's such a buzz to visualise the business actually taking off and to imagine what might be. I'm not really ready to commit but looking is fun. Mrs G thinks that I'm ready for a change of scene and so am subconsciously rejecting the city options. It's possible...

However, as I told Mum over the weekend, I'm considering a more conservative plan for the time being. I'm so attracted to and impressed by what Tess Wood has created at Spring to Mind Spa that I want to put a proposal to her to run my children focussed classes there initially while I build up a reputation and credibility. I need to capitalise on the infrastructure already in place - the clientele, the word of mouth - until I generate a following of my own. I've interviewed more than 10 Pilates and yoga instructors over the past week in search of someone who might share in my vision and passion. I've short listed three! This week after school they're booked to run some sessions with Gracie and Freddie and Helen and Clothilde's children so I can see them in action. Helen's son is primed to be a "troublemaker" to see how they deal with him!

I know I have support and cash behind me but the real issue is not whether this is a good idea – I know it is – it's: will parents buy this service, book these sessions – for which I now have a name! "équilibre" – which means "balance" in French. I've got some rough ideas of the logo turning around in my head right now. The idea is so perfect – yoga, gymnastics and strength classes aimed at helping children develop good posture and core strength as well as flexibility and balance; coupled with the emotional and social dimension – workshops and play-based sessions addressing mental and emotional balance.

I can't run the Pilates or yoga side of things myself – I'd need training - but I've been reading into the non-physical piece and have some fabulous content for the sessions. Once I have the yoga/strength instructor sorted I'll focus on finding a coach/trainer/teacher for the mental balance piece. Again – a shared vision and belief in the importance of this will be the key.

Everyone I mention this too is completely sold on the value of such classes and the viability of this as a business, but, it's still untested.

Before I commit to a studio or a lease I need a safe, low risk testing ground.

Tomorrow I'm meeting Mrs Mellloy at Frobisher to run through the concept and whet her appetite for *équilibre* classes at Frobisher. I'll then work my way through my address book tapping into everyone I know with children in private schools. Look out Mia – I'm going to make use of you after all!

Wednesday, 17 March

I fully expected to be too busy to attend the St Patrick's Day regatta with Beth, but I had a change of heart last week and agreed to go, spurred on by my fabulous meetings with Mrs Melloy (call me Sarah) and Tess at Spring to Mind who both agreed to run my sessions on their premises. Sarah will fit them into the sport programme and pay us very well for our time. Tess has agreed to waive studio hire fees for the first month and is giving us four hours a week in which to test the market. I've booked two yoga/Pilates instructors and Tess recommended two facilitators/coaches who she knows that have worked with children. One is a former lawyer who runs communication workshops for kids – I really like her. The other is very young – more malleable perhaps – but she seems ok. Again, I'll need to see them in action next week. At this rate we'll be in business offering classes after Easter. So far my costs are under control. Instructors will be paid 10% above market rate and receive bonuses based on bookings attributable to them. Not risking any disenfranchised staff.

The next step is to see whether I can fill the week with regular sessions at the schools in the area, either within the curriculum, as lunch activities or after school clubs. I'm also flirting with holiday sessions for a block of time – say 9am-12pm over five days but I'll hold fire til I see where we are after the first month.

George is speechless. He says the old Verity is back and my energy is inspiring. Hopefully more inspiring than Rebecca's radiant beauty, but I won't be asking.

So today, in big hat and emerald green dress bought specially for the occasion with the help off my personal shoppers, Helen and baby Eloise, I graced the yacht club. It was such incredibly good fun. So much so that I have to revise my top three worst fears and my hatred of yachts!

I felt a bit fish out of water-ish on arriving when I saw the dearth of hats. I love hats but one never wants to be the only one wearing one. Claire didn't disappoint – in her massive white floppy number – so I bee-lined her and the rest of the day went fabulously. Claire was a font of ideas and help – really keen to hear about *équilibre* and to introduce me to her friends, many of whom were familiar from charity boards and the opera. Some were just as helpful and I now have a long list of names to follow up with tomorrow.

Beth was conspicuously late. It was her invitation – raising money for juvenile diabetes that secured the huge crowd – but delays at the lawyer's office (dealing with Yves' ex-wife and property in France) apparently threatened her attendance. Yves came too – bless him. So devoted. Thank God Mia was not there. The two have completely busted up, Yves told me – Beth and Mia that is - and the word is that Mia is in detox following an intervention staged by Mitch on a rare weekend in town. We all owe him a huge debt of gratitude. Claire says Mia was crying out for attention ever since her fat and frumpy days in kindergarten where Claire first met her. Claire remembers her as being obnoxious, bratty and a bit of a reject.

It's too messy to write about. Suffice to say I'll go to Mitch direct for access to their kids' schools, should I need it.

Claire and two of her friends asked if I would do themed birthday party entertainment/activities. Wow. That never occurred to me. Yes I will, I insisted. To top it off, Beth's journo contacts sent photographers to capture the event. Snaps will be in the paper tomorrow. Me and Claire alongside the lovely Yves aboard the "Mermaid's Refrain". So glad I wore the hat!

Note to self – share that pic on FB.

Ooh and set up a page for *équilibre*.

And see what Wendy is up to!

Saturday, 3 April

Where is the year going? I can't believe it's April already. Easter holidays are upon us. It's wonderful to have some quiet time at home after the last few weeks of activity. George arrived last night – he'll be home for a week – and has taken the children to the garden centre this morning. The centre has a new child friendly café where he's meeting Harry and Wilbur for breakfast, leaving me this rare lull to catch up with my journal.

George is looking good! After a long stretch away it's great to see him, but even better for the children – hence this outing without me crowding them out. I'm always acting as the conduit or filter in their communication with George. It's time for him to rebuild his relationships with them given his "project" in HK is drawing to a close and he'll be back in 7 weeks. Yes, that's right. All the angst and worry has culminated in a decision to resign from Pharma Co with effect from Christmas and thereafter he wants to divide his time between consulting to NGO's based in and focused on South-East Asia and helping with his mother's environmental causes. With any spare time he is considering helping his father's parasitic disease research foundation. What a lovely, neat and sensible solution.

I owe Rebecca Thompson a huge debt of gratitude – in fact we all do. Her coach friend helped George work through his issues and formulate this plan – facilitating the thinking process and keeping it real. George has been most forthcoming about the coaching and the way he brainstormed the issues and opportunities, narrowed down his preferred options and settled on this new hybrid career path. The plan sounds superb to me. It offers flexibility, plays to his desire to leave a positive legacy, leverages his skills, network and experience, while also allowing him new scope to learn and grow as well. Oh and it lets him keep his family and earn some money too! In a funny way it parallels what I have come up with for myself. Mmm. My way was a lot quicker and cheaper, but then I was not having a mid-life crisis...

Pharma Co is now desperate to keep George and they've arranged several dinner engagements for him next week at which the Board hopes to persuade him that he can fulfil all his dreams in-house. George is not that keen but is playing willing. He'll call his coach tomorrow and brainstorm some ideas he has about what sort of package and role he could live with as a minimum before agreeing to stay, another year to start with – something about heading up their Corporate Social Responsibility function and putting some real substance into it. Whatever happens he seems to feel in control and is the happiest I've seen him in months.

I'm so pleased to see him smiling and joking, relaxing and being genuinely *present*. I don't mind what he does – within reason – as long as he can sustain this newfound *joie de vivre*. Mrs G was here last night to share the first night supper with us. While George took the children up to bed she took the opportunity to say:

"See, Verity. They all come good in the end. He seems to have found some answers, don't you think. You should be very proud of him and yourself."

I would love to take credit for George's situation but I never really *did* anything; just let him be. Pretty passive, really. Mrs G gave me a very stern look when I said as much.

"Honestly, you young girls need to wake up. Without your support he would be dragging himself to that job in town, miserable, going off the rails and chucking all of it in to wander aimlessly around the jungles of Cambodia feeling sorry for himself. "Letting him be" was exactly the thing to do. You deserve a lot of recognition for all you have done this past 6 months, and longer – taking care of the children so well, managing this huge house, starting your business, being here for George when he came back. I don't think *I* could have done it with a young family."

High praise indeed from someone as amazing as Mrs G!

I always thought I would want to find a way to milk it – to cash in all my credit – if he came back. But now that he's here – albeit only for a week – I'm just pleased for him (and me). A quiet Saturday morning on my own is enough pay-back... for now, anyway. No doubt the novelty will wear off at some stage, but at the moment I can't help but feel a mixture of relief and even a little bit of disbelief. I don't want to push things or burst this little happy families bubble.

I've got a lot to be grateful for really. Business is booming – if booking classes and running workshops can be called a "boom". But all the indications from *équilibre*'s first few weeks in business are very positive. Tess Wood has been so supportive – getting the word out about our work so that we have full classes at Spring to Mind Spa 4 afternoons a week from now until the mid-year holidays in June. The sessions at Frobisher have gone beautifully – Gracie loves having me involved at school. It's very different from library duty though. It's hard work keeping 12 little girls focused on their breathing and posture for 45 minutes! I'm helping Julie, my instructor, and learning a lot from her at the same time. We also have bookings for sessions at Fauntleroy (due to Beth) and even a couple of party bookings thanks to Claire. The resilience and mental and emotional balance classes are also exciting interest with at least 10 hits a day on my website. At this rate I'm going to need an admin assistant before long.

I was telling Luscious Larry a little bit about *équilibre* at Montessori last week. He was almost wistful. He basically asked whether I would give him a job. Tempting – he *is* so very luscious – just not sure what his skill set is, apart from being lovely. Come to think of it – that might be rather useful in luring in more clients - mothers (looking for classes for their kids). Might give him a call and see if he's serious about wanting to work with me.

While talking to Larry, Tedious Tabitha tottered over from the Tuckshop – I suspect she was having a snack – she said she was tallying the takings (lovely alliterative prose there). Never keen to miss out on a conversation with Larry, she interrupted and prattled on about her plans to buy new school shoes (yawn) and the machinations within the Parents' Association – hence my uncertainty as to whether he was serious about the work. Apparently no one has stepped forward to take over my former role as Secretary of the Association and *poor* Wendy is run off her feet doing that job as well as being President. I gave Larry a look upon hearing this news:

"Fancy helping Wendy out?" I asked him innocently. "Sounds like she could use all the help she can get." Larry laughed and deflected the comment, saying:

"Tabitha – why don't *you* volunteer. You'd make a great secretary."

I stifled a giggle and enjoyed Tabitha's lengthy explanation (again involving school shoes) of why she's just too busy to do more. The great thing is that the implied criticism from Tabitha that I left Wendy in the lurch, failed to land on or with me. While I could see Tabitha wanted to make that point and possibly force me to step up again out of guilt, I just let it pass me by. So mindful!

But back to business – Gracie has asked if she can have a party later this month so we are trying to think of themes. Freddie suggested Snakes and Ladders – George brought him a game from Hong Kong. Maria suggested water ballet – but the memories of the near drowning thing two year ago are still quite strong. George suggested we have a house party at Mum's and offer pony trekking and beach campfires. Bloody good idea! It wins hands down.

We are going down to Mum's on Tuesday for four days so we can scope things out then.

Can't wait. I miss the place terribly for some reason, even with all that's going on here, and often find myself thinking about the farm, our holiday, the beach and the people that work for Mum.

Sunday, 11 April

Time flies. George has just flown out for Hong Kong. The kids are fast asleep – worn out after a long day in the sun at the club with Harry and Claire and Wilbur. We played tennis and swam all day thanks to Pharma Co reinstating George's membership – it seems they'll go a long way to keep him. It was very relaxing and fun. I can't remember the last time we all got along so well – probably never...

Claire has proven to be great company. Can't really remember why I used to have such a problem with her. I said as much to George. He smugly responded that he would be happy to remind me, given he had heard me complain about her so many times. I replied:

"Don't bother, George. We're in a different place now so let's move forward and focus on the positive." Self-help clap-trap, but apt and true.

We had a fantastic visit at Mum's last week. She was away for most of our stay unfortunately, at various large race meetings. The big Easter Racing Carnival kept her in town so we essentially did a house swap. The beach is so lovely this time of year and the light and the crisp morning air are magical. We made a bonfire on the beach on Friday night and grilled some delectable fish that George caught despite Freddie shrieking at the cold of the waves. It was idyllic. The children played "spotlight" with their torches and chased little crabs down their holes. There's something very special about Mum's property and the beach there. And yes – it will be a brilliant venue for a party for Gracie. The only thing is that her actual birthday is in two weeks and George can't get back again so soon, given he's starting to wind things up with his project, so we've convinced Gracie to celebrate in the June-July holidays with a stay over party for our special family friends. This seems to be the best solution. She's still finding her feet at Frobisher and wants to invite the whole class though! That's not happening. If I can be bothered, I'll make a cake to send to school with her on the day.

This week is going to be a little crazy. As is now always the case, I had several excellent ideas at Mum's. First, I remembered that Luscious Larry played cricket for a time and coached the state schoolboys team before he and Rose had kids and he "retired" to stay at home with them. This got me thinking about his suggestion that he work with us at *équilibre* and I emailed him to ask whether he would consider running some outdoor adventure sessions for us – marrying more physical boy oriented activities with treasure hunts and play based communication skills classes to get boys negotiating and problem solving with scenarios that will capture their imaginations and play to their natural proclivities to learn through movement and doing. I seem to be very connected with the earth and my own creative energy at Mum's – hence these ideas just flowing! Larry was very interested and we are meeting tomorrow with Frances – the communication coach I hired – to workshop where to take this with a market of 8-13 year old boys in mind.

Then I had a brainwave about how to increase our profile using Twitter which I confess is a tool that eludes me. Like Facebook, the way it's used as a confessional through which people post the banalities of their life for public approval and comment, it just anathema to me, but despite that, it's the only way to be visible and be seen as relevant. Problem is, I can't and won't give up any time from more interesting and productive things to spend it "tweeting" tidbits to strangers that I would not speak to in a gym class. So ... who could I ask to do this for me?

None other than Tabitha! I'll offer her a basic rate of $2.50/tweet to post kids/wellbeing and health related tweets that are not complete nonsense and share meaningful and helpful tips and ideas and communicate our ethos. I ran this by Larry who thinks she would be very good at it. She was actually a marketing manager before becoming a full-time mum.

What else – Mah Jong on Wednesday night and lo and behold – having mastering a few more basics of social French over the past couple of months, Clothilde invited me to join *"Le Petit..."*. Can't quite believe it and I'm not sure I have time for it, but I won't offend her by playing hard to get.

Oh yes - Maria wants to play a role in *équilibre* and I've promised to give some thought to where she might be best used and what would best play to her strengths and aspirations. The children are great –

happy, thriving at school and socially – so I can hardly hold her back on the basis that they'll suffer. Certainly don't want to lose her – especially not now that she cooks and cleans like a pro and also given how invaluable she has been to Helen.

What else - I need to see Jorgé this week after missing my sessions with him last week. I also need to prioritise my yoga practice. Won't look good to be running yoga classes and never attend any myself.

Finally, I must see Felicity before she has her baby and see what she plans to do afterwards. She might need some help managing the transition.

Better go to sleep now. Yawning constantly.

Sunday, 18 April

Tabitha is on board. Larry is in. We have party bookings (even some *double* bookings) for the next five weekends. Felicity has offered to provide catering for my party classes – a partnership with Felicitations! Mum is delighted that we want to have Gracie's party at the farm. George is great. Still weighing up his free-lance options against the CSR agenda at Pharma Co. They're saying he can pursue his NGO ideas and his Dad's foundation on their time and dime; they see no conflict, and even think it will be good for morale and their brand. Rebecca is newly engaged to an American venture capitalist she met in HK last year. I am invited to a party in HK for her, but I declined. There is so much to do here that escaping for even a weekend is extravagant. George will have to send my best wishes...

Neglecting journal – feel bad.

Friday, 7 May

Felicity's c-section scheduled for tomorrow. Mum staying to be close and to help mind Jessica while Felicity's in hospital. Have to get back to her downstairs. Just popped up to Skype George and put kids in. Gracie is reading for 10 more minutes while I write this.

Maria is in the garden moving into the summer house - now her suite – be careful what you wish for. Feel a little sad to see it transformed from art and play space – the clay days there were very special. Still, will be better for her to be on-site.

Mum's hinting that Doug might be interested in going into partnership with her. Not going to worry – she knows what she's doing and I know her lawyer will protect her interests. Must get back to her and hear more about it.

George has decided to go for a trek after his project ends. He'll meet up with Harry and Tim and spend three weeks trekking to Everest's base camp. Not sure Harry will make it, but so happy for George! Wish I could go too. When I said that, he promised to take me on the Marlborough winery tour and for some glacier adventures in NZ at Christmas. Yay.

Better sign off. Gracie will stay up reading all night if I don't stop her.

This time tomorrow I'll have a new nephew!

Tuesday, 18 May

398 followers on Twitter. Tabitha is an amazing find and exceeding all my expectations. I really like her!

Claire called today for help persuading Harry to defer the trek with George until next year – she's terrified he'll have a heart attack. Having dinner with both tomorrow to discuss.

Larry's first official class last weekend was excellent. Wish I were a little boy again (as I say to Freddie most days) so I could sign up for a term.

Équilibre is going so well. I never imagined it would attract the following it has. Friday morning I have an interview with the local parenting glossy. It used to be mostly ads but this year it's added some feature articles and food and lifestyle pages. They want me to write a regular piece about balance and wellbeing in pre-teens. So thrilled. Old habits die hard - rang Beth to share the news. It's been weeks since we spoke but since media was her thing I asked her to come along with me. She promised to cancel her manicure and reading at school to be there!

Helen and Eloise are on their way over to help me decide what to wear for the photo shoot.

I need to call Felicity and see how she and little Reggie (named after Dad) are faring. He's so cute – the image of Allan – but not so bad in a baby. She's having him baptised at our old parish, half way to Mum's on Sunday week. Just hanging out for the trip – any chance to get back there and I'm on board. We'll drive down Friday night and spend Saturday on the farm. Mum is like a teenager in love. Doug has virtually moved in – horses and staff divided between his stables and Mum's farm. Can't wait to see what it all looks like now and how they're all getting along.

I'm heading off to the track this Saturday with the *équilibre* team and their partners, Tess Wood, plus Claire and Harry. We're having a little heels up in Mum's box so that I can thank them for all they've done for the business over the past couple of months. Am thinking of setting them a quiz or a treasure hunt to build the team dynamics even more. Tabitha is beside herself about it. She's never been to a race course.

She told Wendy all about her new job with me and now Wendy is livid. With George away all this time, her husband's business case for partnership has disappeared. The acting head of Strategy and BD at Pharma Co gives all their legal work to his brother's firm. Apparently I was meant to do something about that. Alas, I may have lost Wendy forever. Helen reports that her presidency has gone off the boil since Paul was passed over in March and Mrs Blythe is starting to question the viability of her seeing the year out in either the role of President or Secretary. She might need to find something else to do with herself...

The PAMM Facebook page, never a scintillating read, has become a complete joke. Loosy Lude defriended it last week when Helen told me what Wendy was saying to her about Gracie and Freddie at Tuckshop, motivated by revenge for my letting Paul remain a mere Senior Associate for another year. It's pathetic. Sadly for Wendy, Loosy Lude is a bit of a trendsetter and several other parents and a few weirdos that had nothing to do with Mortimer but "liked" whatever Loosy did, have followed her lead and also abandoned it, leaving only die hard recipe sharers and gossip mongers logging on to check the stream on PAMM's page – stream of crap – that is. So glad I'm out of that now. One Loosy follower was so bold as to start a page titled "Enemies of Wendy" until Tabitha (at Loosy's prompting via a tweet(!)) reported it to the Facebook police and had it shut down.

Frobisher is wonderful. Gracie is very settled and engaged. Last week's parent teacher meetings were so reassuring. Her teachers are lovely and speak well of her. Poor George missed the illuminating talk on homework, reading and nurturing curiosity about the world in girls. Largely common sense but delivered to effectively. I'm terribly relieved we did not get a place at Hillmere. I ran into Kate at the supermarket the other day. It's been a while since I saw her and I almost didn't recognise her – she looked really great – new short hairstyle and a whole different look. She told me that Mitch is taking Mia's daughter out of Hillmere and home schooling her for the rest of the year – she's burnt out and showing signs of anorexia – at 10! Whether one can attribute this state of affairs to Frobisher, Mia or a combination of factors, one will never know – but the intense competition at Hillmere will be a thing of the past. Mitch is quite something, it has to be said. It certainly appears he has a few more strings to his bow than fast cars, sailing and making money.

Just as I was starting to wonder whether I would be asked for drugs, advice or the name of a good herbalist, Kate, then dropped her bombshell. After some bitter and acrimonious feuding this year, she has split up with Brad. She's had an on-again, off-again thing with one of Brad's friends for three years. A musician – hence her new look, I daresay. Brad found out and chucked her out. He has the kids and she gets weekend access. I've never seen her looking so good and she did not once ask me for meds or mention her health. What's going on with the world? Too much change all at once.

As well as all of that news, Emma told me when I dropped Gracie at hers to play last week that her entire book club and her well connected friend Sara – the one who told me to run style classes – want her to call me to secure places for them in *équilibre* classes at the Spring to Mind Spa. Sorry girls, join the queue. It's booked solid. They might have to sign up for the special holiday classes that cost a bomb!

It seems that it might be time to consider finding our own premises. Mrs G says I have to gear up or face losing clients or even risk competitors muscling into the space. That has me a bit worried. Our hold is still too new and tenuous to want to lose this ground we have gained so quickly. I find Larry a great source of wisdom – he's lovely *and* clever. Gosh I made terrible assumptions about him just because he's so handsome and his wife is the breadwinner. She rang me yesterday to thank me for taking him on. She recommended to a couple of patients that they send their sons to his class on Saturday and already has heard loads of good things about it. Larry is walking on air – new lease on life. Rose is delighted and things have already improved at home in all "departments". Mmm, lucky Rose.

Anyway, enough musings, time for work!

Monday, 14 June

We celebrated Gracie's Birthday and George and Harry's homecoming on Saturday with a wonderful house party at Mum's. Felicity was there cooking and feeding us all with help from two of her people. Allan and Jessica were a great help with the children, shepherding them to the stables and encouraging the more reticent among them to man up (e.g. Wilbur) and climb up onto a saddle. Then Mum, Doug (his grandkids in tow), and a couple of Mum's stable hands took them all trekking down to the beach. They had to go in fours because of a shortage of ponies and little horses, but no one minded. Ducks and sheep and a big block of land are pretty cool diversions while waiting for a turn.

Hannah and Tim (looking a little peaky post trek) were there with the twins. Claire and Harry (not exactly peaky, but slimmer) came as well. Also Helen and John and all five of theirs, Larry and Rose and their two, and Clothilde and Emmanuelle. Gracie was in Heaven. Her only regret was that Gabriella and Rafaella were not able to come – Skyping from Sweden had to suffice. It was nice to see Desirée too.

Anyway, everyone arrived early Saturday (the new motorway has everyone dashing down in record time) and left last thing. I don't know what has stopped us from doing this before. Poor Felicity is shattered though. Reggie's a poor sleeper so I'm really grateful to her for working so hard to make the day such a success. And George was amazing. He helped everyone have a great time – filling drinks, carrying Reggie around in the baby carrier, making beds, mucking out stalls, building campfires. His trek and his new-found clarity have changed him immeasurably. I'm even a little in love with him again I think. He's fit, happy and great company – even better than when I first met him. Claire remarked wistfully that our separation seems to have done us both a world of good. I said I'd recommend it to anyone! Two weeks with Harry away may have whet her appetite for a little space. You go girl!

While the party was lovely, it was nice to have some peace afterwards. George, Mum and I took a drive around the area on Sunday. It was so quiet and peaceful. We passed a handful of intrepid cyclists out braving the winter winds and a few day-trippers enjoying the winter sun and antique shops along the scenic drive. I can see why Mum never wants to leave.

.....

Yay. George just arrived home – he's been back in Pharma Co HQ for the first time in 6 months today. Better sign off and hear his news.

Thursday, 24 June

Where should I start? I look at the above entries and can't quite believe all that's happened this year.

I'm reeling a bit from the past few days. Pardon the pun.

I just signed the mortgage documents at the bank to finance the purchase of an old building in the little town near the cove, up the road from Mum's. I need premises for *équlibre* and the more I thought about it the more I felt sure that a property outside the city was worth considering – something to capture the holiday makers, the country clients, the children who live in commuter land. The thoughts were just starting to coalesce late last week after the party at Mum's when she called and told me to come down again asap – there was a shop I just *had* to see. George and the children were only too happy to come too. We drove down Saturday morning and met Mum outside the Three Cypresses Bakery – where I took Mrs G all those months ago to discuss my initial thoughts for starting a business. Surreal.

It was a cold and blustery day so we sat indoors and had a delicious brunch as we waited for the real estate agent who eventually clattered in on silly high heels to buy a take away coffee and walk us up the road to the building that was for sale. The agent – Mary – is a woman of a certain age, as so many coastal real estate agents seem to be. She explained that the building had been in the family of the vendors for three generations and has at one time been the general store, a newsagents and most recently, a fishing tackle shop. It's now very run down as the owners were elderly and increasingly spending their time in the city where they could be closer to doctors and their children. Anyway a couple of weeks ago the husband died. He's survived by his widow who wants to sell all their property – a house and this shop - and take the proceeds to buy a new townhouse in the city near her son. The son's in IT, never visits and would love nothing more than having his Mum close to mind his kids!

Why would this shop suit me, I wondered? Well Mary didn't disappoint. Up the street we all went, matching our stride to her little high heeled steps, as she explained the virtues of the central location.

"It's off the high street, but very central Verity. A short walk from the main drag with the cafés and the amenities, with good parking and lots of trees, a short walk to the beach. But best of all, it's a two storey building with permission to go up another level, and the views from the roof are amazing – out across the beach and the cove on one side and over to the hills on the other. It gets great sunshine all winter and catches the sea breezes. It needs some work, a lick of paint and obviously a re-fit for your purposes, but it's a sound building – structurally excellent. All the surveys and inspections have been done and it's a steal at the price she's asking. She's ready to move on and will take an offer lower, I'm sure." Mary had to draw breath then so I asked:

"Any zoning issues?"

"No issues, it's mixed commercial so you can use it for retail, banking, therapies, medical, hospitality. No light industrial though! And you can use the upstairs for living."

Mum was right to call us to come down – I was getting more and more excited as we approached the corner. George and the kids had run ahead and we finally caught up to them outside the store aptly named "Fishing Tackle and Bait Shop". Glamorous. Mum read my mind.

"Now V, don't worry about the fishing stuff. You'd have to redo it anyway. Just wait til you see the views."

We spent the next half an hour scouring the building. Mum was a godsend. She asked all the questions I didn't think of, while pretending to think we still needed to see more properties. I was sold the minute I stepped inside. It was charming, oozing character. I could almost feel all those old men standing around the counter talking about the tides and the catch of the day. It felt imbued with love and calm and the simpler concerns of a bygone age.. I could picture the widow, in younger years, making tea in the little kitchen, a couple of children under foot and a cheerful, weather beaten husband pricing fish hooks in the shop, chatting to city folk down for the weekend looking for new rods and tackle. I was romanticising, I know. I lost track of time for a while. Gracie and Freddie went outside and found an old tyre hanging from a tree in the back yard. They were pushing each other on it, their delighted squeals bringing me back to reality.

The stairs at the front – with their own entrance from the pavement – took us straight up to a massive room with dusty wooden floors and huge picture windows overlooking the street, with glimpses of the sea through the leaves across the road. The wind was picking up and the sheets and towels on the line in the garden opposite billowed and flapped furiously.

I was so caught up in the magic of the place that I lost George and Mary for a while. Mum and I paced out the floor and wandered through the back rooms – formerly bedrooms. It was perfect.

We asked a few more questions but I was ready to make an offer. Mum restrained me with a look and told Mary we would call her. Mary looked happy as she locked up, as if she knew it was in the bag. Shaking everyone's hands and getting out her phone to tee up her next viewing, she reminded us that our first mover advantage would disappear in another week. She predicts that there will be loads of buyers down from the city after the vendor lists it with the city agents on Monday. Bloody city people. Don't want that lot buying up down here!

We found the children befriending the cat next door and headed back to the bakery. Driving to Mum's (the children went with her on the beach road for a treat), I was practically delirious with joy and excitement.

"It's fantastic George. Absolutely perfect. I want it! Shall I make an offer today? Do I need to call the bank?"

"Slow down V!" He laughed, squeezing my knee. "It was great but are you sure you want to own a building all the way down here? When will you use it? How will you use it? What about your staff and all your commitments in town?"

"That's the best part George. I can be down here in an hour and half, as can they – or even less - as some of them live on the south side of town. The idea would be to divide the week between the city and here. Now I have a staff I can keep the bookings going in schools in town and maintain the slots at Spring to Mind – the overheads are negligible. And this will be the expansion pathway - opening up *équibre* for holidays and weekend classes. Imagine a summer full of bookings. People will love it. Mummy can go out for lunch while the kids do a session. They'll come in their droves! And this is so well located for locals, city-siders, the whole hobby farming hinterland and the horse people too. Everything is an hour or less away. It's just off the scenic drive and the antiques tour. Plus it's not expensive. You know what Yves and Beth paid for their place down the coast. This is a bargain. It's not a trendy area so we don't have to pay the fashion premium. It's ideal."

George just smiled. I didn't know what he thought. I sensed he was indulging me – paying out some credit. I didn't really care. I knew he would eventually see the merit of the plan and get on board. Mrs G would get it. And Mum. I also had Felicity in mind. A little café for weekends and summers, taking a step back from the frenetic pace of catering? Maybe Allan could have a little practice at the beach.

Mum and I took a walk when we got back, and we discussed it at length. She was so supportive. Completely saw the vision I was describing, told me not to worry about George and pointed out the scope for developing the top floor into an apartment. She even offered to have us stay any time while managing the refurb.

The afternoon turned cold and dark soon after, so we hurried back to the house to find the kids and George having tea with Doug in the kitchen, drawing horses and seahorses. What a lovely scene!

I announced that I'd decided and hoped that George would be supportive. He got up and came around the table to give me a hug.

"I think this calls for champagne, eh?"

Skipping like a girl through the house I grabbed my phone and called Mary, made an offer £25,000 less than the asking. I then gulped down two flutes of champagne waiting for her to call back. She never called! Two hours later as Gracie and Freddie finished their dinner and I was checking my phone to see if I'd missed any calls in the last two minutes while I was washing the salad, a car came down the drive and two older ladies climbed out. Mary and someone? They came around to the door where Mum greeted them. The other lady was Mrs Harrison – the owner of the shop. She wanted to meet us before agreeing to a sale. Shit!

But she agreed! She loved us. She loved my plan and the energy I feel for it. She loved the kids too, of course. She was so smitten with us that in agreeing terms, she even threw in all the stock in the shop. It was all happening so fast – it felt right and wonderful – but all that fishing crap to offload? I hesitated at that.

"Err. Thanks. So kind of you... You're sure your son wouldn't like it. I gather fishing stuff sells well on ebay."

Mrs Harrison and Mary exchanged a look. Then George cut in:

"I'll make use of it, V. Don't worry." He positively twinkled!

Too much Veuve? It was a lot of kit for George to shift. He likes fishing but even fishing every other week, he'll never use all that stuff. But hell, it couldn't ruin my day.

"Ok. It's a deal!"

And now it's all signed and approved by the bank, fast tracked thanks to Mrs G. And we get the keys in two weeks.

Have to tell the team at our weekly meeting tomorrow. Felicity and Reggie are coming with treats to soften the blow – not sure if they'll be pleased. Maria knows and is delighted – she's in love with one of Mum's assistants.

Now I need to call the architect and discuss the refit.

Saturday, 26 June

Just got inside from an invigorating walk on the beach with George and the children. We're down at the farm. We spent the morning at the new building. George was in Heaven going through all the fishing merchandise while the kids befriended the owner of the cat next door and played happily for two hours. We swept up the dust upstairs and the architect and I started planning the new floor above – an apartment as Mum suggested – and the fit out of the first floor as a yoga/Pilates studio and three smaller workshop rooms, bathroom and kitchenette.

The *équilibre* team took the news very well and are already volunteering to come down and run taster sessions in the next few weeks for local schools and at sports grounds on the weekends. We hope to have the studio and workshop rooms ready by the school holidays in September!

Tonight Doug and his sons and their wives are coming to Mum's for dinner and Felicity, Allan and Jessica should be here any minute. It will be great to meet them. I'm cooking. From scratch – Felicity has promised to stay out of my way!

Sunday, 27 June

Couldn't wait to get away and steal a moment to write in my journal. Mum's getting married again! Such wonderful news – announced last night over my hazelnut gateau dessert. We weren't surprised, but we pretended to be shocked for their sake. They were prepared for fights and resistance. Why? We couldn't be happier. Doug's family is lovely.

Have discussed with Felicity the possibly of setting up a cafe in the shop in town. We'll clear out all the fishing paraphernalia and have a really good clean up and see what needs doing to make a lovely little courtyard bistro. Opening Summer and weekends only, for now.

Oh – hold on. George is calling me.

.....

George has just left me sitting here on my window seat – dear George. He's taken Gracie riding. Now I have to steal myself to speak to Felicity again when he's back.

George came in with wild flowers picked from around the farm and put a proposition to me.

Could he take over the fishing tackle shop – as is – and spend half his week and all his holidays here with me, selling fishing stuff, leading fishing trips and teaching sailing to inner city kids (poor kids who otherwise would never get the opportunity).

He wants to call the shop "Fishing for Meaning", "Drop in the Ocean", "Seachange" or "Kettle of Fish" ... or "Ebb and Flow"...

I cried when he laid it all out – all those names... I thought he'd just been indulging my little dream to have this business, happy to come along for the ride but really only committed to his new CSR role at Pharma Co. How little I noticed. I was so wrapped up in my plans that I didn't see he's been holding back, not wanting to take over, or to influence my thinking. Now with me planning to turn the shop into a café he's in earnest. I've never seen him so alive, brimming with humour and energy. Positively beaming at me like a little boy given the best new bike in the world.

I love the idea! Sailing, fishing, *équilibre*, good coffee. And my little nostalgic vision of the fishing shop circa 1967 with children and family and old men chatting together can become a reality after all!

I just need to sell Felicity on the idea that she'll be relegated to a smaller space with only courtyard dining...

She'll think the compliments on my superb cooking efforts last night have gone to my head and I'm trying to compete with her. George has promised to help me explain it. Also need to think how this will work with the kids' schools... We'll figure it out.

Who is this man? This George Fortescue - father, husband, son and friend. He's just so fantastic. He was there all along and I never knew him. What was I doing with my time? He says he never was this man; that he's become him, grown into him. I suppose I don't care and it doesn't matter. He's here now.

I have to wean myself off this journal. Life is passing me by.

I must find George. I miss him already.

.....

Acknowledgements

Heartfelt thanks to my friends for your support and interest over the past several months while writing "The Inner Child Journal". I thank you in advance for the support I will beg for now that it is in print!

I started this book without a plan; driven merely by a desire to connect and communicate with parents – especially mothers.

I would like to acknowledge the dedication and hard work of all the mothers I know. My own, of course, and my dear aunt, my sisters-in-law and my darling sister, often a mother to so many people. Finally, and by no means least – all of my dear friends.

I hope that something in Verity's story resonates with you; that you laughed a few times and related to some of her thoughts and concerns.

Above all, though, I hope that this book might have made you pause to wonder about your own inner child. To consider your own strengths and interests and the ways in which to be your own best self.